ROMANCE LANGUAGES

A SOUTH ROCK HIGH NOVEL

A.J. TRUMAN

Cover by Bailey McGinn

Proofreading by Kate Wood

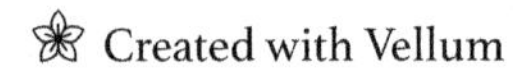
Created with Vellum

1

JULIAN

So how did I become an almost thirty-five-year-old virgin? Believe me, it wasn't planned.

No kid grows up wishing to hold out on physical intimacy for his adult life. Even kids forced to wear purity rings counted down the days until they could have sex.

I wasn't celibate. I wanted to have sex. Lots of it. The occasional cramping in my right hand could attest to this desire. Sex was always on the docket for my life.

But then it just...didn't happen. As Ferris Bueller warned us, life moves pretty fast. Days turned into months which turned into years, and suddenly I woke up one morning and found myself one month away from being a thirty-five-year-old virgin.

How did I let myself down?

Like many gay guys, I was closeted in high school. While my classmates were letting their hormones run wild, I held mine back for dear life, lest anyone find out my secret. I wasn't one of those lucky closeted teens who had a neighbor kid he could experiment with or who secretly got it on with the closeted jock, like my friend Amos. I was a chubby, awkward kid with acne who had a tendency to blend into the background. Even if every guy in my school had magically become gay, I doubt I would've been at the top of their boyfriend wishlist.

It took me until my senior year of college to find the courage to finally come out as gay.

There were some guys who went through a slut phase when they came out. (The empowered version of slut! No shaming here.) They wanted to make up for all the action they'd missed while in the closet. I didn't have that urge. I didn't want to toss my v-card to the first breathing homosexual available. I wanted to find someone I could fall in love with. The closet was lonely, and navigating openly gay life was its own kind of solitude. I wanted to find that person who would make the loneliness disappear.

Unfortunately, while I wanted a boyfriend, potential boyfriends did not want me. I went to LGBTQ+ nights and gay bars, but things never progressed past a first date or some guy taking down my number and never texting me. Was it because of how I looked or my personality or a combination?

Guys on apps were much more direct: *sorry, no fatties.*

Oh, the power of not having to look someone in the face when you reject them.

At least they said sorry.

I existed in this gray area where I wasn't big enough to be considered a bear, and I wasn't muscular enough to be considered an otter. I was garden variety overweight, with most of my weight pooling in my stomach, hips, and ass. I'd received compliments on my lush brown hair (my best feature) and dark eyes, but those assets couldn't outweigh what was happening below my neck.

As more of the gay dating scene migrated to apps, I focused my attention on grad school and then teaching. I held out hope that I'd meet someone in person, someone who could get to know me first, rather than judging me based on a thumbnail image. But eventually, that hope slowly eroded, disappearing into the wind.

The years passed.

Once I hit thirty, I was determined not to fool around with guys in random hookups. I'd waited this long; I couldn't throw away my virginity. It became this thing that unintentionally grew in stature. I couldn't bear the thought of finally having sex with someone and then having them ghost me.

Voilà! Virgin for life!

On the bright side, I could still be used for ritual sacrifices and lighting the black flame candle in *Hocus Pocus*. Who wouldn't want to hang with the Sanderson sisters?

It was a secret I seemed destined to take to my grave. I hadn't even told my friends. They wouldn't kick me out of the group chat for being a virgin, but that didn't mean it wasn't humiliating. Especially because two of them had serious boyfriends and were likely having sex on a regular basis.

Amos: Happy one month until your birthday, J!

Chase: Are we counting a month as four weeks or thirty days? Technically, his birthday is thirty days away.

Amos: Chase, stop being such a party animal.

Amos: Get ready for an epic birthday celebration!

Julian: Epic? I'm fine with something lowkey.

Everett: J, what are your thoughts on mechanical bulls?

Everett: And how do you feel about go karts?

Julian: Um, not really my cup of tea.

Amos: Ignore him.

Everett: We're just putting together your birthday festivities.

Chase: They don't involve either. I would say more, but I'm sworn to secrecy.

Everett: Lordy, excuse me for trying to drum up anticipation and throw in some red herrings.

Julian: Has anyone told you you have a flair for drama?

Everett: GASP.

Amos: We're busy planning. It's going to be epic, in a lowkey kind of way.

Julian: You really don't have to do anything big. It's just another birthday. We can have a birthday at your condo, like we did for Chase.

Everett: Save it, lady. We won't settle for anything less than strippers slapping you in the face with their dicks.

Julian: Please tell me that's not it.

Amos: That's not it.

Amos: Or is it?

Chase: Would it hurt if you were hit in the face with a dick? More or less than a hand? I suppose whether it was erect or not would make a difference, as well as the flexibility of the stripper's hips to create a suitable range of motion for the dick.

Julian: Chase, I love how your brain works.

Everett: I don't.

Amos: Yes he does.

Everett: Bottom line - we're cooking up something good for you, J. You're going to love it. And I will continue to tease you with hints and red herrings because I live for drama. Now, is there anything special you want for your birthday?

I thought about it for a moment, then typed out my answer: *I want to lose my virginity.*

I stared at the group chat screen where my text sat, not yet sent. Of course I wasn't going to send it, but seeing it spelled out in plain English turned it from a wandering thought flitting through my head into something real, something tangible, something I could achieve.

Julian: If there's something special I want, I'll let you guys know. Although now that you mention it, I've always wanted a mechanical bull for my house.

Somehow, I was going to have sex with a guy before my birthday. It was time to get over the hump. Or under the hump depending on the position.

2

JULIAN

I was a goal-oriented person. That was how I'd pushed myself through undergrad and grad school.

New goal: rid myself of my metaphorical hymen.

On Monday morning, I arrived extra early at South Rock High School, before the sun was fully up. South Rock was where I'd met Amos, Everett, and Chase. We'd all started here around the same time and bonded as nerdy, gay teachers. Our group chat was endless and the Holy Bible of our friendship. On rough days, when school bureaucracy or obnoxious students were getting me down, those guys were my saving grace. They were the family I happily chose.

I was close-ish with my actual family. There were no fights or estrangements, but everyone in my family was slim and trim and thought they were being helpful by constantly talking to me about my weight.

My grandma and I were tight, though. She was eighty and spry and lived life with no filter.

At South Rock, I taught French. I sat in my classroom, surrounded by posters of French sayings and touristy pictures of

France. The Eiffel Tower. Vineyards. Cannes. I did a study abroad trip in college, and I forever fell in love. There was a reason why they called French a Romance language.

But this morning was not the time for romance. It was about lust. About two bodies coming together in a sweaty heap of passion.

With a heavy sigh, I reactivated my Milkman account. It was a gay dating app supposedly for finding love, though all the shirtless pics and mentions of DTF (down to fuck) said otherwise.

I scrolled through the seemingly endless options of attractive gay men in my area. Why couldn't I bump into them at the supermarket or in the literature section of the local bookstore? I found a few who had charming things written in their profiles and sent messages. I figured I'd launch arrows this morning before they started their day and hopefully hear back by the time school was over.

Yet it seemed men on Milkman were hotly watching their notifications because not even five minutes later, two blocked me and two replied back before blocking me.

Not interested, said one.

Sorry, no fatties, said the other.

I laughed under my breath, trying to find the humor in the insanity of online dating. The gay men of fifty years ago would find it ironic that we could date openly now, but we were all too busy rejecting each other.

I exited Milkman and let my finger wander to a more pleasurable app. I opened up BlingBling, the social media app du jour that abounded with micro videos, usually of people lip syncing or joining in some dance craze. I basked in the glow of a new Mr. Shablahblah video.

"*Things my students are totally embarrassed by*," he said, facing the camera as the text popped up above him. His blue eyes reached through the screen and held me in place.

Cut to him wearing a jacket, and looking side-to-side, mortally humiliated.

"*Wearing a jacket when it's cold.*"

Cut to him tossing a crumpled piece of paper into the waste-basket, missing, then scurrying out of frame.

"*Not making a trash shot.*"

Cut to him sitting at a desk, raising his hand, and muttering "Here."

"*Saying 'here' during attendance.*"

Cut to him dropping a book, then panicking, picking it up, and trying to play it cool.

"*Accidentally dropping things.*"

Cut to him staring into the phone's camera, zooming in on his eyes.

"*Making eye contact with literally anyone.*"

I paused the video, pretending Mr. Shablahblah was making eye contact with me. I got a tingle up my spine and had to look away for a second.

The video cut to him standing in front of his markerboard giving a big smile to his fans. "If you enjoyed this video, make sure to like and subscribe."

Trust me, I was already subscribed.

How was it possible that these twenty-second videos could lift my spirits on a regular basis?

"You really don't have to watch those." Seamus hung by my door, looking even better in person.

Yes, twenty thousand people might follow Mr. Shablahblah, but only I got to teach in the classroom across the hall from Seamus Shablanski himself.

Things I am totally embarrassed by: getting caught watching my coworker's BlingBling videos which I blatantly swoon over.

I shove my phone into the top desk drawer. "I was just scrolling."

"It's getting a lot of shares. I may turn it into a series because my students are embarrassed by *everything*. Were we this strange when we were their age?" He quirked an eyebrow, which rested on his beautiful face.

Seamus had a shag of dark hair that couldn't decide if it wanted to be curly or straight. His eyes were an icy blue hue that was powerful enough to scoop anyone into their orbit. There was a near-constant lazy grin on his thin lips as if an inside joke were playing in a loop in his head. He'd recently grown a close-cropped beard that gave him an added layer of sex appeal. His tall frame was all toned, lean muscle. He was one of those guys who was probably scrawny as a kid, and no matter how much they worked at it, they'd never be bulked up.

And if cataloging his cuteness wasn't obvious enough, I had a crush. A big one.

Seamus was straight, though, and I was more than happy to be his coworker and friend. Who needed gross guys rejecting me when I could have a one-sided flirtation with a sweet, funny ex-fratbro?

"You're here early," I said.

Seamus stepped into my classroom. No matter what the temperature was outside, his outfit was constant: a polo tucked into a pair of chinos, black Chuck Taylors on his feet. He hadn't quite gotten the memo about teacherly dress code, and he was all the better for it.

"I have to do inventory of our baseball equipment. The season is starting up soon. Somehow, we lost like a hundred balls last year."

"Home runs?"

"I guess so."

Seamus was the baseball coach for South Rock. Knowing him was the closest I'd gotten to playing sports since I was forced to play soccer for two years as a kid. Because I was on the bigger side,

I was always stuck playing goalie. The coach—a real, actual human adult—thought it was good strategy telling the fat kid that since he was bigger, he naturally covered more of the goal area.

"Do your students ever jump up and hit the doorframe?" I asked him. "I feel like every guy in my class does that when he leaves. And when they miss, they shuffle away."

We shared a chuckle. Our students had no idea, but they were our biggest source of entertainment.

"I'm putting that in my next video." Seamus sat on the edge of my desk and knocked on the wood. He was close enough that I could smell his citrusy, musky scent—some alchemy of cologne, soap, and his natural Seamusness.

"So Jules, can you help me with something?"

Seamus was the only person who called me Jules. I didn't know how it had started, but every time he said it in his thick Staten Island accent—heavy on the U—my stomach did a flip like a rickety Coney Island roller coaster.

"I'm having trouble saving my lesson plans on the new system. It's not saving, even though I hit save."

"Yeah, it's kind of confusing. I don't know why the administration insists on making life more difficult for us." I pulled my laptop from my bag and opened up the program Cyllabus—with a C, because the tech world must always be different. To improve transparency with parents and students, we had to upload lesson plans regularly to the Cyllabus portal. It was supposed to help kids stay on top of assignments, but like most educational software, it had zero impact and only led to more work for us teachers.

But at least it meant that Seamus could come in, sit on my desk close to me, and ask for help. I turned the laptop so he could see. He hunched closer, our shoulders touching, my stomach flipping. I pointed out how you had to click save, then submit, then save again.

"Why do we have to hit save twice?" he asked.

"I have no idea."

He let out a raspy laugh. When he found something really funny, like this thing I just said, his laughter cracked in pure joy.

"I hate this system." He scribbled a note to himself on his pad. Even his handwriting was sexy. It was a messy, boyish scrawl.

Lusting after a straight guy's handwriting? I *really* needed to get laid.

"It takes some time to get used to, but you'll get the hang of it."

"Unless they bring in something new." He flipped his notepad shut. He used it to write down ideas for videos. There was something charmingly old school about him using pen and paper.

"Don't worry. We'll figure it out."

"You'll figure it out, Jules. You always do. I swear, I don't know how I'd survive at South Rock without you."

My heart had the audacity to read more into that than it damn well should have.

I shrugged. "Whatever."

"Seriously. I remember my first day at South Rock, my first day ever as a teacher. I was so nervous. I had no fucking idea what I was doing." He looked around to make sure the coast was clear, something he always did when he cursed. Again, endearing and charming somehow. "I thought I was going to faceplant and be outta here by the end of the week. But you showed me the ropes. I'm so glad we wound up in the same department and across the hall from each other."

"Romance language teachers have to stick together."

Seamus taught Spanish. How a part-Irish, part-Russian kid from the New York outer boroughs wound up a Spanish teacher was a mystery I ascribed to the randomness of life. That, and he was fucking hot when he rolled his R's.

"I was happy to do it. You were kind of a lost puppy those first few months," I said.

Truth was, there was something lost puppyish about Seamus

even now. He was kind and loyal, without a mean bone in his body. Even if he wasn't fit, even if his eyes weren't impossibly blue, I'd still be hopelessly attracted to him.

"Thanks for everything, Jules."

"Anytime. That's what colleagues are for."

"Come on. I think we're past only being colleagues. We're buds." He shrugged, like he was embarrassed for even having to say this.

"Definitely."

He hopped off the desk. "Well, I'm going to enter in lesson plans that parents and students won't look at."

"And then they'll blame you when they fall behind."

"Like clockwork. Don't work too hard, Jules." Seamus studied me for a minute, his gaze a flaming hot spotlight. "You okay? You seem a little blue."

"Blue? I mean, I just realized my birthday is in one month. It's a big one."

"Nice! I'm definitely getting you a gift. Anything in particular you want?"

You. On top of me. Thrusting. Kissing. Confessing your love.

I shook out the thought before it became a full-fledged horny daydream.

"Nope."

"I'll think on it." He put a hand on my shoulder. "I know birthdays can be stressful. I had a little freakout when I turned thirty last year. But don't let it get to you. You're doing great, Jules."

He peered down at me, freezing time for a moment.

"Thanks, Mr. Shablahblah."

"Shh. Don't reveal my secret identity."

He was joking. Everyone at South Rock who knew how to use BlingBling was well aware of his videos. I'd tried showing one of his videos to Mrs. Darling, my fellow French teacher who was on the verge of retirement. She'd let out an annoyed sigh and said "I don't get it."

"Good morning, gentlemen!" Principal Aguilar joined our conversation.

"What's good, Principal Aguilar?" Seamus asked.

"I just added two new cacti to my collection over the weekend. They're extra prickly!"

Principal Aguilar was almost fifty and equally obsessed with corny jokes and his cacti collection. And yet even he was probably having regular sex with his boyfriend Clint.

"Do you mind if I talk to Julian for a moment?"

"I was just on my way out. Off to upload my teaching plans to our sterling new software." Seamus pivoted around and shot me a smile. "Thanks again for the help, Jules."

"Anytime."

The air changed once Seamus left the room, like a party that had lost its coolest member.

"Julian, do you still have your health certification active?"

"Yes. I took courses on it in college and post-grad."

"Good." His brow furrowed, making my stomach tighten with concern, but I didn't know what to be concerned about.

"It was easy to add on the certification to my course load since I already had distribution credits." I found myself rambling, not unlike my friend Everett, who was much more of a conversationalist.

"Mrs. Stockman broke her leg skiing, so she's going to be out for a few weeks."

"Is she okay?" This was reason number one why I never got into skiing. I preferred to stick to activities where people weren't prone to tumbling down mountains or crashing into trees. Like attending museums. Nobody ever broke their legs at a museum visit.

"She's recovering at her family's cabin. I'm going to send her some baked goods and flowers from everyone to hopefully cheer her up. But since she's going to be out, I've been looking for teachers to cover her classes. We're short on subs. I see that you have fourth period open. Would you be up for teaching her health class?"

"Sure. Whatever I can do to help out." The material wasn't challenging, and I could read up on her lessons. Health class was about discussing physical, social, and emotional changes that came with adolescence. None of the kids took it seriously.

"Excellent! I'll update the schedule. Thank you for pitching in."

"Of course. What's the grade and current lesson?"

"Eleventh graders, and they're up to..." He referred to his printout. It seemed he wasn't one hundred percent onboard with the new software either. "Sexual education."

"Sex ed?" I asked and hoped my voice didn't crack.

"Yep. So you'll be teaching the unit all about different kinds of sex and safe sex. It's like that Salt-N-Pepa song. Get ready to talk about sex!"

He cracked himself up, while I could barely muster a grin. Because of all the things I could teach about, sex was nowhere on the list. Whoever came up with the expression "Those that can't do, teach," hadn't taken into account my predicament.

3

SEAMUS

I look into the camera lens. Smile. Chest out. Give 'em that influencer swagger.

"Okay, I'm Mr. Shablahblah and these are random things that my students love to touch."

Cut to me strumming my fingers on the corner of my desk.

"My desk. Whenever they pass by, they have to touch the corner. For good luck, I guess?"

Cut to me running a finger over random notes scribbled on my markerboard.

"Markerboards. They literally can't get over the fact that they can erase words with their fingers."

Cut to me sliding my finger across a row of World Book Encyclopedias as if they're piano keys.

"Old books. For some reason, there's an old set of encyclopedias in my classrooms. They don't like to open them. Just touch them. And last."

Cut to me hopping up to touch the top of my classroom doorframe.

"The doorframe. Every guy has to jump up to touch it when they leave, and if they don't, they will be cursed with immortal humiliation.

If you like this video, make sure to like and subscribe to see other weird things my students do."

The sound of exaggerated slow clapping snapped me back to the present. I pulled off my headphones.

"Nice! Oscars for everyone." Greg hung in my bedroom doorway. The sleeves of his Browerton University hoodie were pushed up his arms. "Dinner's ready."

"I think I'm gonna just grab some snacks and continue working tonight."

"What? You can't do that. Your dads cooked you a delicious, nutritious dinner, and we're all going to eat like a family."

"Dude, you gotta stop saying stuff like that. It's weird." I strummed my fingers on my desk. The aroma of a warm, cooked dinner from upstairs made me reconsider. "What is it?"

"Spaghetti and turkey meatballs."

"The ones with the breadcrumbs?"

"You know it, son."

I rolled my eyes.

"You and Ethan are only two years older than me." I hopped up from my desk chair and sucker swatted him in the stomach. "Race you upstairs!"

No, I didn't have gay dads. Although that would've been cool.

Greg, Ethan, and I had all gone to college together back in the day. Greg was my big brother in our fraternity, showing me the ropes of university life, and continuing to look out for me in the adult world. I'd done an absolute shit job of adulting in my twenties and was hoping to turn things around in this new decade.

They'd let me move into their basement so I could shore up my shitastic financial situation. And if living here rent-free meant I had to put up with their dad/son jokes, I could handle the good-natured ribbing.

Plus, these guys could cook.

The pull of the salty aroma of Greg's turkey meatballs was like a tractor beam yanking me into my seat at the dining table. Greg had remembered to buy fresh garlic bread, which meant I'd have something to clean my plate with this time.

I set the table while Greg and Ethan did their little dance in the kitchen, working in unison to make dinner. This was their thing, cooking together, and it illuminated how crazy in love they still were with each other. Greg gave Ethan a little pinch on his ass; Ethan held out the wooden spoon for Greg to taste. It was all a bit nauseating, but ultimately very adorable.

In college, they came from different worlds. Ethan was a strait-laced academic, Greg was all about frat life. But they'd found each other and made it work.

Their relationship almost gave me hope that I could find a love like theirs.

Almost.

"This is incredible," I moaned when the first forkful of food hit my tongue. Who needed love and sex when I could have two gay guys cook for me on the regular?

"I added a little more basil this time," Ethan said, taking his cooking as seriously as his casework for his big, fancy law firm. He was still in his dress shirt with rolled-up sleeves, his dirty blond hair combed in neat waves.

"Yeah, you did." I spun a thick glob of spaghetti on my fork. I knew how to eat like an adult, but perhaps all their jokes were making me revert to my teen self.

"How was school today, Shay?" Greg asked. "Were the kids nice to you?"

"Ha," I deadpanned. "Let's see. One of my students found a

Reddit thread of sexual idioms in Spanish that he decided to share with the class."

Having my students ask each other to *mojar el churro* (wet the doughnut) right as Principal Aguilar, who spoke Spanish, walked by was something I wouldn't likely forget. Fortunately, he wasn't up on Spanish slang because he asked if we were having churros and if he could have one. My life and teaching career had flashed before my eyes.

"I won't be including that in my next BlingBling video."

"Do we actually get to see a sneak peek of the next Mr. Shamwow video?"

"It's Mr. Shablahblah."

"I should've trademarked that name when I gave it to you in college." Greg turned to his husband. "If Seamus becomes a mega-famous and wealthy BlingBling influencer, do I have any legal claim to his fortune?"

"Well, that depends. Is there documentation of you giving him this nickname?" Ethan fought sarcasm with cold, hard legal facts.

"We'll have to look at our old videos." Greg darted his eyes left and right. I had the same thought. We shuddered to think what shit we might find from old party and frathouse footage. "Or not."

"Yeah, or not." I gulped down my water.

"I don't want to know," Ethan said.

"I was a lost man before I met you." Greg went full sappy Hallmark card, kissing his husband's hand.

"Please." Ethan rolled his eyes, but his blushing cheeks said otherwise.

It was still strange to see Greg with his husband. In college, Greg was known for getting with lots of chicks. He was proud of his manwhore status. Then one day, he told the frat he was dating this nerdy, kinda uptight guy. It was like a lightswitch had been flipped, and he was gay. Of all the people who I'd suspected might bat for the other team, Greg had been at the bottom of the list.

Greg pulled off the crispy end of the garlic bread. "So what's your next video about?"

"It's about the random things my students are obsessed with touching in class. Books on shelves, the corner of my desk, hitting the top of the door when they leave class."

"That's...accurate." Greg taught in middle school, a hell I never wanted to subject myself to. He was able to gain their respect and get on their level, though. His charm knew no bounds. "My students don't like to read books, but they love touching them. Is it the same thinking behind dogs peeing to mark their territory?"

"Maybe, maybe. I just report on what I see," I said with all the seriousness of a news journalist.

"That one about touching the doorframe is really spot on. I never realized it, but yeah, most of my guy students love jumping up and trying to touch it. I'm secretly rooting for them."

"The junior associates in my office do it, too," Ethan said.

"Jules gave me that idea."

"She's a keeper," Greg said.

"She's a he. Jules is Julian." I felt myself blush a little, for some unknown reason.

"Oh. Huh. The way you talk about him, he sounded like a girl you were into." Greg wiped garlic bread across his plate.

"What?" Okay, now I was blushing *a lot*. "What are you guys talking about?"

"You're always like 'Jules this' and 'Jules that.' 'Jules had this great idea' or 'Jules helped me with that.' I can deduce that you spend a lot of time together." Ethan's crazy memory and lawyering skills were not to be fucked with. I pitied all opposing counsel.

"That's because our classrooms are across the hall from each other. We both teach foreign languages."

"Helping each other learn a new tongue?" Greg cocked a giddy eyebrow.

I didn't know why the back of my neck was suddenly hot...and why Greg's joke about tongue made my mind go to an interesting place for a second. I flipped him the bird.

"Son, what did we tell you about flipping off your parents?"

I flipped him off with both hands.

"Ethan, can you send your husband to the doghouse?" I got up for seconds, grateful the kitchen wall could provide some separation.

Jules was a good friend who helped me find my way at South Rock. Maybe I did talk about him in the same way I might have talked about a crush, but only because he was an interesting person that I enjoyed being around. I wouldn't let Greg corrupt our friendship.

"Just because you're gay doesn't mean everyone's gay," I said when I returned.

"Don't be homophobic." Greg sucker swatted me in the gut.

"Don't be heterophobic." I smacked him back.

"Heterophobic isn't a word, dipshit." He smacked me again in the gut, making me double over. So much for being older and more mature.

"Is this how you discipline your students?"

"No, just underclassmen who step out of line."

Some things never changed.

"Hey!" Ethan jumped between us. "Can we try to remember that we're adults? Hands to ourselves."

Greg and I got back in our seats. He was smiling and having fun. And I should have been, too. Why did his joking about Julian strike a nerve with me?

"Just for that, you both can clean up."

AFTER DINNER, I manned the sink while Greg loaded the dishwasher. Ethan was adamant that we clean off and pre-wash all dishes before loading. Something about extending the life of a dishwasher.

"I was kidding back there. You know that, right?" Greg was good at picking up on when something really affected me.

"I guess." I didn't fully believe him.

"I feel like all you do is teach, coach, work your second job, eat, and sleep."

My second job wasn't that taxing. I did data entry for a real estate office in town, helping them digitize their files. It was easy to zone out after a long day at school. But I got what he was hinting at.

"You can make room for someone else," he said, the hint becoming more pointed.

A girlfriend.

"I'm not focusing on that right now." I let my hands soak in the warm, soapy water. "I have bigger fish to fry."

"How's it going with the debt?"

My jaw tightened. "It's going."

"Look, I wanted to bring up what I said in the past. The offer still stands. Ethan and I can give you a loan."

I shook my head in a firm no. They'd already been incredibly generous allowing me to stay here rent-free. I wouldn't let them help with anything else.

"This is my mess. I will handle it." I handed him a fresh plate.

"It's not mess, Shay. You had an addiction, and now you have it under control."

"Addictions are for mind-altering substances like drugs and alcohol. Not for dumb twenty-five-year-olds who can't stop playing online poker."

"Actually, numb nuts, there's a word for it. Gambling addiction. Are you still attending meetings?"

I nodded yes. Another embarrassing point. I went to a local church once a week for GA meetings, where we shared and shared about what we'd done wrong, never letting me forget it. Not like I would.

"Good. I'm proud of you. Seriously, I am. You had a problem, but you're getting help and working to make it right."

"I have a long way to go before that happens." A wave of shame washed over me like it regularly did.

"In the meantime, you can open yourself up to the possibility of a lovely girl coming into your life."

"No. Hard no." I threw down the sponge. "Greg, do you realize what I did? Not only did I blow my savings and dig myself into credit card debt, I ruined Lauren's life."

"You didn't ruin her life."

"I didn't? How would you feel if you were engaged to Ethan, and then he convinced you to combine finances, then wiped out most of a modest inheritance you received from a dear aunt?"

Greg stiffened. No charming response on that one.

It had been two years ago, but I still felt like a fresh piece of shit for what I did. Lots of young guys played online poker; why did I have to be the one who let it ruin their life? I'd been so sucked into the online gambling world, so utterly convinced one big play could turn things around, that I'd nearly decimated the savings of the girl I loved.

I was doing this for us! To give you the life you deserved! I'd had the nerve to tell her.

We didn't talk anymore, only to make sure I continued to pay her back on an agreed-upon schedule. I hated myself for what I'd done, for how I'd let myself completely lose control.

"I don't want to date, Greg. I'm damaged goods."

"You're not." His comforting hand on my shoulder couldn't change my mind.

"A part of me hopes that my BlingBling can take off, so that I can start getting sponsorships and be able to pay her back sooner."

I wanted all this guilt and shame off me, but deep down, I knew it'd never go away.

"You're going to burn out if all you do is work."

"It's what I deserve."

"Shay. Come on, man. You went through a bad period. That doesn't mean you're damaged goods. That doesn't mean you don't deserve to be with someone."

Greg could be so convincing. Look no further than the shit he'd had me do in college. But I couldn't ride with him on this one.

I'd hurt someone I cared about. I wasn't going to risk that again.

4

JULIAN

On top of having to teach a subject I had no business teaching, I was late on my first day as substitute health teacher. The power imbalance swung hard to the students.

I entered the classroom to find all of my students seated, chatting amongst themselves and checking their phones. All heads looked up at me, twenty-four sets of judging eyes.

"It's a good thing they don't give detention to teachers for being tardy," I said and flopped my bag on the desk.

Mrs. Stockman hadn't updated her lesson plans in Cyllabus. Was I the only teacher in this school who had? I'd tried texting her to get a sense of where she was in the curriculum, but she'd never responded. She was taking her sick leave *very* seriously.

I recognized a few students from my French classes, but it didn't hold back the wave of embarrassment cresting in my gut.

"Welcome to health!" I said, which only made things more awkward. "Or should I say, thank you for welcoming me. Because Mrs. Stockman is recuperating, I'm pitching in for the next few weeks. I'm Mr. Bradford. I usually teach French, so should I say bonjour?"

I didn't know why I turned to making jokes when I was nervous. Funny wasn't my forte. My poor comedic timing had the effect of tossing buckets of blood into shark-infested waters.

"Does anyone know where she left off? Unfortunately, I haven't been able to get ahold of her lesson plans yet."

Avery, one of my top French students, raised her hand, an ally in the mist. "We were about to start our lesson on contraceptives."

She blushed a little, and I thought of one of Seamus's videos where he described how students raise their hands. Avery was doing the nervous, I-hate-that-everyone-is-looking-at-me raise.

"Thank you." I flipped open the textbook to the contraceptives lesson. Diagrams of condoms and birth control filled the page.

"She was supposed to show us how to put a condom on," said a kid in the front row who had the swagger of someone meant for the back row. My suspicion was that Stockman made the kids sit alphabetically. His dark, judgmental eyes narrowed at me with that menacing grin that was eerily common with teenage boys.

"Okay," I said. "Condoms. Condoms are good."

Woof. I was off to a fantastic start.

"Does anyone know where she kept her condoms?"

"The nightstand, probably," said the Front Row Menace to murmured laughs. He held a hand behind him for the guy in back to high-five.

"Well, since there is no nightstand here, my guess is she kept them in her desk." I searched the drawers, trying not to be frantic. I pulled open the bottom drawer and my heart officially stopped.

I found a box of condoms. An extra-large, overflowing box of condoms. And what could only be described as a school-approved sex toy. A dildo attached to a stand.

I'd never owned a box of condoms or a sex toy. I was in deeply uncharted waters.

The dildo felt weird in my hand. Did other dicks feel this

thick? It was real enough to make my virginness seep through my pores.

I plunked it on the desk, which elicited unavoidable gasps and murmurs from the students. But I was in control here. I was the teacher. I knew more. I was certified in health. Were they?

Perhaps those health certification courses were further in the past than I thought, or maybe I had missed the lesson on prophylactics, because I suddenly drew a big blank.

"Today, we're going to learn about proper forms of contraceptives, which can protect against unwanted pregnancy and STIs. The easiest form of contraceptive is the condom. Whereas female contraceptives can be complicated with medication and intrusive devices that have to be implanted, the condom is simple to put on and is incredibly effective against unwanted pregnancy and disease transmission. It stops the sperm from entering your partner."

A flash of embarrassment hit me as I said sperm, even though it was the technical term. We were all little kids at heart when it came to sex. I blamed our Puritan ancestors.

"Guys, this is a no-brainer. Wear a condom." I held the packet up for all to see.

Then I looked down at the demonstration dick staring up at me, waiting to be sheathed.

"So, I suppose Mrs. Stockman was going to demonstrate how to put this on?" I asked, my eyes cutting to Avery for support.

She nodded yes.

"Putting on a condom correctly is important to it functioning properly. If the condom breaks, then it's useless."

I was holding a condom. Was my hand shaking? I looked at the circular piece of rubber, I realized that in addition to never owning a box of condoms, I'd never put one on. Not even out of curiosity. Mrs. Stockman had been teaching this class for years. She could probably roll it on in her sleep.

"Okay, well the next step is for me to demonstrate, to ensure that you're doing this correctly."

"I always do it correctly," said the Front Row Menace with a sneering chuckle. I couldn't be mad at him. I was too relieved that he actually used condoms.

"That's great that you care so much about safe sex!" I said earnestly, yet my students thought I was joking. He turned bright red.

The condom shook in my hand as I ripped open the packaging. I tried to roll it down the demo dick, because that was what condoms were supposed to do. They rolled. This condom did not roll.

"Sometimes they can get stuck." I exerted more force. "Some come pre-lubricated. Others don't. You should check before you buy. It's worth it to spend the extra money for lubrication."

The rubber of the condom made a high-pitched squeak against the plastic of the dick. Every guy in the class clamped their legs together.

"Oops." I let out a nervous laugh. "Technical difficulties."

"What about leaving some space at the tip?" Front Row Menace watched on, amused.

"Some...space."

"Yeah. When you blow, you need somewhere for it to go," he said to guffaws from his classmates.

"The proper term is ejaculate," I said.

The condom was pushed flush against the head of the demo dick, wrapping it tight like a sausage.

"Right. Yes. You should leave some space at the top for collection," I said, pulling up the condom slightly. I continued to try and push the rest of it down, causing another squeak of rubber on plastic.

"I think the plastic of the model is causing some issues." I grabbed the sides of the condom and pulled down as hard as I could.

It split in two. Pieces tumbled down the shaft like a sad, deflated balloon.

"I think we all just got pregnant," Front Row Menace deadpanned.

"That's why..." I started, but the laughter and murmurs were drowning me out. "Excuse me," I said, finding my teacher voice. Being a teacher meant living in a constant power struggle that you could never relinquish. "That's why you always want to make sure you have extra condoms. If the first one breaks, you want to have back ups."

I ripped open another condom and this time, made sure to leave space at the top. I wrapped my fist around the shaft and tried pulling the condom down again. Again, it got stuck. More laughter came from the students, and when I followed their eyes, I discovered my fist was twisting and moving up and down to hold the model steady.

I was jerking off the demo dick.

I yanked my fist away. I could feel the red take over my face.

"Do you two need a room?" asked the guy behind Front Row Menace, who then held his hand up. Without turning around, Front Row Menace gave him a high-five.

How did guys put these on so easily? How did they stay hard while figuring out how to put these on? Maybe they didn't and this was why unplanned pregnancies happened. Guys just gave up.

Front Row Menace hopped up and joined me behind the desk. "Mr. Bradford, let me help you out."

I thought this was going to lead to some devastating prank, but Front Row Menace refused to live up to his nickname. He grabbed a condom packet, ripped it open, applied the condom to the dick, and rolled it down with such delicate ease I thought I was watching Picasso paint a masterpiece.

"Getting over the head is the tricky part. Fellas, you gotta fight through the weirdness. Then you roll it down," he said.

"Thanks?" I said, equal parts humiliated and gobsmacked.

"I'm not used to working with regular condoms. I only use magnums." He dusted imaginary dirt off his shoulder. "There you go." He pointed to his creation, a perfectly sheathed dick. "We are ready to smash."

The class gave him a smattering of applause as he took his seat. I stared at the demo dick, and from this angle, it looked like a sheathed middle finger.

5

JULIAN

It took no time for word to spread that Mr. Bradford didn't know how to put on a condom. As I walked through the halls, I got thumbs-up and laughs and "Better luck next time" from students. I was back in high school—the worst parts of high school.

Rather than eating my lunch in the teachers lounge and facing their comments, I escaped to the roof. There was a section with old benches. Decades ago, it had been a smokers lounge for students and teachers. I pictured teachers bumming cigarettes off students, and students providing lighters to teachers. The '60s were wild.

It was the first days of March and the last weeks of winter. Spring was around the corner and would make an appearance every so often like it did today. A balmy breeze swept across the roof. The mountains stretched in the distance, framing the Hudson River and the downtown cluster of businesses. I'd grown up not too far from here and always loved coming to Sourwood. It had more going on than the average suburb. It had preserved that quaint small-town feeling.

"Found him!" I heard behind me.

Amos stood at the heavy door, yelling into the stairwell. Everett and Chase soon followed. As much as I wanted some solitude, I'd never turn down hanging out with my friends. We forged a bond thicker than the layers of cigarette smoke that had once clogged this roof.

"I hope you don't mind some company for your brooding," Everett said. As South Rock's drama teacher, his personality was as fiery as his red hair. He was a fan of barbs and wasn't afraid to use them. I admired how direct he could be.

"What are you guys doing here? Don't you have class?" I asked, making room for Amos and Everett on the bench. Chase had hidden a bleacher cushion up here and sat on the ground.

"We wanted to check on you. We heard about your first health class," Amos said, biting his lip. "Apparently, it didn't go so smoothly."

"Perhaps using some lubricant next time would help that," Chase said, pushing his thick black glasses up his nose.

I buried my face in my hands. "It was a disaster."

"If it makes you feel better, I suck at putting on condoms, too." Amos rubbed my back.

"Not to brag, but I'm quite good. I can put them on guys with my mouth," Everett said, sitting up a little taller. "Well, not anymore. That's one of the benefits of having a serious boyfriend. No more contraceptives."

Recently, Everett and Amos had both begun dating fellow South Rock gym teachers. In a perfect, not-at-all realistic world, I could one day join them with Seamus. I shook that fantasy out of my head because it would make today feel even worse.

"Thanks for rubbing it in," I said with a wry smile. While I wanted what they had, I was happy for them, not jealous. I loved seeing my friends having it all.

Amos put a hand on my knee. "How are you feeling?"

"Is everyone in school talking about it?"

"Pretty much," Everett said. "I even heard some freshmen laughing about it."

I looked around the roof and wondered if I could live here permanently.

"I can't believe that happened." I rubbed a hand over my eyes. That class was going to be one of those moments that I thought about randomly at three a.m. twenty years from now.

"You taught those students a valuable lesson: sex is an inherently awkward experience," Amos said. "Like, I seriously don't know how our species survived this long knowing how awkward sex can be."

"I blame straight men. They have no shame." Everett shrugged.

"We've all had awkward sexual experiences. Hell, I climbed a tree, almost fell to my death, and tried to justify using expired condoms to have sex with Hutch," Amos said.

"And I once squeezed a bottle of lube too hard and hit Raleigh in the eye," Everett added. "We almost had to go to the emergency room."

"I also have an embarrassing story that takes place during sexual activity." Chase raised his hand.

"Yes, Chase?" Everett called on him. Force of habit.

"When I was in college, a guy was doing a terrible job at oral sex in my dorm room. On my wall was a poster of the periodic table. I shut my eyes and tried to list off all the elements by memory to distract myself. When I got stuck on tungsten, I came, and he started choking because I didn't give warning. Ironically, that night was anything but a W." Chase fixed his glasses and chuckled to himself. "Get it? Because W is the symbol for tungsten." He laughed harder, fully embracing that he'd cracked himself up with a chemistry joke.

Amos and Everett started laughing, too, though for a different reason.

"Chase..." Everett messed a hand through Chase's hair. "Never change, buddy. Never change."

I feigned a smile, but I couldn't join in the laughter. Chase was a total science nerd who made periodic table jokes, and *he'd* been with multiple guys. They all had stories. Awkward stories, sure. But they were stories. They were experiences. It was as if I was stuck waiting outside a club I'd never be cool enough to enter.

"What about you, J?" Amos asked.

But they didn't know that. So the lie had to continue.

"Me? Well, I don't have anything as crazy as a periodic table blow job, but..." I scrambled for an anecdote. Something, anything that could be spun. "Actually, I think all of my experiences have been pretty tame by comparison. I can't think of anything off the top of my head."

"Consider yourself lucky," Everett said.

"It makes sense. You're the classiest one of us. You're the real gentleman. You never kiss and tell," Amos said, something I was sure he meant as a compliment, but which made my stomach turn all the same.

I didn't kiss and tell because there was never anything to tell. I hated having this secret among my friends. Like all lies, it had started small and innocuous. They assumed I'd been intimate with guys, and I didn't correct their assumptions. I didn't want to be the odd man out. During our first New Year's Eve together, we'd got drunk on champagne and shared the story of our first time. This was one of those nights when friendships solidified from *work friends* to *bonded for life*. Even in the moment, I could tell that memories were being made.

I hadn't wanted to ruin that. I wasn't someone who made friends easily. If I'd told the truth about being a virgin, it could have been a record scratch stop on the night, a wall shoved between newly bonded friends.

When it came to me, I'd spun a tale about a guy in my English Lit class who I'd bumped into at a party and yadda yadda yadda sex in his twin bed. Even though they bought it, I felt embarrassed, a total fraud who blatantly lied to his friends. I wished I could take it back, but that would make things even weirder. I had wound up erecting a wall myself.

From then on, I kept mum about sexual escapades, preferring to be the gentleman they all thought I was. The French thing helped.

"Did you want to hang out tonight? We can start watching that show about the missing woman who was probably killed by her boyfriend," Amos said.

"Actually, I have a date."

"Oh?" Amos asked. "Why didn't you lead with this?"

"It's just a first date. I've been on lots of those. We've been chatting on Milkman. We're going to meet for a drink."

"Where? Stone's Throw? Remix?" Everett asked.

"I'm not telling you. You'd probably show up."

"Oh Julian. Of course I would."

"He's cute. He's a police officer."

"That means he has handcuffs!" Everett blurted out.

"There are some police precincts that don't use handcuffs anymore as cuffs can escalate altercations that don't need to be escalated." Who needed the internet when we had Chase?

"God, think of the role-playing," Amos added, gazing out into the ether. "Can we see a picture?"

I felt myself beaming as I handed over my phone to show off his Milkman profile. I'd been trying to downplay it to myself, but we'd been messaging the past few days. He was funny and very flirty. Maybe finding a guy out there wasn't as difficult as I was making it out to be.

The three of them huddled around the phone and oohed and aahed as if I were showing off an engagement ring. They dutifully scrolled through his pictures and read his profile. I stared at them, as if I were an Olympic athlete waiting for my scores.

Their reactions were tens across the board.

"He's cute!" Amos said.

"And judging by the dense proliferation of winking emoji and ellipses in your messaging, there's a strong probability that he intends to jump your bones," Chase said, handing back my phone. "I recommend you sharpen up your condom application skills."

"Thank you, Chase." As I reached for my phone, a notification popped up. My three friends, nosy as could be, looked at my screen.

"Mr. Shablahblah has posted a new video," Amos said. "Hmm. Interesting."

"You have notifications set up when Mr. Shablahblah posts new videos?" Everett asked. "That's *very* interesting."

"What? You guys don't have notifications on your phone? When I downloaded the app, I forgot to uncheck the box for notifications." I shoved my phone into my pocket.

"I would take a guess and say you only have notifications set up for Mr. Shablahblah. That's *very, very* interesting." Amos was way too pleased with himself.

I loved my friends, but I also hated them, in a loving kind of way.

"Fine. I have notifications whenever Seamus posts. Big deal."

"I'm excited for this date tonight. Hopefully, this cop can get you to end your crush on Seamus once and for all," Amos said.

"I don't have a crush."

"J, you do so much pining for this guy you could repopulate a forest," Everett said.

I made a production out of stopping notifications for his videos for my audience to see. "Shouldn't you guys be in class?"

Everett waved off my concern. "I put on the Leo version of *Romeo plus Juliet*. They're fine."

I MET Erik at a wine bar on the edge of town. Like most suburban haunts, it was located in a strip mall, but this bar had a gorgeous outdoor patio in the back decorated with trellises and candlelight and a cellist playing in the corner. It was a perfect first date spot.

I walked onto the patio and found Erik on his phone at a corner table. He'd already gone ahead and ordered us two glasses of red wine, since I'd said in our messaging that I preferred red over white.

He was hot. Really hot. A big, muscular guy wearing a button-down shirt one size too small, which accentuated his arms. Amos was right. I couldn't wait to role play with him.

This was it. We were going to have a great date, go back to my place, then do all the sex, banishing my virginity to the depths of hell.

As soon as Erik looked up and saw me, something in the air changed. I couldn't place it, but his face went from excited to something more reserved. I chalked it up to nerves.

"Erik, right?" I held out my hand. "Julian."

"Hey." He remained seated and gave my hand a halfhearted shake. I'd expected a tighter grip, but perhaps he didn't want to crush me.

"Hi. When did you get here?" I asked, sitting down.

"Few minutes ago." He typed something on his phone. Did cops have to answer a lot of emails for their job?

"Cool. Usually, I try to arrive early, too. You know, if you're not ten minutes early, you're late. Which is a good lesson to abide by. I can't tell you how many of my students waltz in late to class."

"Yeah. Huh." He flicked his eyes to me for a second, then back to his phone. I hadn't dated a ton, and I knew we were all addicted to our phones, but this felt...off. And rude.

"Thank you for ordering for me!" I took a sip of the wine. It was exactly what I wanted. Crisp and dry. Point for Erik. "This is fantastic. I love a good red."

"Yeah. It's good," he said, yet by the volume in his glass, I had the feeling he hadn't tried it at all.

"How is life on the force?" I asked, hoping to find a way to break his attention from his phone.

"It's good." He looked at me, gave me a discerning stare, then back to his phone. "I can't really talk about it, though."

"Yeah. I get that. Um, is everything okay?"

"What?"

"You're just on your phone. A lot. In the middle of a date. Technically, the beginning of one." I summoned the directness of Everett, who would've called this out instantly.

"Sorry. My mom, she had to go to the hospital today. She collapsed. So I'm checking in with my family. They're keeping me updated."

"I'm so sorry! Is she okay?"

"That's what I'm trying to find out," he said sharply. "It all happened so fast."

"I'm really sorry." I had no idea what else to say. The date ground to a halt before even leaving the station.

A sense of urgency hit me. This woman could be my future mother-in-law.

"Do they know why she collapsed?"

"Don't know. Maybe we should reschedule this date."

"Okay. Of course. You need to be with your family." I flagged down the waiter for the check. Worry seized me. This could happen to any of us. I was going to call my parents as soon as I got to my car.

The waiter put the check in the middle of the table. Erik and I both reached for it at the same time (cute), and when he did, his phone tipped out of his free hand, showing the unmistakable interface of a Milkman chat window.

"You're on Milkman right now?"

"What? Uh, no."

I grabbed the phone from his hand, my heart turning colder as I scrolled. "You're messaging with guys to meet up later while you're on a date with me?"

Erik took his phone back.

"I take it your mother is just fine."

"I don't think this is going to work out."

What an understatement. A few seconds ago, I was worried about my potential mother-in-law; now I was reeling with anger.

"Why?" I asked, my insides turning to ice. "Just tell me why. You were flirty and interested in our messages. You were the one who wanted to meet up."

"I didn't feel a spark."

"I sat down a minute ago."

His face hardened. "You don't look like you do in your pictures. I'm into muscular guys, and you looked kinda buff in your pictures. But I guess that was just the angle."

I knew what picture he was referring to. I was at a barbeque, and by the way I was turned and the tightness of my shirt sleeves, the angle hid my stomach, flattened my chest, and accentuated my arms. It was an optical illusion that I shamefully embraced.

"You deceived me," he said.

"I didn't deceive you."

"I said what I was and wasn't looking for in my profile."

"No fatties," I grumbled.

"I take fitness very seriously. Look, let's not waste each other's time."

"Right," I said, my jaw tight.

When I stood up, I hit the table with my knee, tipping over both of our wine glasses onto his lap. It was petty, but at least I could smile once on this god-awful date.

"Thanks for the wine."

6

SEAMUS

After another long day, I drove home in my usual daze, zoning out to some Maroon 5 song on the radio. They all kinda blended together, didn't they? I'd stayed late after school first to help a student who struggled on his latest test, then to work on more videos. Social media was a gremlin that had to constantly be fed.

I detoured through some of the more scenic areas with upscale stores and bougie developments. Maybe one day I could live in a place like this. The trees were sprinkled with buds, their exposed branches twisting up to the sky.

Everything in this part of town was neat and proper. No grass or shrubs out of place. Trees lined both sides of the road in perfect symmetry. Except tonight, there was a curious exception: a guy sat on the curb, very out of place. This wasn't a neighborhood where people sat on curbs.

As I got closer, I had to wonder if I was seeing things because there was no way that could be Julian.

His flowing brown hair and sweet face were unmistakable.

I stopped and rolled down my window. "Jules?"

Shock registered in his eyes as if I'd caught him in the shower or something. "Seamus? What are you doing here?"

"I was about to ask you the same thing. I decided to take the scenic route. Did your car break down?"

"No. I live down the street. I was taking a walk."

Julian lived around here? Not that any teacher was loaded, but I knew he was comfortable. He was an immaculate dresser and enjoyed the finer things in life. He was the guy who spent more than five bucks on a bottle of wine and like, did the thing where he sloshed it around in his glass and smelled the bouquet.

"Did you injure yourself?"

"No. I just needed to sit down."

I glanced down at his dress shoes. Definitely not ones suitable for walking. Nor was his blazer and shirt combo, although he looked snazzy.

Something was off about this whole thing, and my concern grew.

I put the car in park and joined him on the curb. I squatted down to his eye level.

"Jules, you're sitting on the sidewalk at night in fancy-ass clothes. What's going on?"

Julian turned to me with his warm brown eyes, the kind of eyes that could break your heart without saying a word.

"I had a bad night."

"What happened? Are you hurt?" I put a protective hand on his shoulder.

"Just my pride." He tossed a pebble into the street. "I had a bad date. A really bad date."

"Eh, we all have shitty dates. Did the guy chew with his mouth open?"

"He said he couldn't stand to be near me because I was too fat. He was on his phone messaging other guys during our date."

What. The. Fuck.

A surge of anger lit me up. I was not a man prone to violence. I was a lover, not a fighter. But I wanted to track this asshole down and pound his face in.

"What a fucking piece of shit!"

Julian's eyebrows rose at my reaction.

"Jules, you're not fat."

"This," he motioned to his chest and stomach. "begs to differ."

"Well, *I* beg to differ. You look good."

"You're just saying that."

"Am not."

He turned to me, only half-amused. "You're straight, Seamus. Your opinion comes with an asterisk."

"I mean it. You're a good-looking guy." Fuck asterisks. I gave him a once-over and stood by my assessment: Julian was attractive. Yes, he was on the bigger side, but that made him cuddlier. Who wanted to cuddle with a skinny person? Their shoulder blades could poke your eye out. "If I were gay, I would totally stick it in you."

We burst into laughter. It was good to see him smile again. He had a great smile, which in my book, was a more valuable asset than all the abs in the world.

"How romantic. Have you thought about writing Hallmark cards?"

"I'm too busy making stupid videos." I believed that if you could make someone laugh, then all was not lost. I still wanted to find that date and whoop his ass, though.

"Things are different in the gay world," he said. "Guys only care about how jacked you are. The more you can look like Captain America or Thor, the better."

"Have you read about what those guys had to go through to look like Captain America and Thor? The grueling workouts that nearly destroyed their bodies and minds? The diets where they were only allowed to eat boiled chicken and steamed broccoli?"

I shuddered at the thought of ever having to get into superhero shape. I would forever be a scrawny kid at heart, and I was okay with that. While I'd put on muscle as an adult, I was still on the slim side. That was just genetics at play. I wasn't going to mess with supplements and excessive workouts to change that. I watched student athletes obsess in front of the mirror after workouts, and it broke my heart a little.

"Maybe I should try that," Julian said.

"No!" I knocked him with my elbow. "Please don't. There's no guy out there worth a diet of boiled chicken and steamed broccoli."

Julian nodded that he understood, but it was one of those bullshit nods that my students gave me when I asked if something made sense. I hated seeing my friend crushed like this. Julian had so many wonderful qualities. He was so fucking intelligent and kind. Who cared what the scale said?

I rubbed his back. "You know what I like to do when I want to work through a shitty day?"

"What?"

"Drink."

A LITTLE BIT LATER, we found ourselves in Stone's Throw Tavern, Sourwood's local watering hole, kicking back beers.

"Hmm," he said, his face twisting as he gulped down another Bud Light. It reminded me of being a kid and having to take a spoonful of cough syrup. "I usually don't drink beer. I'm more of a wine drinker."

"But some things are better suited for beer."

In other words, it was easier to chug beer than wine.

"I don't want to think about wine," he said, pounding down

another beer. "I met my date at a wine bar. It's my favorite wine bar in town, and he's now ruined it for me."

"Fuck him," I yelled, letting my New York accent really come out.

"I spilled wine on him." He rubbed an embarrassed hand through his hair. "It was not my best moment."

"He deserved it."

"I technically assaulted a police officer." He laughed and burped at the same time. It was adorably sloppy, his refined exterior slowly slipping off. "Nobody told me dating would be this hard. I thought since we're all out and open nowadays, it would be easier. Closeted men a hundred years ago probably got more play than me." He chugged the remaining third of his beer. "Can I have another one of these?"

I signaled the waitress and through hand gestures ordered another round.

"Jules, don't be so hard on yourself. You have a lot going for you."

"Like what?"

"You're a great teacher. You have a great group of friends. I see you fuckers cracking each other up in the bleachers at assemblies." Julian's friends had the buzzy energy of guys enjoying one long-running inside joke. They were always fun to be around.

"And not just that. You have your shit together more than anyone else I know," I said. "You're acing this adulting thing."

Unlike me, whose life was a semi-disaster. The only thing I was good at was hiding the mess.

He shrugged. "I don't really know what I'm doing."

"It's better than most of us. I'm still hoping some of your togetherness can rub off on me. Seriously, I never would've survived teaching without your help. You're an awesome guy, Jules."

"Then how come no one will sleep with me?" His eyes bulged, like he knew he'd crossed some line.

The waitress brought a fresh round. He scooped up his bottle and took a big swig.

"That's not true."

"It is. Excuse me." He burped into his sleeve. "If you were gay, would you have sex with me?"

Jules sure had the asking-awkward-questions-directly part of being drunk down pat. An explicit image of the two of us in bed popped into my head...and I didn't hate it.

"Of course I would. You've got it going on, Jules." I gave him another look, and you know what? I probably would.

"Can I tell you a secret?" He motioned for me to come closer. "I'm a virgin."

"Wait. What? Seriously?"

He nodded so hard his head was going to detach.

"I'm turning thirty-five in a month, and I still have my hymen intact. Do guys' butts have hymens? Well, my metaphorical hymen."

I couldn't resist laughing. The man was trashed yet still had the wherewithal to say shit like *metaphorical hymen*. Julian didn't realize how hilarious he could be.

"It's not funny!"

"I'm not laughing at you. I promise. So when you say you're still a virgin, does that just mean sex?"

"It means everything. Seamus, I've never even touched another man's...you know."

I held in my surprise. No wonder Julian had no idea how to put on a condom, according to the rumors flying through school.

"You've probably gotten further than me during a fraternity initiation."

"That's a big-ass nope. Shutting that thought down." There'd been a frat brother who loved walking around naked, but that was the extent of the homoeroticism. When it came to man-on-man stuff, I was as much a virgin as Julian.

"My students have gotten further than me."

"Who cares? It's not a race. Fuck what other people think. And if any of our students are having sex, I guarantee you it's lousy and unmemorable."

He hung his head. "You can't tell a soul. I haven't even told my friends. I've been lying to them. I've been lying to them for years. What kind of friend maintains a long-term lie?"

I put my hand over his to keep him from spiraling. "Hey, hey. Jules." I made him look me in the eye. Behind the drunken exterior, my wounded friend was still there. "It's okay. Whatever you've done or haven't done is up to you. It's nobody's business. When you find the right guy, it'll all happen."

"But I've been looking for the right guy for years, and..." Julian overdramatically looks to his left and right and up at the ceiling. "I can't find him. I don't want to be a thirty-five-year-old virgin. I have a month to ditch the hymen. No, I have..." He did the math on his fingers. "Twenty-six days."

"You can do it. You're a driven person. Look how you were able to learn Cyllabus."

My joke was met with a thundering thud.

"The thing is, if I wanted to, I could ditch my hymen like that." He snapped his fingers. "There are guys online who want to have anonymous sex with strangers. There are even guys who post their address online and say that they'll be bent over and ready for any stranger to have a go at it. Which, you do you, no judgment here, but that's not what I want my first time to be like. What if it's a rainy night and these strangers don't take off their shoes and they track mud into my apartment? I have this light beige carpet. It picks up everything."

I snorted. My beer almost shot out my nose.

Julian sighed and peeled the label off his beer bottle. "I've waited this long. I want my first time to be with someone that I know and trust. Someone who doesn't see me as a piece of meat."

"So your plan was to find a boyfriend in the month leading up to your birthday and have him cash in your v-card?"

He nodded yes.

"But then what if you're dating someone for what? Like three weeks, and then you have sex, and then you break up? How will that be anymore memorable?"

"Um." He shrugged and a burp escaped his mouth. "I don't know."

"What if you start dating someone a week before your birthday? You're just going to have sex with him?"

"It'll be better than nothing."

Julian deserved better than better than nothing. If he wanted to lose his virginity to someone he trusted and someone who knew him, that wasn't going to happen with someone he met this month.

"I can help," I said.

Julian looked at me as if I were crazy, then laughed when he assumed I was. "Funny."

"I mean it."

The idea gained steam in my head...as did the explicit image from before. Julian had been such a good friend; it was time I repaid the favor and gave him a helping hand.

"Yeah. I'm serious. I'll help you check off those things before your birthday."

"Seamus, you're straight."

"But I'm also someone you know and trust. I'll make sure you have a good first time."

Julian cocked his head and continued to give me the crazy stare. "But...you're straight. Why would you want to have sex with another man?"

He had a point there. Watching my friend Greg turn from

ladies man to dudecentric had made me a bit bicurious. What would it be like to have the hard, hairy body of a man entwined with mine? What would it be like to have those big, brown eyes stare at me inflamed with lust?

But this wasn't about me, though. It was about being the right kind of friend and providing the right kind of friction. And if I happened to enjoy that friction, then so be it.

"Did you know I can bat righty and lefty? I'm right-handed, but I trained myself to bat left, too."

Julian, totally drunk, bless him, held up his hands in front of his face to better comprehend.

"This is a little more involved than swinging a bat."

I shrugged. Was it? Learning how to swing a bat correctly was a skill. Sex was something stupid people did all the time.

"It'll be kinda weird, but everyone's first time is always kinda weird. I'd rather you have it be weird with a friend than a stranger."

"And when you say sex, you mean..."

"All of it. Everything on your list. Let's run the bases."

Julian stared at his beer bottle, then at me. He wasn't trying to hide his confusion at all, which was adorable.

"Dude, I gotcha covered." I might've fucked up other areas of my life, but I still knew how to be a solid friend. I could help Julian gain more confidence while scratching my bicurious itch. Win-win.

"Sure." He grabbed his beer for a much-needed swig.

I clinked our bottles together. "That's what friends are for."

7

JULIAN

Was there such a thing as a conversation hangover?

The next morning, I was regular hungover. That wasn't in question. An anvil had lodged itself into my skull, clanging against the bone. I thought beer wasn't supposed to give people hangovers because they drank it all the time.

Oh, how wrong I was.

But...was I so drunk that I imagined Seamus offering to deflower me?

That's what friends are for.

Friends were for giving you a ride when your car broke down, not letting you ride *them*.

My brain ached from the alcohol and from wondering if that had happened. Seamus must've been even drunker than me, which meant he probably shouldn't have driven me home.

Oh God. If he'd offered to deflower me, that meant I'd told him I was a virgin. *Oh God.* He knew my deep, dark, terrible secret. He'd been supportive, but who the hell knew what he was thinking on the inside.

Speaking of mistakes, I'd forgotten to set my phone to silent last night. The ringing of an incoming call became a loud blare rattling my brain.

"Morning." I put the phone on speaker because I didn't have the energy to hold it up to my ear.

"Am I on speaker?" Grandma asked in her raspy voice.

"I'm getting ready for school," I said as I shuffled to the kitchen.

"Are you okay? You sound sick."

My grandmother didn't need to know that I was hungover on a Wednesday...and everything else that had happened last night.

"I haven't had my coffee yet."

"Don't drink too much coffee. It'll either make you piss like a racehorse or give you the runs like you've never experienced."

Grandma reveled in her role as saucy grandmother. She didn't have a filter and had no interest in one.

"I'll have an adequate amount." I measured out slightly less coffee than I usually make in the morning. "What's up?"

"Have you ever had to rent an outdoor tent for parties? I think I remember you doing that for school once."

"Yeah. When I used to be the adviser for South Rock's student council, we had to organize an end-of-year barbecue. I made us get a tent because the weather can be iffy in June." I hit start on the coffeemaker with a satisfied smile. "And I was right. It saved the day."

"Of course. You're so smart and organized, Julian. You definitely didn't get that from your mother. Or me, for that matter. Can you text me the company you used? I've been going back and forth with your mother about renting one for the party."

"Why are you involved in planning? I thought it was something Mom, Dad, and Uncle Dale were doing for you and Grandpa—the kids throwing their parents a fiftieth wedding anniversary party."

"Dale is on a Mediterranean cruise with his new boyfriend,

your father is tied up with work. and your mom...well, I love her to pieces, but it's a good thing she married your father."

I bit back a guffaw. Grandma and Mom got along fine on the surface, but the tension between mother- and daughter-in-law never fully went away. It wasn't the first dig on Mom that Grandma had made, and it wouldn't be the last.

"Remember when Grandpa and I were moving into our condo, and you all came over to help us pack?"

I laughed to myself. Mom had sat on the couch and directed my siblings and me. Despite not having lifted or packed anything, she'd claimed she was exhausted by the end.

"I remember."

"To make sure my anniversary party isn't a belly flop, I'm helping her out with planning. Don't be surprised if I reach out to you with more questions."

"Grandma, I'm happy to help however I can. Seriously, call me with anything."

My grandparents deserved a party for the ages. They were still healthy, together, and crazy about each other after half a century. Their unconditional love for all parts of me was a saving grace growing up, as I always felt like an outsider in my immediate family. I was the gay, nerdy fat kid in a family of straight athletes.

"I mean it. Call me with anything," I said in a raspy voice to match Grandma. I needed some kind of hydration. I poured myself a large glass of water.

"I'll make sure we have a birthday cake for you, too," she said.

"Don't worry about it."

"I'm not going to do to you what that family did to poor Molly Ringwood."

"Ringwald," I corrected.

My birthday was one day after their anniversary, so not an exact *Sixteen Candles* situation. Not like I had much to celebrate... unless Seamus was serious.

Was he serious?

He *couldn't* be serious.

"I gotta go, Grandma. I love you."

"You, too. Is your coffee ready yet? You sound like shit."

THE SCHOOL DAY WAS A BLUR. First, I got to South Rock exactly one minute before home room. Then, I had my French classes pair off for the period and practice conversational skills with each other while I sat at my desk in a daze.

It had to have been a drunken mistake.

Seamus.

Friend.

Crush.

Fuck buddy?

"Mr. Bradford, how long are we supposed to be doing this exercise?" asked Mikayla, my top student in third period, a girl who was already fluent in French thanks to her hot French Canadian dad and used this class as an easy A.

"I want you to practice having a long-form conversation in French. You'll all reach stumbling points, but you'll have to learn to get through them. Imagine you're in Paris. You can't have a conversation with someone while peeking at your textbook every three seconds. You have to go with it."

"Everyone in Paris speaks English," said Seth, a student who preferred to coast with a C-average.

I exhaled a breath, the anvil pushing harder against my head. "Then pretend you're in a quaint French village."

"They probably speak English, too, especially if they want that sweet American tourist cash," he said.

Sometimes, I really hated how smart my students were.

"I heard that teachers make students do activities like these when they're too hungover to teach." Mikayla narrowed her eyes at me with all the confidence of a teenager who believed they knew how the world worked.

In this case, she wasn't wrong. Even a broken clock was right twice a day.

"We don't have to do this exercise. I could give you all a pop quiz right here and now. Is that what you want?"

My students groaned, except for Mikayla, who was guaranteed to ace it.

I almost cried when I reached the coffee pot in the teachers' lounge. A teacher without coffee was a medical emergency.

I poured myself a large cup and sat with Chase in a pair of comfy arm chairs, or as comfy as furniture in a public school teachers' lounge got.

"Do you ever wonder why we don't call salt N-A-C-L?" he asked. His brain was working fine today. No anvils there. "I think it should be shorthand for salt, the way we call water H-2-O. 'Hey, pass me the N-A-C-L.' What do you think?"

I had zero opinion on this. I wanted to crawl back into bed.

"I, uh, like salt?"

"And why is H-2-O a nickname for water anyway? It has more syllables than water, and thus by definition defeats the purpose of being a nickname. It would be like Julian being a nickname for J."

"Yeah." My head pounded. I longed for an exit ramp off this conversation. "You're right."

As Chase launched into more examples of chemistry equations that should be colloquial sayings, Seamus entered the lounge. I slumped down in my chair, hoping the cushions swallowed me whole.

He greeted another teacher by the coffee machine. I peeked over my chair. Damn, he looked good. His polo clung against his chest, and his chinos framed his tight butt. He didn't have some gymrat body, but real ones knew what was under there.

What did he look like naked? Had he actually offered me the opportunity to find out?

"What do you think about that?" Chase asked.

I whipped my head back to him. "What?"

"Let's stop calling it carbon monoxide. Just call it C-O. It's cleaner. Like how Facebook dropped the *The*. 'Oh, we have to install a C-O detector.' I just saved you three syllables!" He slapped the chair arm.

Even hangover-free, I couldn't handle this conversation, not when Seamus was in the same room as me less than twenty-four hours after offering to deflower me.

Why was I using the word deflower? He offered to fuck me.

"Chase. I need coffee."

"You're drinking coffee."

"I need more." I peeked over my chair, but Seamus was still by the coffee machine, probably regaling Mrs. Rogalsky about how he discovered South Rock High employed a thirty-five-year-old gay man who'd never seen another cock up close.

I remained locked in my seat and poured the last drops of my drink into my mouth.

"Hello, gentlemen." Seamus's voice rattled behind me. I clenched my eyes shut.

"Seamus, it's a good thing you're here," said Chase. "The next time you need to borrow salt, say 'Pass me the N-A-C-L.' I want to start a movement."

"You got it, Chase."

I stared down at my empty coffee cup, even though Seamus's beautiful face was directly above me.

"Maybe in your honor, we should blast some N-A-C-L and Pepa," Seamus said. Bless him for playing along. He was always such a good sport.

"Yes! What's that song they sing again?"

Seamus sat on the arm of my chair and stared directly at me. It was inevitable to meet his eyes. "*Let's Talk About Sex*."

"That's it! Putting that on my Spotify playlist in three, two, one," Chase said as he pulled out his phone. "I need a refill. You want one, Julian?"

Seamus was still looking at me with his oceanic eyes, and I let myself get swept out to sea. "No. I think I'm good."

Chase went to the coffeemaker, leaving us alone.

"Here." Seamus handed over his coffee cup, sensing that I really needed it. "So..."

"So." I gulped down the coffee, hoping it washed away this awkward lump in my throat. "Was I super drunk last night or did we agree to..."

"Yes to both."

"Oh. Okay. Um, I was joking. You were joking, too. When people drink, they...joke." I tried giving him a not-so-smooth out.

"Jules, don't worry. Your secret is safe with me." He zipped his lips, lips that he'd offered to put on my body in the fog of beer. "How are you feeling?"

"Crappy on multiple levels."

"Hangover that bad?"

I leaned in. "Seamus, you were joking last night, right?"

"Nope."

"You're serious?"

"Yep."

"People who are serious don't use words like nope and yep."

Seamus's face brightened with a smile. "Jules, I meant what I said. I don't flake on a promise. Come over to my place tomorrow night for our first session."

"Session?" I shook my head in confusion.

"Yeah."

"Session implies this will be a multi-pronged process."

"It will be. We're going to run the bases. First base, second base, third base, home run. You haven't done any of those things, right?"

Blush permanently moved onto my face. "Correct."

"We'll check those off your list first, then end with a fireworks show, just like at Disney World."

Had he just compared his lovemaking skills to a fireworks extravaganza? A Disney fireworks extravaganza that spared no expense? The confidence on this man...

Yep, I was hard.

"Deal," I said, crossing my legs.

8

SEAMUS

"Guys, please don't embarrass me tonight."

"Us? Embarrass? Not possible," Ethan said. "We just want to meet the mysterious Jules."

Greg joined us in the living room wearing a chunky knit cardigan that belonged to every grandfather on the planet. He wrapped an arm around Ethan, and with his other hand, stuck a pipe in his mouth.

"What the hell is that?" I pointed at Greg's whole...everything.

"Language, son." Greg smirked, the pipe sagging on his lips.

"What are you wearing? Is that a pipe? You don't smoke."

What kind of 1950s *Leave It to Beaver* bullshit was going on?

"It relaxes me."

"Just...stop."

Ethan shook his head. "Teenagers. Always embarrassed by every little thing their parents do."

"You're not my—"

The doorbell rang, sending me into a panic for multiple reasons. Nerves tingled up my spine. I heaved out a breath. Why was I nervous? I was helping out a friend.

I yanked the pipe from Greg's mouth and shoved it in between the couch cushions.

"Hey." A small wave of relief came when I opened the front door, and Julian nervously smiled back at me. "Come on in."

"Hi. Nice place." He looked around, hands clenched on his messenger bag. Greg and Ethan lived in an older house with high ceilings and big rooms. The foyer had an elaborate light fixture at its center that had to be at least fifty years old. It made a statement.

"It's not mine. I share it with—"

My friends marched over. Greg stuck out his hand. He'd retrieved the pipe.

"Nice to meet you. I'm Greg, and this is Ethan. We're Seamus's dads."

I threw a hand on my face. I loved *and* hated my friends.

"They're not my dads. They're just being assholes."

"Son, what did we say about language?" Ethan said.

"We all went to *college* together." I tried to signal with my eyes for them to get lost, but of course, they ignored it.

"We like to look out for Seamus." Greg clapped a hand on my shoulder.

"He speaks very highly of you," Ethan said.

Technically, that was true, but it still caused a fresh surge of embarrassment to heat up my face. Julian was amused, at least.

"I told them that you help me keep my shit together." I shot a look at Greg warning him against another comment about my cursing. It was a miracle Julian hadn't run away screaming by this point. "Anyway, we've all met. We're gonna go."

"It's great to meet you. You guys look way too young to be fathers." Julian laid it on thick, which my friends got a kick out of.

"We like to give Seamus a hard time." Greg broke character, letting Julian know that he and his husband were actual normal people. "So what are you guys up to tonight?"

Without intending it, he managed to embarrass me all over again. Julian and I shared a nervous smile.

"We're going over plans for the foreign language cross curriculum." Each word was pulled out of my mouth, and I hoped that lie was enough to satisfy them.

"We want to strengthen our students' understanding of Romance languages. Since French and Spanish have the same root, it can be a way for our students to pick up another language. I came over with lessons." Julian tapped his messenger bag.

"Huh. Smart." Ethan nodded at Greg, who agreed.

Julian remained cool, his ability to spout believable bullshit a surprising turn on.

"We don't want it to be a late night, so we should get to it." He looked to me for confirmation.

"Yes. We need to do it."

"Cool. Well, we'll be up here if you need anything," Greg said before slipping back into his dad voice. "And remember the rules of the house: bedroom door open and four feet on the floor at all times."

I darted my eyes at Julian, promising that he was kidding.

"Okay, then. Bye!" I snaked an arm around Julian's waist and led him to the basement door.

I shut the door tight behind me. The basement stairs creaked and led to an open space that was filled with boxes. Both my room and the bathroom were finished. If I squinted, it felt like I had my own place.

Julian looked around, taking in every detail, which caused me to feel self-conscious. How the hell did this compare to his cushy apartment?

"Ignore the surroundings. They're going to get around to finishing the basement in the future." I opened the door to my bedroom. Julian stepped inside. We both avoided sitting on the bed.

"Did you really bring school stuff to go over?" I gestured at his bag.

"This? No." He chuckled as he removed a bottle of tequila. "I brought drinks."

"Sweet."

He pulled out a Tupperware filled with pre-sliced limes. "Tequila shots!"

"Um, okay. Yeah, get this party started." Never in a million years had I expected Julian to do tequila shots. But then again, this situation was one we'd never in a million years thought we'd be in.

"I figured a little liquid courage wouldn't hurt."

"Love it." I needed some, too.

I had a row of shot glasses on the hutch above my computer desk. I grabbed two Cancun-branded ones, memories of a wild spring break flashing in my mind.

"We need salt," he said.

I searched my desk drawers for salt packets. No way was I going back upstairs to retrieve a salt shaker and field questions from Greg and Ethan.

"Yes." I unearthed a cache of packets from old takeout orders. I tossed them on the desk.

Julian immediately got to pouring us shots.

"Cheers!" I clinked my glass against his, some of the tequila sloshing onto my wrist. Down it went. It burned like a mother. When was the last time I did shots?

"Jules, I didn't take you as a hard alcohol drinker."

"I'm not. It usually doesn't sit well with me. But isn't this whole thing about first times?"

"Salud." I wiped lime juice off my lips. My dick thickened in my pants, anticipating what was to come.

"I loved your latest video, by the way!" He poured another shot. His hand shook slightly. "*Questions my students asked me this week.*"

One of my students had asked if I knew Colin Farrell because of my Irish first name. Another wondered if I used a nose hair trimmer. I truly did not understand how teenage brains operated.

"Maybe one day you'll be doing sponsored posts. Although I hate when influencers suddenly get serious in their videos when they hawk a product."

"Oh, God. Does this mean I'm an influencer?"

"You're on your way. You may get big enough to leave teaching behind."

"I wouldn't do that. I love teaching too much." It was the saving grace in my shitstorm of a life. I was adrift in so many areas of my life, but I had found a professional calling to anchor myself to. Each year, I got more comfortable in front of the classroom and more confident in the material. My teaching skills would continue to improve until I became one of those all-timer teachers that they made inspirational movies about.

"What made you get into it?" Julian took another shot.

"Pace yourself, Jules."

"I'm good." He leaned against my desk and sucked on a lime. I plopped into my desk chair and swiveled back and forth.

"I wasn't sure what to do after college. Greg switched from pre-law to education in college, which was a total surprise because his dad's a judge and shit. But he inspired me to think about teaching. I had some rough times a few years back, and he and Ethan helped me through it. They're letting me live here rent-free."

I supposed I couldn't give them a hard time about the whole dad/son stuff. They were looking out for me more than my actual parents, who firmly believed once you were eighteen, you were on your own.

"I know it's corny, but I wanted to make a difference in kids' lives," I said.

"It's not corny. That's why we all do it. We have to deal with stuff like Cyllabus and parents, but every once in a while, we're able to get through to a student. We're leaving them better than when they entered our classroom."

"Those moments, brief as they are, make it all worth it."

Our knees touched, causing my dick to continue to swell. I was surprised at how easily I was able to get it up.

"I had a student decide to major in French at college because of my class."

"That's awesome."

Our conversation turned to a thick silence that turned into a game of chicken. When people weren't talking, they were supposed to be getting busy.

I took his hand and led him to the bed. Electricity crackled between us. *Okay, let's get this party started.*

I leaned in for a kiss. Julian lurched back, as if my lips were radioactive. Not the kickoff I had intended.

"Actually, I don't want us to kiss."

"Oh. Is it my breath?"

"No. It's not you. I've already kissed guys before, so that's been checked off my list." He made the check finger gesture. "A kiss isn't the same as sex. It's more intimate, more sacred. It's romance, not lust."

"I guess I've been doing it wrong." Kissing was about turning up the heat, preheating the oven. Did he expect us to jump in cold?

"What we're doing is more technical," he explained. "It's just one friend helping out another, and a kiss might make things weird."

And there it was, a stark reminder that we were on the same page. One friend helping another. Why did I feel a bit let down then?

This time, I poured another round of shots for us. We skipped the salt and limes.

"I'm sorry. I'm sure you're a great kisser, Seamus. But honestly, that's something I'd like to save for the right time and right somebody."

"I gotcha. That makes sense." I was nobody's right somebody. "It's like in *Pretty Woman* how the girl won't let the guy kiss her on the mouth."

"Exactly! You've seen *Pretty Woman*?"

"Jules, c'mon. I've had to watch that movie with all of my ex-girlfriends."

"You were really going to make out with me?"

"Yeah. This is all about giving you good firsts, but if kissing isn't needed, that's cool. I am here to help you out however I can." I was straight. I shouldn't be wanting to kiss my friend. But then again, I was a good kisser, and it was a shame he couldn't get to experience that. "Onto the next!"

"What's next?"

I thought for a moment before the no-brainer answer popped into my head. "Hand jobs!"

Julian poured himself another shot and gulped it down.

"You're really taking those shots like a champ," I said. "Tequila always makes me sick."

"I have a strong stomach." Julian returned to the bed. "Okay, let's do it."

"First, you gotta get a guy revved up, get him stiff. Wait, what am I talking about?" I snorted a laugh. "You are a guy. You know what's up. Man, this is going to be easier than I thought."

I leaned back and jutted out my crotch, my legs in full manspread position.

"Why don't you rub me?" I said, grabbing myself through my jeans.

"Right. Touching and rubbing are cornerstone methods used to get people aroused."

"Don't overthink it. And don't be freaked out when I pitch a tent. It's friction."

I said that for my own benefit as much as his. Just because I was getting harder with each second I spent around Julian didn't mean I was suddenly gay, right? My bicurious itch was flaring up and needed to be scratched, preferably by Julian's big hands.

Julian skimmed his warm hand over my bulge. My breath hitched in my throat as my erection quickly went rock hard. Kissing wasn't needed to prime my pump, apparently.

My dick rose, responding to Julian's grip. He tightened around me, moving to slow strokes up and down my shaft.

"How's that?" he asked, his voice thick, his eyes heavy-lidded. The lustful side of my classy, intellectual friend came out to play.

"That's...that's good."

I flopped back on the bed, eyes closed. A blissed-out smile perked on my lips. It'd been so long since I'd been with someone, I'd forgotten how good this felt when it wasn't my hand doing the work.

A light moan escaped my lips. I clenched my lips shut. I didn't know how much I was supposed to be enjoying this.

I pushed my hips up to meet his hand. Julian's assured hand stroked my cock up to the head and down to the base. His free hand rested on my stomach.

"Is this okay?"

"Yeah," I breathed out.

Julian moved up to my chest, fingertips gliding across my shirt. I flexed for him.

He gave my cock a light squeeze. Another moan escaped my lips.

"Are you enjoying this?" he asked, as if the moan wasn't confirmation enough.

"Yeah. Is that weird?"

"No. It's friction, like you said."

Friction...right.

Speaking of friction, I couldn't take any more over-the-pants action. I needed to feel his hot palm wrapped around me.

I popped open my top button and unzipped my fly. My cock twitched in anticipation.

Yet as I reached into my boxers, something shifted in the air. The bed became lighter.

The sounds of our breathing were replaced by the clomping of Julian running out of my bedroom.

And then the sounds of the bathroom door swinging open.

And lastly, the sounds of Julian wringing out his stomach.

9

JULIAN

I woke up to darkness. The glow of moonlight provided the barest illumination. I turned to my side, letting my head sink into the warmth of the pillow.

The pillow?

I looked down and discovered that I was lying on a bed. A bed that was not my bed. My bed had a billowy burgundy comforter. This blanket was thin and it's-a-boy blue with a starchy feel under my fingers.

The steady sounds of breathing came from behind me. I turned to the other side, the springs of the mattress creaking under my weight.

Seamus was fast asleep on top of the bed, a small New York Yankees blanket draped over him. His toned arms and broad shoulders peeked out. Bare skin I'd dreamed about many times over was now in full view.

I peeked under the blanket to see how nude he was. He was clad in boxers. White boxers. The same ones I'd glimpsed last night before I gunned it for the toilet.

What was I doing in bed with Seamus? I looked down, and I

was fully dressed. My shirt and pants were wrinkled from sleep. A disgusting taste permeated my mouth.

I glanced at the clock on his nightstand.

4:54

Fuck. My head pounded with excruciating pain. And I thought beer was bad. The tequila had hardened into a bulldozer knocking a wrecking ball against my skull. My stomach was no better, queasy and empty.

Tequila, thy mortal enemy. Never again.

With all its squeaking, the mattress made it nearly impossible to sneak out of bed unnoticed. I crept to the bathroom, the scene of the crime. Fortunately, Seamus had a large bottle of mouthwash on the counter. I leaned my head back and poured it in without the bottle touching my mouth. It burned as I swirled, but the grossness on my tongue was being sterilized away.

Objectively, I looked like shit. The mirror did not lie. My skin was pale, eyes bloodshot, hair sticking up in loops and swoops.

Gross.

My plan was to sneak out the door, pray his roommates weren't up, text Seamus a beautifully crafted apology, and then go about transferring schools and leaving the continent as soon as possible.

"Jules?" he called from the bedroom, his voice raspy.

Busted.

Shit.

I did a walk of shame back to his bedroom. It wasn't the fun walk of shame my friends loved to brag about. This was actual shame.

"Hi." I waved from the doorway.

"Morning." He sat up in bed. The Yankees blanket fell, revealing his naked chest and the small tuft of dark hair between his pecs. Now was not the time to lust over his body. Now was the time to put my tail between my legs and get out of there.

"How ya feeling, bud?" he asked with such concern in his voice that it scuttled my plan to run away.

"Not so great." The sharp pain in my head and stomach, as well as overall weakness in my legs, confirmed this.

"That was epic last night."

"Epic? Did we..." A sinking feeling added to the overall yuckiness inside me. "Did we have sex?"

I felt like an idiot as soon as the question popped out. Was I that drunk that I didn't know my virginity had been taken? Seamus snorted a laugh.

"No. You passed out in the bathroom. I was talking about your puking. I've never seen someone throw up that much, and I lived in a frathouse for two years."

Change of plans: run away screaming.

"I thought your stomach was going to get ripped out of your mouth. I'm glad you're still alive."

"Me, too."

"If I were you, I'd stay away from tequila."

"Agreed." From now on, I was going to be a mature, responsible adult and only get drunk off wine.

"How did I wind up in..." I pointed to his bed.

"You passed out on the bathroom floor. I couldn't leave you there, so I carried you in. I figured you needed a good rest."

Another wave of mortification mixed with nausea hit me. Seamus had to carry me? He had no choice but to put me in his bed. No way could he have lugged me up the stairs. I'd essentially forced myself into bed with him.

"I'm really sorry," I said.

"Don't be. I'm actually impressed that you got all the puke in the toilet bowl. I didn't need to do much cleanup."

Much. Meaning there was some. He'd cleaned up *some* of my mess and then carried my fat, drunk, blacked-out ass to the bed. I was a person who preferred to keep his mess tidy and to himself. I was the friend who helped friends with their messes.

"This is why I never drink hard stuff."

"Why did you bring it then?" His lips pouted in beautiful confusion, making my stomach find the strength to flutter.

"I thought it would relax us, make things less awkward."

"I watched you blow chunks like I've never seen chunks blown before. I think we're past awkward."

I hung my head. I couldn't admit that I'd needed to drink alcohol to calm my nerves last night, because agreeing to lose your virginity to someone you were secretly in love with was a very nerve-racking proposition.

"You don't want your first time to be in a drunken haze. Plus if you drink too much, then you might get whiskey dick. We don't need alcohol to enjoy this."

I hoped that Seamus found some enjoyment in this odd arrangement. We were not off to an auspicious start.

"Come here." He nudged his head, inviting me over.

I wasn't going to overthink this one. I sat next to him and let myself admire his chest and the hazy smile hanging on his lips.

"Thank you for...all of your help last night. With everything."

"How was it, from what you remember?"

What I remembered before I threw up? How amazing it felt to touch another man. How hard he was. My hand vibrated with lingering heat.

"Good. It was cool."

"Yeah, you were great."

"I was?"

"The girls I've been with don't know how to hold it, or they pull too hard or too soft. You're a natural."

"I've had practice." I shrugged.

A memory from last night: hearing that low rumbly moan

escape my straight friend's mouth. I'd made a straight man moan. My face deserved to be carved onto Gay Mount Rushmore.

"Hand job." I made a check motion, crossing it off my imaginary list.

"That was just over-the-pants action." He rubbed his fist in the air in a gesture I couldn't translate. Did we as a society change the signal for hand job while I was drunk? "I just erased your check mark from the board."

"Damn."

"Did you want to try giving a hand job?"

"Right now?" I followed his eyes to the boner tenting his blanket. It stuck straight up, like someone dressing as a Yankees ghost for Halloween. "We were just talking about epic puking and you're hard?"

"I always get one in the morning," he said.

"No matter what, it seems."

The boner hardening in my pants could not be blamed on the morning. That was all for Seamus.

"Did you want to give it a try?" Seamus remained his chill self, but a hint of curiosity dazzled behind his sleepy eyes.

My hangover was raging. I was tired. And as previously established, I looked like shit. But time was a-ticking. The golden rule of life stated that we should grab opportunities when they arose. Welp, Seamus's opportunity had risen straight up. That meant only one thing.

Time to grab.

I gave a terse nod, the same nod I imagined astronauts gave when they were ready to be blasted into space.

Seamus removed his Yankees blanket. His dick stretched against his boxers like a wild animal trying to escape. The sight of it lit a fire in me.

I pulled down his underwear before he had a chance to reach for the band.

And there it was. Another guy's cock. Live and in person.

It looked like mine, only thicker.

Yep. I was gay. Definitely gay. Seamus's cock re-confirmed that for me.

"Are you just going to stare?"

I curled my hand around his erection. It pulsed, hot and thick. I began with slow strokes, getting a lay of the land. I moved up to the head, then down to the base, his pubic hair prickling at my fist.

Seamus leaned his head back, arms crossed behind his neck.

"How is this?" I asked, though I already knew the answer. I wanted to hear him say it. I was a slut for positive feedback. (The empowered version of slut!)

"Good. Really good, Jules."

My name on his tongue. Was there anything hotter?

He bucked his hips to meet my hand. I loved how his cock looked in my grip.

"Just like that." He let out another low moan through his blissed-out lips. "That's good."

I reached down and cradled his balls. He spread his legs to provide better access. He heaved in heavier breaths, his relaxed demeanor fading away as he got more into it. He squirmed under my touch. *My touch.*

Seamus licked his lips, making them red and glowing. I wanted to lean over and kiss him, taste him.

Lust, not romance, I reminded myself.

I used two hands, one on the shaft and one on the balls. Stroking and rubbing and causing more shaking of the man underneath. I gazed at his pale thighs and the dusting of dark hair that stopped just above his knees, another part of him I'd dreamed about.

"Fuck," he emitted in a deep groan that hit me square in the crotch. "You feel so fucking good."

"You like this?" I asked in my huskiest voice. "You like getting jerked off?"

(Dirty talk: a bonus item checked off the list.)

"Fuck yeah. So fucking awesome." Seamus opened his eyes and directed his heavy-lidded, carnivorous stare at me.

Without saying a word, and without taking his eyes off me, he brought my hand to his mouth and spat in my palm. That singular move might've been hotter than anything else I'd experienced this morning.

I wrapped it back around his cock, slick with his lubrication. My fist slid up and down his shaft with greater speed. His eyes closed in ecstasy only to reopen and stare at me like for a second, he actually wanted me.

"Jules," he croaked out. He writhed under me, this manly, laid-back jock turning to putty thanks to my hand.

I dribbled more spit onto his cock. His face lit up in absolute shock and hunger. Pre-come pooled at his head.

I got high off Seamus responding to my moves. His every grunt and thrust electrified me. The push/pull of being intimate with someone else, the anticipation and unpredictability, was worth the wait.

"Yes. Oh, shit. Jules..." He was holding onto the last shreds of control. His chest rose and fell with labored breaths.

I leaned into his ear. "Come for me."

He threw his head back, hips leaving the mattress as he arched into the air and shot loads of hot come streaking onto his stomach. Come dribbled down my fist as I pumped the last drops from him. He finally had to lightly push my hand back.

The air was heavy between us, the smell of sex blanketing the room. Still in a haze, I brought my hand to my mouth and tasted Seamus.

Color flushed his face. His bright eyes blinked at me as he caught his breath. I felt as powerful as a sex god.

"Wow."

"Are you okay?" I had to ask.

"Yeah. I, uh, I can be really intense when I come. It's kinda weird, I know, but I can't control it, especially in the heat of things." It was adorably Seamus.

"Which is ironic since you're usually so laid back."

"My orgasm has no chill."

"It's hot." I felt myself blush. *Did I just call Seamus hot to his face?* I had to be careful to toe the line of our friendship, especially when we weren't in the heat of sex. "How was it for you? How did I do?"

Once a straight-A student seeking approval, always a straight-A student seeking approval.

He tipped his head at me. "Seriously, Jules? I think your work speaks for itself." He gestured at his come-splattered stomach. "This is going to be a fun month."

10

SEAMUS

Other teachers had it easy. They could teach English or woodshop on autopilot as their minds checked out. As someone who taught a foreign language, I didn't have that luxury. I couldn't zone out in my lesson because I was constantly translating English to Spanish—very broken Spanish for most of my students.

It sucked, because today, I wanted to zone out. I wanted to zone out hard.

Look, I'd gotten plenty of hand jobs in my life. Most I'd given myself. It was a miracle I could still use my right hand for anything. Jerking off was nothing new to me.

But this morning would not leave my mind. Was it possible that I'd received the best hand job of my life?

I wanted to keep thinking about it, indulging in how good it felt to have someone else's hands on me, someone who had an incredible ability to read my body. It'd been a while (years!) since I'd been with anyone (by choice!). Was it a problem that I was thinking about a guy instead of a girl?

It was friction. Really, really good friction.

I'd always known Jules was an intelligent guy, but he was also like...sexually intelligent.

I should've had sex with more smart girls in college.

It wasn't just that, though. My mind kept going back to the way he looked. Darker, hornier. Buttoned-up, kind, smart Jules was a sexual animal underneath that refined exterior. And his fiery stare? That signed a long-term lease in my brain.

Had I ever been looked at that way? Like I was craved and meant to be devoured?

Devoured by a guy. What would *that* be like?

"Senor Shablanski?" one of my students called from her desk, while I stood idly at the markerboard.

"What?" I asked, like I was the student caught flat footed by the teacher.

She pointed at the board. My Spanish sentence turned to English halfway through.

"Lo siento," I said. I shook off any thoughts of Julian.

I was reading into things that weren't there. It was the heat of the moment. Julian's intense gaze was no different from my intense orgasm. He needed a friend to help him run the sexual bases. Just because I'd been wandering in a sexual desert of my own making didn't mean I had to make shit weird.

When the bell rang, my students darted out of class before I realized I'd forgotten to assign them homework. Shit. Damn hand job messing with my lesson plans.

I strolled into the hall and watched kids and teachers scurry to third period. The halls were abuzz for these few precious minutes. I high-fived current and former students passing by.

Across the hall, I peeked into Julian's classroom. He leaned over his desk skimming papers. He glanced up and caught me looking. *Busted.* I gulped back a lump.

Why did it feel different now? We said hey to each other across the hall millions of times. That was before he'd held my cock in his hand and made me Old Faithful all over myself.

He gave me a half-wave, half-salute with a genial smile. I stared at his waving hand, the same hand that only hours ago...

You're making it weird. Don't make it weird.

I waved back and almost smacked a passing Principal Aguilar in the face.

"Easy there," he said.

"Sorry."

Julian chuckled at the scene. I took a small bow.

LATER THAT MORNING, I settled in the teacher's lounge trying to grade papers, which I was supposed to do last night.

A pair of teachers from the history department hung by the coffee station chatting about concert tickets they were planning to buy. These types of conversations were common at the start of the month. Teachers' bank accounts were flush with cash from fresh paychecks. Their minds swirled with possibilities. I'd heard teachers discuss plans to go shopping, remodel kitchens, book trips.

A part of me deflated whenever I listened. I didn't have that luxury.

As soon as my paycheck hit my account, a large chunk was deducted to chip away at my massive credit card debt repayment plan, a smaller-but-still-substantial chunk taken for student loans, and another chunk was transferred to Lauren to pay back the money I had taken. Add in the chunks for car payments, gas, and food, and poof, the money was gone before I knew it. Even with the extra cash I got from my second, mind-numbing data entry job, things were tight. I was still worth negative dollars. No concert tickets or trips for me.

It sucked, but what could I do? I'd put myself into this mess, not to mention an innocent woman, too. I'd fucked up majorly, and the scars of how I'd treated my ex-girlfriend would last longer than the debt.

Once I got out of the hole, I'd feel comfortable dating again. But deep down, I didn't trust myself. I had an addiction. Addictions didn't go away. It scared me how easily I could fall into another mess.

"Hey. You seem deep in thought." Julian stood behind me. Talk about someone who was mess free...

"Just grading papers."

"How many of your students forgot accent marks? It's inching up to forty percent for me Not like I'm keeping track." Julian poured himself a cup of coffee. My eyes naturally watched his hand. Julian knew how to hold things.

"How are you feeling?" I asked as he gulped down his drink.

"Still a little hungover, but the coffee helps."

His eyes were clearer now, no longer bloodshot. Their bright brown hue was like a warm hug from an old friend.

We stood there silently, awkwardly drinking our coffee. I'd promised him things wouldn't be awkward with our arrangement. I had to hold up my end of the deal.

"This is good coffee," I said. "Sometimes, the coffee sucks, and sometimes it's good. I don't know why that happens."

"It's like the coffee maker has a mind of its own." Julian sipped his coffee, and for a second, I wondered what his mouth would feel like on my dick.

You're making it weird. Don't. Make. It. Weird.

Mr. Claffy, an older English teacher, joined us. "Seamus, you're handy."

I choked on my coffee. "What?"

"Can you help me? My Snickers bar is stuck in the vending machine."

"That's been happening. I thought they brought someone in to fix it," Julian said, cool as a cucumber.

"Some guy was in here last week to fix it, but he was on his phone like a total jerkoff," Mr. Claffy said.

My coffee cup fumbled in my hands, but I saved it before it spilled.

"Are you okay, son?" he asked.

"Yep."

Julian snorted. "I'll help you out."

He got on his knees and reached into the vending machine. He grabbed the Snickers bar, but it wouldn't come loose from the bit of metal it was stuck on. Julian kept moving it around to loosen it.

Moving it up. And down.

Julian's fist wrapped around the candy bar.

He let out a small grunt.

Up. And down.

Was the heat turned up super high in here? Was anybody else sweating? Was anybody else sprouting wood?

Just me?

"Here." I charged forward and banged on the glass until the Snickers bar fell, along with two bags of Doritos and a Kit Kat.

Julian handed over the Snickers to Mr. Claffy, who gave me a puzzled look.

"Thanks, Seamus." He slunk away, looking over his shoulder at me.

"Teamwork," Julian said with a nervous laugh.

I waited for the door to shut behind Mr. Claffy.

"So when did you want to plan our next session?" I asked.

"Oh." Julian raised his eyebrows.

"We are on a deadline, right?"

Did I sound calm and collected or like a complete fucking horndog? Judging by Julian's reaction, the former. Thankfully.

"About three weeks." Julian strummed his fingers against his coffee mug. "What are you up to afterschool?"

My dick twitched. Another session less than a day after our first. Hell, I was ready.

"Shit." My responsible brain overrode my crotch. "I have my second job, then I have to shoot some videos in the park. It's been more than a day since I last posted, which is like a month on BlingBling."

"I didn't know you had a second job. That sounds tiring."

"It's not too bad." I wanted to veer away from this line of discussion. If he knew about my shitty financial situation, Julian would probably want to keep his distance. "I'm shooting some videos in Renegade Park to switch things up. Doing a video about students on field trips, one about promposals."

"Do you need help? It's the least I can do considering you're helping me."

I wasn't sure what I'd done to help except provide a willing cock. I literally lay back and let him go to town. But it would be fun to have Julian there with me. I had only made videos by myself.

I gave him a thumbs-up.

It was one of those March afternoons that made you believe spring was here, even though tomorrow, we'd be back to cold and gray weather. People took advantage of the sunny weather, walking and biking through the park trails.

I had us settle by a small patch of trees on one of the walking trails, then set up the tripod and phone.

"What's today's video?" Julian asked.

"Things my students do when they're in nature."

"I love it. What made you decide to start your page?"

"I don't know. My students said the weirdest things. I was lost when I started teaching, so I made these videos to see if there were other teachers who were dealing with the same weird kids. Turns out yes."

"You're already at twenty thousand followers. If this continues to grow, you might get approached for sponsored posts."

"I'm probably a long ways off from that." I could only imagine what influencers with millions of followers were raking in. Actually, it was better not to imagine or else it'd depress me.

"Not necessarily. There's an account I follow. He's got ten thousand followers, and he does sponsored posts. He's probably not making much, maybe a few hundred dollars, but if he's already making the videos..."

Julian might be unimpressed with a few hundred dollars, but that could be a game changer for me. That could provide a cushion each month, help me clear away debt faster and get out of Greg and Ethan's basement.

"Good to know." I made a mental note to do some research later.

"It could maybe replace that extra job you have." Julian shrugged.

That'd be nice.

I took my position in front of the phone; Julian cued me. First, I would say all my lines. Then we'd film me acting them out. I'd bring them together for maximum comedic effect in editing later.

"I'm Mr. Shablahblah, and this is how my students act when they're in nature. They try to climb trees but can't. They freak out whenever they see a bug. They ask why everything is so dirty. They get bored and go on their phones. If you liked this video, make sure you like and subscribe."

"Cut," Julian said, stopping the video and chuckling to himself. "Are all those true?"

"Yeah. I volunteered to take kids on a nature hike last year. It was an experience."

It was nice having an audience. I never knew whether my videos sucked or not before I posted them.

For "They try to climb trees but can't," I jumped up to grab a branch and yelled, "Yo! Look at me!" at the camera right before it snapped, and I fell on my ass. Oh yeah, that was definitely going into the final cut.

I pretended to be a too-cool student who yelps when he thinks a bug is on him. I acted like a prissy girl who looks at the dirt under her shoe in disgust. For the last one, I sat against a tree and pretended to scroll through Julian's phone bored out of my mind.

Each time, I glanced over to find Julian holding back laughs, a hand over his mouth as his shoulders shook so he didn't mess up the audio. I enjoyed his responses more than all the comments from followers.

When I was done, I looked over Julian's shoulder as he replayed the video footage for me.

"This is perfect," he said with a snort.

I rested my chin on his shoulder and continued to watch.

"Did you plan for that branch to break?"

"Nope. That was dumb luck."

"You should do a video about high school kids sitting on park benches. Because they never actually sit on the bench. They sit on the top part, or they do stretches against the bench, or they put one foot up."

"Excuse me, are you trying to push me out of the job?" I teased playfully in his ear.

"I'm merely offering up a suggestion."

"I'll have to credit you to make it fair. Mr. Brahbrahbrah."

"I'm not being referred to as a bra."

"We'll figure out a name for you."

"Julian." An old lady called out to him. She was dressed in

oversized sunglasses and a red and blue warm up suit with dumbbells in each arm.

"Grandma!" Julian gently stepped out of our bubble and hugged the old lady. He kissed her on the cheek.

"What are you doing at Renegade Park?"

"Getting my exercise in. When you're eighty, you can't fuck around with your health."

My eyebrows jumped. I'd never heard old people spout off curse words so easily. I thought when you got older, you learned to stop cursing. That whole maturity thing.

To her credit, she was in great shape. She was small, but not frail.

"Usually I do my walk at Hudson Park, but Shirley Millberg is playing tennis there, and we're not speaking. She bowed out of our canasta game at the last minute with no explanation, and we couldn't find a replacement. We had to cancel. Bitch."

"I'm sorry. Hopefully, you can play next week," Julian said.

"When you're my age, you never want to put something off until next week."

Made sense.

I got a kick out of her. My grandparents had passed away when I was a little kid—one of the downsides of being the youngest child. I remembered a candy dish filled with Werther's Originals in their apartment, and that was it.

"Where's Grandpa?" Julian asked.

"He's fishing in his usual spot. Here, let's walk and talk. I want to keep my pace." She continued walking on the trail. Julian and I bundled up the equipment and caught up to her. Grandma waited for no man.

"Grandma, this is Seamus. Seamus, this is my Grandma Judy."

"Great to meet you!" I held out a hand to shake, but it was no use. She wasn't letting go of her dumbbells.

"Likewise. Julian, it's a good thing I ran into you. Your mother is going on and on about the color of the tablecloths for the shindig. I think she's trying to give me a heart attack, an actual heart attack. She thinks white is too plain, but going with a color is too bold. Neutral would be best, but she can't decide what kind of neutral. Eggshell, champagne, on and on. I told her it's a fucking tablecloth. As long as the food is good, nobody will care."

I snorted. Old people cursing was fun.

"You know your mother." They shared a knowing eye roll.

"She's not good with making decisions," Julian said. "I'm surprised she offered to help."

"She means well." Grandma Judy shook her head, a pained look on her face. "It's a good thing I ran into you. I'm taking you up on your offer to help. This party is turning into a disaster."

"Of course."

"I know you're busy with school, but..."

"Grandma, I got it covered. I'll reach out to Mom." Julian didn't hesitate, just like he hadn't hesitated to help me this afternoon. He really was a thoughtful, kind person. Why the hell didn't other guys see that?

"You're a gem, Julian. You really are."

"It's my pleasure. I want to celebrate you and Grandpa. Fifty years is a huge milestone."

"Eh, it's no different from forty-nine, but I'll never turn down a party."

We rounded a corner that led to a long bridge that went over a pond. The water reflected the trees and sky like nature's mirror.

Grandma Judy switched to pressing her weights overhead without her pace lagging.

"I'll keep you updated on party planning," Julian said.

"I know spending all that time with your mother isn't your favorite..." Grandma dipped her head, an unexpected silence taking over for a beat.

"It's fine. She isn't the best with filtering what she says, but I'm used to it." Julian waved it off, but I detected a tightness in his voice.

"Thanks again, sweetheart. I'm going to go. You two are slowing down my pace. Seamus, a pleasure."

Grandma Judy power walked forward, leaving us in her dust.

I wanted to recommend her to South Rock's cross-country coach. With some hair dye, she could totally pass for a high schooler.

"Thanks for rolling with that," Julian said. We turned around and walked to the park entrance where we came from.

"She's awesome." It made me wish I had a cool, saucy grandmother. "What's the deal with you and your mom?"

"She likes to make comments about my weight. She means well; she just has a weird way of showing it."

"I'm sorry." For some reason, I'd thought Julian's family was perfect. I didn't have any hard evidence, but he seemed so well-adjusted. Showed how little I knew.

"It is what it is." He laughed it off, but I could tell it stung.

We spent the rest of the walk talking about future video ideas and weird things other students did. I could've talked to Julian for hours more, but we reached our cars, and I had a data entry job to get to. The grind never stopped.

"Thanks for today," I said. "What are you up to on Thursday? Did you want to get together for our next session?"

"I love how you call it a session."

"What else should I call it?"

"That's a good question." Julian smiled down at his shoes. His smile was hypnotic, like ASMR for the eyes.

"Are you free?"

"Yeah, I can do Thursday."

"Nice. Get ready. Because this time, it's your turn."

I got in my car and heaved out an *oh shit* breath. In two days, I was going to jerk off a guy. And I was...looking forward to it?

11

JULIAN

The most important element of a party was the food. People never forgot a bad meal. Whenever I saw my cousin Molly, I remembered the undercooked chicken and watery vegetables I'd had at her wedding eight years ago. She wound up getting divorced less than three years after that night.

Coincidence? I think not.

I arranged a tasting session with a caterer for Grandma and Mom. I was still dreaming of their beef short ribs that I'd had at a faculty dinner last year.

We met at their headquarters nestled in an office park. They set a long table in the front room, making us feel like judges on a cooking show.

The bell on the door rang as Grandma and Mom entered.

"I'm ready to eat!" Grandma said.

"Judy, this is just a tasting."

"They're not going to give us crumbs, Elizabeth. They want to make sure we truly savor each dish," Grandma said back to Mom.

They each kissed me on the cheek.

"Thank you for helping out," Mom said to me. "I'm so busy with everything. It's good to have an extra set of hands."

Grandma and I exchanged a look. The only thing she was busy with was tennis and remodeling the kitchen.

"Just give us another minute, and we'll get started," said Tilda, the catering coordinator running today's tasting.

"How's school?" Mom asked. She had the wavy blonde hair and wrinkled beauty of a fading beauty queen. I'd seen her high school yearbook, and she'd been at the top of the social food chain, not to mention the cheerleader pyramid.

"Going well. Spring break is in a few weeks. Once that comes, all my students zone out for the year, so I really have to make March count."

"I remember that. Spring was when I did most of my ditching. We'd go tubing on the river, or take the train into New York City. My boyfriend at the time had a Corvette, and we'd drive with the wind blowing through my hair, Jefferson Starship blasting."

Mom's high school memories always sounded like the plot of some teen drama or a music video. Also, her high school boyfriend, per his yearbook photo, was a stone-cold fox. My high school experience had been vastly different. I actually went to class. It was disconcerting for her.

"Fun times," I said.

"They were, they were."

"I'm going to hit the head before we eat. I don't want my bladder interrupting things." Grandma waltzed to the bathroom.

Mom eyed my outfit, a striped shirt tucked into khakis. Before she opened her mouth, I knew what was going to come out. Her face pinched every time she was about to say something critical. "Julian, can I give you my opinion on something?"

"Sure." I gritted my teeth, knowing she'd say it anyway.

"If I were you, I would avoid horizontal stripes in the future.

They, well...they aren't flattering on your body type." She moved her arms out to demonstrate what my body type was. "I'm just being honest. Visually, they stretch bodies out, make them seem wider."

I loved this shirt. I'd been so excited when I saw it on a mannequin in the store window, and even more excited when they had it in my size.

"Mom, it's fine."

"It's not," she said firmly. "I know about these things. I see people wearing awful, unflattering outfits all the time, but I can't say anything to them because they're strangers. That would be rude."

Because I was her son, she could be honest with me. In her own twisted way, this was her way of showing love. It had to be hard for her having a son who she would've made fun of in high school.

She gave my shirt another once-over, making me wish I had a parka I could bundle up in.

"How are things going with the diet and exercise?"

"I'm not on a diet. I just had a physical, and my doctor says I'm healthy. My blood work and everything came out great."

"Who is this doctor?"

"Weight isn't the only signifier of health. There are skinny people who are unhealthy."

Mom rolled her eyes. My scientific facts were no match for her uninformed views. Round and round we went.

"You're going to be thirty-five. It gets harder to lose weight as you get older."

Maybe she could see me floundering, but at that moment, Tilda interrupted and had us sit down, derailing Mom's train of thought.

She gave us the menu for today. Because we were leaning toward going buffet serving, she had the chefs come up with multiple options for each course. My mouth watered at what was to come.

"That's a lot of food," Mom commented.

"We're getting our money's worth," Grandma said, rejoining us. She sat in the seat between Mom and me.

"Well, we don't want to go overboard. All of these tastes can add up. So let's be careful," Mom said, and I knew exactly who she was saying it to.

The first course came out. Three different types of salads. Mixed greens, Caesar, and a Waldorf. Each one was fantastic. Grandma would have to make the final call, as I couldn't decide. They brought out fresh rolls and butter balls. I took two and felt Mom's eyes on me.

Next came the main courses. Grilled chicken, roasted vegetables, and the beef short ribs that had captured my heart. When Mom turned away to check her phone, I took an extra serving of them.

"Helena Burstyn just RSVP'd. She and Edward are a yes," Mom said. "I've gotten mostly yesses. It's going to be a full party. People want to celebrate you two."

"Of course they do." Grandma shimmied her shoulders. She was never one to shy away from praise. "Julian, are you going to bring your boyfriend to the party?"

I whipped my head up.

"Boyfriend?" Mom asked.

I choked down my short rib.

"Yeah. Julian has a boyfriend. I met him the other day. Seamus. They teach together."

Now was the time to say something, to set the record straight. I needed a glass of water first, to clear the piece of meat stuck in my throat.

"Oh, don't look so shocked. My eyesight may be going downhill, but I saw you two canoodling when I came upon you during my walk."

"I'm not—Grandma, we're not dating."

"Jesus H, I'm so confused with your generation. You like to keep it casual. You don't like labels. Well, in my day, you were either going steady or you weren't, and you two are going steady." She plopped a piece of broccoli in her mouth.

"I didn't know you were seeing someone, Julian," Mom said with a confused look.

"He's cute! He's a baseball player. He's got a nice butt." Grandma wiggled her eyebrows. Heat raced up my neck. I mean, she wasn't wrong about Seamus's butt...

"Oh. Well, I hope he can make it to the party." Mom managed a supportive smile, but her initial reaction stuck in my craw.

"He'll be there. You're going to love him." I flashed her a victorious smile. Watching her head metaphorically explode over the fact that I was dating a sexy jock was a victory that tasted better than anything we'd eat today.

Now I just had to pray that Seamus was up for a little ruse.

SEAMUS CAME over that night for our next session.

"I have a favor to ask you," I said. I brought two cold cans of La Croix to the living room and joined him on my sofa. Our sessions would be alcohol-free from now on. "I know what we're doing is already a huge favor, so to ask you for another favor on top of this one is a lot..."

"Jules." He put his hand on my shaking knee. "This isn't a favor what we're doing."

"I mean, it is. It's literally sexual favors."

"A favor implies that you'll owe me in the future."

"And I will. If there's anything you need from me, even if it's ten years later, just let me know."

He squeezed my knee, sending a jolt of calm and heat coursing up my body. What was I more nervous about? That I needed him to be my pretend boyfriend or that we were going to do more sex stuff after I shut up?

"What is this new favor?" His full lips rose in a lazy smile. Why did his smile have to be so transfixing? It was distracting.

"Will you pretend to be my boyfriend for my grandparents' anniversary party?" I explained how Grandma had confused us for boyfriends in the park, and the lie began. "We'll stick to the *Pretty Woman* no-kissing rule, but maybe there'll be some handholding."

I flashed back to Seamus resting his chin on my shoulder in Renegade Park. It had been natural and comfortable and gave me a fuzzy feeling when I replayed the moment in my head.

"Sure." He shrugged, as if I'd asked to borrow a pen.

"Really?"

"Yeah. Will there be food there?"

"The catering will be immaculate. Do you remember the food from the faculty dinner last year?"

"I'm still thinking about those short ribs."

"Me too!" Damn, too bad Seamus wasn't gay because we could have the best dinner dates.

"Why didn't you want to tell them the truth?" he asked.

I sank into the sofa and sipped my seltzer. "Grandma was so excited for me. And my mom, too. I've never brought home a guy before."

Even if Seamus was my fake boyfriend, I could enjoy the pomp and circumstance around bringing a guy to meet the family and having a plus one.

"It'll be fun. Your grandma was a trip. What's your grandpa like?"

"Quiet. Reserved. He prefers to stand back and let her shine."

They complemented each other perfectly. I wondered if that was fate or something cultivated through decades of life together.

We fell into silence. Seamus rubbed his hands on his thighs. We both remembered why he was here.

"I have some leftovers from the tasting session. Did you want something to eat?" I asked.

"Nah, I'm good. Also, you have an amazing place. It's so nice. Like, you have real furniture that matches. I'm sorry I had you come over to my dungeon room."

"I liked it. It was cozy." Seamus's room was very much him. Shaggy but warm. And there was something hot about fooling around while people were upstairs sleeping.

I chugged the rest of my La Croix, which didn't have the same impact as downing tequila shots.

"What's so funny?" I asked when Seamus began chuckling to himself.

"What did I tell you about being nervous? We're just two friends fucking around, getting you some experience."

I chanted that in my head as a constant reminder.

"If you're going to go through this whole performance every time we're about to get busy, then I'm gonna need to rework my schedule."

I put down the La Croix. He closed the distance between us, his fresh, musky scent doing wonders to my head.

"You've proven adept at giving. Now it's your turn to receive."

"Receive? As in, with your hand?" I asked, sounding as clueless as I did leading health class.

"Yep."

"And you're still sure you're okay doing this? Because it's one thing to receive a hand job, but to be the one giving it...Some guys might be weird about that."

"We're not making it weird," Seamus said adamantly. "Yeah, I wouldn't normally give guys hand jobs, but it'll be fun to try."

"Right. Two friends fucking around."

"Get comfortable and relaxed."

I sank back into the sofa and closed my eyes. Seamus massaged my shoulder, which was enough to get me hard. *Dear Lord, please let him at least touch my dick before I come.*

"Relax, bud." He rubbed my chest in firm circles, sending me to a zen place. His hands were already doing A-plus work.

I melted under his touch. Bliss radiated throughout my body. I hadn't realized how much I craved the touch of another man. This was—

What the hell was he doing?

My eyes snapped open to find Seamus unbuttoning my shirt.

"What are you doing?" I asked. My hand clamped around his.

"Undressing you?"

"Why?"

"To set the mood?" He snatched back his hand and rubbed out the cramping from my grip.

"Why do I need to be shirtless for a handjob? That seems severe." I sat up straight and buttoned my shirt faster than the speed of light.

"I don't know. It's hot. I was going to take off my shirt, too."

"Why? You're the one giving." None of the porn I'd watched in my life had explained these clothing etiquette rules to me.

"I do my best sexual work when I'm naked. Clothes can be very constricting."

Seamus and his gorgeous body could get away with a comment like that. Me? Not so much. My life had been firmly lived in clothes.

"Jules, have you ever been naked in front of anyone?"

"Aside from birth? No."

"Just pretend you're home alone hanging out."

"Why would I hang out in my house naked?"

"You don't? You mean, when you're home alone, you don't walk around naked or jerk off naked or sleep naked?"

"No!" I said, horrified. "Do you?"

"Yeah. I love being naked. It's what God intended." He rubbed a confused hand through his hair. "Okay, new question: have you ever seen yourself naked?"

"I...Probably."

"You never looked at yourself in the mirror?"

Was my friend a secret exhibitionist? These questions had to be sourced from outer space, far removed from the realms of sanity.

"No! Why would I stand in front of a mirror and look at myself? That's conceited."

"What about when you get out of the shower? You ever catch a glimpse of yourself?"

I was too embarrassed to tell him the truth. As soon as the shower was done, I grabbed a towel, wrapped it around myself, and bolted into my bedroom for a T-shirt before I could give myself a chance to look up.

I knew what I looked like. I knew in the way Mom studied my body like car crash footage, in the way guys would bolt when I tried striking up a conversation, in the way the gay dating world put me into the fatty box. I didn't need a mirror to tell me what I already knew.

"God did not intend for us to be naked. He gave humans brains and opposable thumbs so that we could have the good sense to manufacture clothing and cover ourselves up." I wrapped a throw blanket around myself. "I like wearing clothes. So sue me."

"You understand that in a few sessions, you're going to have to be naked. Unless you intend to cut a hole in your jeans, I don't know how else we're going to have sex."

I hadn't thought that far ahead, but the realization sent a shiver up my spine.

"We're...That's a long ways away."

"Well, we gotta get comfortable. So, let's get naked." He began to unbuckle his own belt. I used my vice-like grip to forcibly remove his hand.

"We can cross that bridge later." *Much* later.

"It's okay, Jules. We'll get naked, it'll be a little weird, then it'll be fine."

That was like saying we'd do some heroin. *Sure, it'll be weird at first, but then shooting up will be old hat.* Anger began to rise within me. How could he be so chill about disrobing? Did he realize how fortunate he was?

I hopped off the couch. I needed some space.

"I *really* don't have to get naked. Maybe the hole in the jeans is the best idea. Trust me, Seamus, you don't want to see what's underneath here unless you feel like gouging your eyes out immediately after."

I let out a laugh, but he didn't join me. Concern crossed his face.

"What does that mean, Jules?"

Did I really need to explain it?

"Seamus, come on. Guys like you are meant to be naked. You give good naked. Guys like me...we should keep our clothes on."

"That's bullshit."

"Is it? Nobody wants to see someone like me naked unless they have a fat fetish."

"Even more bullshit. You look good, Jules."

"That's because I know how to dress for my body." I changed into a new shirt when I got home, unfortunately bending to Mom's advice about horizontal stripes. "It's like wearing concealer. And I'm concealing a lot." I was on a roll with the fat humor. It was a natural defense mechanism honed from a lifetime as the fat kid and fat friend.

"You have a great body." The sincerity in his voice grated on me like nails on a chalkboard.

"Oh please. Don't treat me like I'm an idiot. I don't need one of those body positivity talks. I don't have a six pack abs and guns. I have rolls and more rolls and man boobs. Trust me, you don't want to see that."

"Don't talk about my friend that way! You have a hot body!"

"Seamus, stop."

"You do! You're sexy and you don't even know it."

"Will you stop!" I kicked my coffee table, leaving a chip in the thick wooden leg. I wanted to scream. I wanted to wipe that look of pity off his beautiful face. "Don't give me this bullshit about how sexy I am, when we know the kinds of bodies people like. Is it really some mystery why I've never had a boyfriend or why I have to resort to a straight guy pity-fucking me? Here's your answer." I gestured at my chest and stomach, my lumpiest parts. "And for you to sit there and pretend like we live in a world where I have a hot body...it's insulting. We both know what I look like. I'm a fat ass. My third-grade classmates had it right all along." I shrugged, fighting back tears. "That's the truth."

Too bad saying the truth didn't make me feel any better. Maybe this whole arrangement was a mistake.

"It's probably best if you go," I said before making a beeline to the bathroom so I could be alone with my fat ass self.

12

SEAMUS

I couldn't leave him like this.

Julian wasn't the only one hurting. Anger surged in my chest. My fists were tight and coiled. I wanted to punch every person who'd made him feel this way. Every guy on every app. Every Instagram model. Every superhero Chris. Hearing Julian talk about himself with such disgust broke my heart. He was ridiculously smart, and caring, and funny, and loyal. Why did none of those qualities matter more than having a stupid six-pack?

A few moments later, I knocked on the bathroom door. No answer.

"Hey, Jules?" I knocked again. "Can you give me a sign that you're still alive in there?"

After a painful silence, he knocked back.

"Can we talk about this?" I asked, leaning my head against the door.

"I'm sorry I'm being dramatic. Can we just talk tomorrow?"

I hated hearing him sound so dejected. Even at his lowest, he was self-aware. His brain was always going. How many times had he beaten himself up about his weight?

"Can I let you in on a little straight guy secret, Jules? But you have to promise not to tell anyone." I imagined he was listening, his big brown eyes focused on me. "We're not looking for stick figure girls. We like women who have curves. Yeah, the media pushes these super skinny girls on us all the time and makes us *think* that's what we want, but it never sticks. Hooking up with someone with a perfect body is only fun the first time. Then after that, the high wears off, and you need something else about them to get you excited. They need to make me laugh, or have a good smile. I promise you, if you hooked up with some hot guy model, it'd be good the first time, and then you'd be bored. I once hooked up with a girl who was a model, but she was so boring that I couldn't get it up. Seriously. That doesn't leave this apartment."

I couldn't hear anything, but I liked to believe Julian was smiling.

"I meant what I said. You are a good-looking guy. But you're so much more than that, too. You're interesting and funny and sweet. I love talking to you. You make mundane subjects like Cyllabus fascinating. Those qualities have way more lasting power than a ripped body. And I might give good naked, whatever that means, but I'm not boyfriend material. I'm...kinda fucked up. I live in a basement for fuck sakes."

I got off this track before I derailed my whole pep talk.

"If there's a guy who rejects you right away because of your weight, then you dodged a bullet because that guy sounds like a loser. Who wants to be with someone who places so much value on how many muscles you have? Who's constantly rating what you look like?" I rested my head on the door. "I wish you could see what I see. I wish you could realize how beautiful you are. I wish you could see what a fucking catch you are."

I wanted to tell him more. I wanted to tell him that I didn't need to picture a hot girl to get hard around him. Not like he would believe me. I closed my eyes and got lost in images of Julian.

I used to feel weird for thinking about him this way, but fuck that. I celebrated him the way he should be celebrated.

When he opened the door, I pulled him close to me, my hands sizzling with heat on his hips. I meant what I said. Julian was attractive. His broad chest and shoulders could wrap around me like a soothing weighted blanket.

"Jules, you're sexy," I whispered into his ear.

"How?" he asked, almost as a dare.

"Let's see. You have penetrating eyes. And this faint stubble on your jaw shows me you have a dark side." I skimmed my finger over the prickly hairs. "And you have broad shoulders and chest." I rubbed his shoulders, feeling their heft. "And we can't forget this big ass back here." I gave his ass a pat. "There are guys out there who are ass men, and they are going to eat it up."

"Are you an ass man?"

"Hell yeah." I gave it a squeeze with my whole hand. My dick immediately went hard. I had never openly admired a man's body like this, but I took my time savoring all Julian had to offer. Not just for his sake.

I brushed my hand over his crotch where his dick pressed against his fly. Julian leaned against the door, eyes closed, breathing heavy.

"You're so hot," I murmured in his ear as I unzipped and reached into his jeans. I massaged his erection through his underwear. "You got a nice dick. All those losers on the apps are missing out. More for me."

I maneuvered my hand and reached inside his underwear. Fuck, I was grabbing a man's dick, and I liked it. I liked how powerful I felt giving pleasure, how I was the one turning my friend on. Julian maintained a calm, refined composure all day long. Only I got to see this wild side in him get unleashed.

He moaned, his eyes still closed. I wanted him to look at me, but I understood why he couldn't.

"Jules, you are so sexy," I whispered into his ear as I gripped his cock. I wanted him to feel his power...because I was feeling it.

He leaned back against the doorframe, short breaths escaping his lips. I stroked him in his underwear. With a shaky hand, he unbuttoned his pants. They dropped to the ground.

I pulled down his underwear, fully freeing him. Damn, this was so hot. I loved watching my friend become unglued by my touch.

"You feel so good," I said, my mouth right against his ear, making the hairs on his neck stand up.

Julian let out a low moan. Pre-come slicked the tips of my fingers, providing lubrication. That had to mean I was doing a good job. I jerked him faster, listening to his heart race.

"You are so fucking hot," I told him, over and over.

"Want you...want you so bad, Seamus." He reared his back and exclaimed with abandon. "Fuck, Seamus!"

My name had never sounded sexier, especially as it cracked in his voice. I was rock hard in my pants, but it would've been selfish and weird of me to whip it out. I tried to stealthily rub myself over my jeans, but I made sure my main focus was on my friend.

Julian seemed to intuit what was going on. His eyes were closed, but he reached for my crotch and rubbed me, just as he'd done the other day. I nibbled on his ear lobe as I jerked him off at full speed, doing everything to him that I secretly wanted done to me.

"You want it, baby?" I asked. I didn't plan to call him baby, but as soon as it left my lips, it stuck. I undid my pants and he instantly grabbed for my cock. I was ready to blow the second his hand made contact with my flesh.

Must not come in under two seconds.

We stroked each other. I went fast, and he followed, getting into a synced-up rhythm, our grunts filling the silence. My legs had trouble keeping me upright. Heat built up in my core.

"Jules," I practically whimpered, desperate for his touch to give me release. I leaned toward him, letting our cocks touch. We both emitted moans of approval.

"Seamus, don't stop. I'm so close."

I jutted my hips out to give him a clear grip. He did the same.

I cracked out a groan as I shot my load, waves of release wringing me dry. His balls tightened under my grasp, and he shuddered as he came.

We blinked open our eyes at the same time. His pupils were blown wide open, his round cheeks flushed with color. I looked down at the mess we'd made on his floor. Our releases were mixed together. There was something a little romantic about it.

Lust, not romance. I reminded myself of the cardinal rule of this arrangement.

He gazed at me, lost in the hazy afterglow. It'd been a long-ass time since someone looked at me that way. He ran his finger down my beard, savoring each bristle.

"Jules's first handjob. Check," I said with the accompanying finger motion.

"When did you decide to grow a beard?"

"It was really cold in January. I needed to keep myself warm." I was proud of myself for being able to grow one. When I'd tried in the past, it had come in patches, as if I were forever going through puberty.

"I like it." His voice was scratchy, as if he just woke up. It threatened to make me hard again.

"Jules, you're half-naked in your apartment." I nodded at his exposed bottom half.

"It's a start."

Julian brushed his palm over my facial hair, like I was all his.

Was it normal to regularly get hard over a guy? A guy who was my friend, first and foremost? I knew I would get some type of enjoyment out of this arrangement. A hand on a dick was a hand on a dick. But was I enjoying it too much?

"Do you have paper towels?" I asked, nudging my chin at the mess on the floor. It was better than thinking of the mess currently happening in my head.

We eventually got the floor and ourselves cleaned up. Now that we'd gotten all the sex out of the way, I had built up an appetite. We split the leftovers from his catering session while watching a rerun of Julian's favorite show *Frasier.* It was nice just hanging out together, no school talk, no sex talk. We could just be.

"I'm sorry again for exploding at you earlier," Julian said during a commercial break. "Whenever I see my mom, she gets inside my head."

It wasn't the first time he'd alluded to this. "What's the deal with you two?"

He swirled the roasted vegetables around his plate. "She's been on me about my weight forever. I went to a fat loss summer camp when I was a teenager, but it didn't stick. I gained the weight back by Christmas. I think..." He let out a heavy sigh. "She's always been gorgeous and popular. My armchair shrink opinion is I don't think she can process having a child who isn't as gorgeous. I think she blames herself for me having weight problems, like she failed as a mother."

"That's a lot to put on you," I said. And I thought my parents were a lot because they yelled all the time, though that was normal for big Staten Island families. It was better than the passive-aggressive thing that seemed to permeate Julian's family.

"I've gotten good at tuning out her comments. And I know she means well. She does, deep down. Even though we're mother and son, we come from different worlds."

"Jules, I meant what I said earlier. You are a sexy bitch. For a sexual newbie, you are very talented. You just gotta get better at believing your own hype."

"Can I ask you something?"

"Make it quick before *Frasier* comes back on," I cracked.

"Even though I've checked off certain items from my sexual to-do list, would it be weird if we continued doing them?"

My dick immediately perked up. "Like practice?"

"Exactly. I didn't know if our arrangement only allowed for one time for each thing."

It probably should since I was mostly straight and shouldn't be enjoying this so much. But fuck that. Rules were made to be broken.

"It doesn't."

"So if when this episode of *Frasier* is done, I wanted to go again...that would be okay?"

"Yeah." I shrugged. Fortunately, as a guy, I'd had lots of practice staying calm while savagely horny. "I'm here to help you out. I mean this from the bottom of my heart, Jules: use me for my body."

13

JULIAN

Tonight, I wasn't meeting up with my friends for a night out as the regular, normal Julian Bradford.

I was transformed. This was a Julian Bradford who was sexually active on the regular. This was a Julian Bradford who had given and received multiple handjobs.

Over the past few days, Seamus and I had gotten lots of practice.

Handjobs at my apartment.

Handjobs at his place.

Handjobs in the car.

Handjobs in the classroom before school.

Handjobs for everyone. Handjobs for Algernon.

To say it was amazing was an understatement. How much joy had I been missing out on? How bleak had my life been without the touch of another man?

I'd thought Seamus was eventually going to do the whole straight guy thing of getting weirded out by the whole arrangement, but it never came to pass. The only thing that came was each other. Multiple times.

If I didn't know any better, I'd say he liked it. Sure, on a purely physical level, he was enjoying himself. A hard dick didn't lie. But he really got into it. The moaning, the mumbling of my name like it was a religious chant, the way his eyes blazed into me.

He got lost in the pleasure. I was *that* good. Was I a sex God in training?

I knew better than to read too much into it. A guy liked getting jerked off. In other news, the earth was round.

When I met up with my friends at Remix, Sourwood's biggest gay club, I strutted into the club like it was my personal catwalk. Usually, I'd slink in with my head down, avoiding the inevitable way guys would turn away when they saw me.

But not tonight. Tonight, I strolled through the main floor of the club feeling like a boss, deserved or not. I was getting it on with a hot straight guy, a hot straight guy who was absolute putty in my hand, a hot straight guy who I reduced to muttering in tongues.

Bow down, bitches.

"J, you seem different tonight," Amos said around our usual table next to the dance floor, a table that gave us a perfect line of sight through the whole club.

I sipped my mai tai and shrugged. "I do?"

"Oh, you totally fucking do." Everett sipped his vodka Sprite. "Did you get a raise and not tell us?"

"Nope." I made a hot straight guy get a raise. *Ba-dum-bum. Thank you. Don't forget to tip your waitress.*

Amos and Everett stared at me like two detectives on the case.

"Something's up with you," Amos said, mixing his drink with his straw. "I like it, and I'm intrigued."

"I guess it's Friday, and I'm happy it's the weekend?" I offered.

"Frankly, you're never this happy to be at Remix," he said.

I couldn't help but take that as a small dig.

"Not that you've been miserable or a drag to be around,"

Everett said, backpedaling for our friend. "It's just that you seem… I can't describe it. Here, let me act it out."

"You really don't have to," I said. Everett was a trained actor and prided himself on his charade skills, but I wasn't ready to be his next project. Yet I knew better than to try and stop Everett from being his dramatic self.

"This is how you used to be at Remix." Everett dipped his head, then lifted it to signal the start of the scene. He had a neutral look on his face, a fake smile that hid a poor time. His shoulders slumped as he hunched over the table swirling his drink.

This was supposed to be me? I flicked my eyes at Amos, who had no notes.

"And this is how you are tonight." Everett dipped his head again, then popped it back up. New scene. New Julian. He stood up straight, had almost a cocky, genuine smile. He looked around at guys in the club. He might as well have worn sunglasses, too.

I couldn't help but grin. I never saw myself like that. What was it like to walk through the world with that kind of confidence? Maybe the key was not realizing you had it.

I gave him a round of applause.

"Ev, what are you doing?" Raleigh, his boyfriend, joined our table. He, Hutch, and Chase had come back from the bar with beers. "Are you doing that thing where you have to be the center of attention?"

"You're one to talk, Raleigh. Your ego knows no bounds." Everett shot his boyfriend a loving glare. They had started out the school year as mortal enemies, and even though they were very much in love…they were still kinda enemies.

"That was quite a line for beer. This establishment should look into hiring a second bartender. Surely, they have the volume to justify the expense," Chase said, leaning against our table. I remembered when it was just the four of us. Now it was a tight squeeze with Hutch and Raleigh, making for a cozy feel. I loved that our crew was expanding.

"What are we talking about?" Hutch threw an arm around Amos.

"I was merely demonstrating to Julian how he seems different," Everett explained. "A good different."

Raleigh studied me now, too. "Did you part your hair a new way?"

"No, Raleigh." Everett rolled his eyes. "It's not the hair. It's his whole demeanor."

"Can you guys stop talking about me like I'm not here?"

"I believe they're talking about you like you're the only one here," Chase corrected.

"Julian looks great. Leave the guy alone," Hutch said, sipping his beer. "Let him enjoy his night."

"Thank you!"

"This is all a good thing," Amos said. "You have an aura of confidence."

Everett's eyes bulged open with realization. "Oh my God, you're having sex aren't you?"

It was a good thing I wasn't mid-drink because I would've spat it out. Was Everett a drama teacher by day and demon psychic by night? All eyes turned to me, hungry for the truth.

"What? No. Everett, that's your answer for everything," I said. "Oh, the mail is late. The postman is probably getting some. Oh, Principal Aguilar is in a good mood. He must be having great sex. You've been hanging around our students too much because you have sex perpetually on the brain."

"I'll take some credit for that," Raleigh said with a puffed-out chest.

"It's a simple yes or no answer," Amos said.

But it wasn't so simple, not so simple at all. I couldn't tell them about Seamus, because then I'd have to tell them why Seamus and

I were fooling around in the first place. I'd have to untangle the years of lies I'd fed them about my fraudulent sex life and then untangle the sticky gray area of me getting it on with a straight friend. No, this was all too much for a night out on the town.

And I kinda liked that Seamus and I had this secret. Amos and Everett didn't reveal every detail of their sex lives with their boyfriends (although Everett got *real* close at times). Why did I have to just because I was single?

"No," I uttered, getting a tiny spark of excitement over this secret that Seamus and I shared.

Maybe it was in my head, but I thought I saw them all deflate at the news.

"Well, don't waste whatever you're feeling on us," Amos said. "Take this newfound confidence and unleash it."

He waved his hand at the myriad of gentlemen before us.

Wild thoughts swirled in my head. I was...attractive. I was...a catch. I was...sexual. Why *wouldn't* a guy in here want me?

I scanned the room and locked eyes with a tall, burly guy who'd just gotten a beer from the bar. He had a thick beard and dark eyes that told me he was soulful but also capable of getting down.

I gave him a sly smile. He smiled back.

At me.

This had never happened before. Was it really this easy?

Before I could second-guess myself, I nodded back at him.

And he smiled again. At me.

My friends were courteous and didn't gawk, but I could feel their eyes on me still.

"Damn, J. Get it," Everett said under his breath.

And then I was off, making a casual beeline to this new potential Romeo, liking what I saw the closer I got.

"Hey, how's it going? Julian." I held out my hand. I didn't have a suave line, but I didn't need it.

"Dylan," he said back, his voice deep and relaxed.

"How's your beer?"

"I haven't had it yet."

"Well, something tells me this isn't your first one of the night," I said with a flirty smile. I recalled the flirting lesson our friend Charlie had given us back in the day. When I felt my confidence falter for a moment, I remembered that I was cool and sexual, so why wouldn't this guy want to flirt back?

"Are those your friends?" He nodded behind me. When I turned around, my friends all scattered, busted.

I sighed. "For the time being."

DYLAN RAN A MUSIC SHOP. He played the guitar, piano, and harp of all things, something he'd learned from his mother.

We'd found a small high-top table in the corner to talk, and the time had flown. We were clicking as we discussed music and high school and commenting on songs the DJ spun. Our hands kept touching, and we kept looking at each other. The flirting was on.

I alternated between living in the moment and standing outside myself shocked that this was all happening. Maybe real life was kinder than the apps because people had no choice but to get to know me. Or maybe it was as Seamus had said, that the only thing stopping me was me.

"You know, I've seen you here before, but I've never had the nerve to talk to you," Dylan admitted while scratching his beard. I ran my fingers through it in a move of sheer boldness. Seamus's felt softer...

...which was an irrelevant point because Seamus wasn't here. He was likely at a sports bar or a strip club or buying a lawnmower or whatever straight guys did for fun.

"Do you ever run into old students?" Dylan asked.

"It hasn't happened yet. But I'm hitting the point in my tenure at South Rock where my first students will soon be old enough to get in here. I'm so not ready for that point."

"I once saw one of my regulars at the music shop here. I remember when he used to come into the store with his mom when he wanted to buy his first guitar." Dylan turned red, cringing at the passage of time.

"What's your favorite instrument to play?"

"Banjo."

"Banjo?" That was a left turn I hadn't seen coming, but the beard should've been a hint. "I'm a Yankee through and through. I don't think I've ever met someone who played the banjo."

Dylan brushed his hand over mine and gazed at me with those warm, dark eyes. He leaned in, letting me take in how good he smelled.

"So, I don't live too far from here. We can go back to my place, and I'll give you a private concert."

My breath caught in my throat. Even a kindergartner could read between those lines.

"How does that sound?" he asked, his voice a low growl.

This was the goal. This was everything I wanted. I could go home with Dylan and check off every item left on my list. I would have a night to remember, and he seemed like the guy who'd take me to brunch in the morning.

He waited for my answer, and his confident stare slipped a bit as the seconds ticked by.

"I, uh—I drove tonight, so my friends are depending on me for a ride home. Maybe we can hang out another time?"

"Yeah, cool. Can I get your number?" He handed me his phone to enter my number. As I typed in the numbers, I knew I'd never hear from Dylan again. The window had closed.

He called me so I'd have his. I held up my phone to show I got it, but I knew that I'd never contact him.

And so our flirtatious banter devolved into who could find the exit first.

"I'm gonna get another drink," Dylan said. "It was good talking to you."

"Same." I held up my beer and watched him go. I took a beat before I returned to be grilled by my friends.

"What happened?" Amos asked when I rejoined the group, the question on everyone's minds.

"He was nice. He owns a music shop a few towns over."

"Is he going to play you like an upright bass?" Everett asked, impatient.

I shook my head no. "We had a good chat, but there wasn't anything there. Maybe we'll hang out in the future," I said with barely mustered enthusiasm.

"I find this perplexing because you both had very positive body language from what I ascertained," Chase said.

"Not like we were looking," Hutch said.

"You ran your fingers through his beard, which is a 'come fuck me' signal if there ever was one," Everett said.

"Not like we were looking," Hutch repeated.

Was that why I like rubbing Seamus's beard? *Ugh, Seamus isn't here. Lawnmower strip club, remember?*

"He seemed into you." Amos shrugged, getting to the simple heart of the matter.

Unfortunately, things were simple this time. Dylan was into me. And I...was somewhere else.

"He was nice. Maybe we'll see each other again. Who needs another round?" I pointed at Chase's empty glass and Raleigh's empty bottle. "Anyone else?"

I headed for the bar before I could get any more looks of confusion from my friends.

It seemed every gay man in New York needed to let off steam tonight. Men danced with abandon, singing along to the music. Every table was packed with groups of bros having the time of their lives. This was what it felt like when a place became thrillingly alive. And yet...I found myself standing just outside the revelry, peeking through the window but unable, and maybe unwilling, to open the door.

I left Remix sometime after one, pushing through throngs of men into the cold air of night. Instead of driving home, I changed course and found myself parked on a familiar curb.

Julian: Can I come in? I'm outside.

I waited painfully long seconds until the front door cracked open. Seamus sleepily grinned at me in nothing but gym shorts.

"Hey, Jules. What's going on? You go out tonight?" he asked with his bright smile, a salve from the weirdness of tonight.

"I'm ready to move onto the next session," I said, breath catching in my throat.

I cupped his dick. He instantly let out a husky sigh.

I closed the front door behind us, walked us backwards to the dining room, got on my knees, and pulled down his shorts. I ran a hand over the outline in his underwear of his throbbing, rock hard dick.

Seamus stumbled, falling onto a dining chair. His cock stood straight up, his eyes wide and alive.

I took him in my mouth, not sure how to give a good blow job, but feeling my way through by instinct and lust. If men could figure out how to fellate each other over the course of millennia before the internet, then so could I. I was smart and a fast learner. I listened to his moans and felt the way his hips shifted under my mouth.

His cock was hot and salty. I swirled my tongue around his shaft and head.

"Fuck. Jules, this is so fucking hot." He threw his head back and threaded his fingers through my hair.

I drowned out thoughts of tonight by bobbing on Seamus's cock. I couldn't get enough of how good this felt, hearing and feeling him get so turned on by my touch.

He pulled on my hair and arched his hips to get farther down my throat. I took him all the way to the base, letting bitter precome hit the back of my throat. I moaned with delight, which made him groan even louder.

"Feels so good. Suck that dick." He thrust into my mouth.

I alternated fist and mouth, proud of myself for building on our previous lessons.

"Yeah, just like that. Just like that, Jules."

I put my free hand down my pants, where I was already hard. One or two pumps would be all it took. Nothing turned my crank like Seamus saying my name.

"Shit. I'm coming." He reached for a stack of napkins on the table. They wouldn't be necessary.

I sucked him harder, sucked him until his whole body shook underneath me, a centralized earthquake rattling the apartment. His chest rose high, then collapsed, then high again as he struggled for air. I stroked myself faster, my balls tightening with orgasm.

"Fuck. Fuck, I'm coming. I'm coming." His fist tightened on my hair as he came down my throat. I sucked him dry, taking his hot, bitter load as I soaked my pants with my own release.

I fell back, hitting my head on the china hutch as I came back to reality. "I think I need the napkins."

He tossed the box to me, and I cleaned off my hand.

"You jerked off while..."

"Yeah. is that okay?" I asked.

"That's so fucking hot." He took my hand, brought it to his mouth.

His eyes lit up and gazed at me with heat and tenderness, cutting through the silence. Seamus had never looked at me in this way, in this way I'd only dreamed about, like he was seconds away from leaning in and kissing me.

I had to get the hell out of there.

For the second time tonight, I made a hasty exit from a guy.

14

SEAMUS

"Uh...what just happened?"

"I'll tell you what happened, Seamus. Ashley isn't playing the game correctly," Ethan huffed.

Greg and Ethan had let me tag along to their friend's party, held in a beautifully restored Victorian house, one of those houses people aspired to when they were in their fifties. Ashley and her wife Jill were living the double income, no kids life and were able to live in their dream house by the time they were thirty.

We were all sitting in a circle on Ashley's living room floor playing Shock and Awe sometime just before midnight. Shock and Awe was like playing fill in the blank, but the blank had to be filled with either the dirtiest or most ironic answer available. It was a fun party game that I'd played in high school, college, and as an adult.

Nobody I knew took it as seriously as Ethan, though.

"The rules of the game clearly state that the person whose turn it is is supposed to pick the most outrageous, but *logical* answer. Ashley's picked an answer that makes absolutely no sense for the sentence." Ethan was a lawyer by day, and apparently a lawyer by night, too.

He pleaded his case to the group in the hopes of getting Ashley to pick another card, preferably his. Ashley wasn't having it, though. She crossed her arms, standing firm on her choice.

"Ethan, you need to calm down. This is just a friendly game," she said.

"And games have rules, no matter how friendly they are."

"Babe, I love you, but you're being a sore loser." Greg rubbed his husband's shoulder, which did the trick of calming him down. "I know you love to win. I think it's sexy. But losing gracefully is also sexy."

"Fine. I will admit defeat. Though don't be surprised if I write a letter to Shock and Awe corporate to get an official ruling for future games." Ethan took a picture of the cards being played for evidence. This was my first game night with Greg and Ethan, and I had a feeling it would be my last.

Greg looked at me from across the circle, and his eyes crinkled with an apology. It took me a second to realize what was going on. I was somewhere else.

"You good?" he asked, arching an eyebrow.

"Yeah. What?"

"Seamus, are you even paying attention? It's your turn," Ashley said.

"It's—what? My turn? Right." I shook my head, getting myself back in the present. Greg suppressed a laugh.

Ethan held out the stack of fill-in-the-blank cards. I blinked at them.

"Pick one," he said impatiently.

"Right. Sorry." I took a card from the middle of the stack and tossed it into the center of the circle. Everyone reacted and guffawed, as it was an especially raunchy fill in the blank. *Oh, I almost forgot. I need to put my _____ in _______.*

I gulped back a hard lump when I read the card out aloud. The other players combed through their response cards to find the funniest, dirtiest, and according to Ethan, still narratively logical answers. I would have to pick the best choice, but the only response I could think of was *Oh, I almost forgot. I need to put my dick in my gay, virginal friend.*

Was it hot in here? These old houses had poor ventilation.

"You okay?" Greg asked. Was he watching me all the time?

"You seem very deep in thought considering nobody's turned in their answers," Ashley said.

"That's because he's taking the game seriously," Ethan huffed.

"Ethan!" Ashley and the other players threw their hands up.

Usually, Ethan was a fun, sweet guy. His competitive spirit truly took over his body like that demon who made the girl's head spin in *The Exorcist*.

As people contemplated and submitted their response cards, I kept thinking about my own answer.

Oh, I almost forgot. I need to put my dick in my gay, virginal friend.

Something I did exactly twenty-four hours ago. I was still riding a confusing high. Good Lord, for being a newbie at blow jobs, Julian was preternaturally talented. This was the American dream, right? Having somebody come over in the middle of the night, suck you off no strings attached, and then leave? That was why Washington crossed the Delaware and all those dudes signed the Declaration of Independence.

Ethan snapped his fingers in front of my face, pulling me out of my post-blow job high.

"What just happened?" I asked, shaking my head.

Everyone in the circle chuckled. Well, everyone except Ethan.

"Seamus, are you on drugs?" he asked.

"If you are, then you gotta share. It's only right." Greg had an ear-to-ear grin, getting a kick out of this whole scene.

I managed through my round, ultimately picking Greg's

response card since it got the biggest laugh. We broke for a bathroom and drink break right after. I hustled to the kitchen and grabbed another beer from the fridge.

Greg clapped his hand on my shoulder. "Have you been in their backyard? It's so nice. Let's go check it out."

"Isn't the game starting back up?"

We craned our necks toward the living room where Ethan and Ashley were continuing their heated discussion of the rules.

"I don't think they'll miss us." Greg tried to act nonchalant, but he lovingly watched his husband argue before leading us through the back door.

We stepped into Ashley and Jill's expansive backyard, filled with two mighty oak trees. In the corner was a greenhouse, moonlight glinting off the panes of glass. Greg walked to it. He was never afraid of a challenge. He figured it was better to be asked to leave than to never venture at all. Like a good little brother, I followed him.

"This thing is awesome." He marveled at the rows of plants growing around us. Fragrant flower smells filled my nose. I dipped my head back to take in the height of one impressive, purple flower in full bloom. "This lets Jill garden year-round."

"Sweet."

"So what the hell is up?" Greg asked, no segue. He held up a hand to block the response coming out of my mouth. "And don't tell me you're good. You're not on drugs. You're not tired. You haven't been paying attention all night. You've been on another planet. Something is up with you." Greg took a step closer. "Is it a girl?"

Oh, how I wished it were that simple. Why had *nothing* felt simple about this arrangement?

"It's actually...about a boy."

As predicted, Greg's eyebrows flew up to his hairline. Greg

Sanderson liked to act cool and collected; it took a lot to shock him.

"I got a blow-and-run last night."

"Is that the opposite of a come-and-go?" He chuckled. "I thought I heard the front door open as I was falling asleep."

He had on a poker face, but I truly hoped Greg hadn't heard any other noises last night.

"Who was the girl? I mean, guy? Are you on Milkman?"

"No. This wasn't a stranger." I ground the tip of my shoe into the grass. "Do you remember my friend Julian?"

"Dammit." Greg threw his head back, silently cursing at the sky.

"What? Is this bad?"

"No, I just owe Ethan twenty bucks."

I smacked his chest. I wasn't a race horse. My life wasn't up for betting on.

"He had a feeling Julian was into you and that you guys might hookup."

"Jules isn't into me. He's never been with a guy, so to help him out, I offered myself up. Like a cadaver, but still alive. And for sex, not surgery."

"Huh. I didn't know you swung that way." Greg leaned against a table lined with small pots filled with dirt.

"That's the thing. I don't, for the most part. I offered to do this for him because he's my friend, and I didn't want him to cash in his v-card with some random guy who'd pump him and dump him."

"You offered to have gay sex, but you don't swing that way?"

"I have a slight bicurious itch. I was intrigued, and Jules is a good-looking guy, so I thought YOLO."

I paced in the tight quarters, my shoes crunching on the dirt and matted-down grass. "I thought that I could get hard from the friction, and that'd be enough to do stuff with him. But I've been...

enjoying it. A lot. And last night, he came over in the middle of the night and gave me head and *I can't stop thinking about it.*"

"A good blow job will do that to you."

"But it's not just the blow job, man. I can't stop thinking about all of it. The way he looks at me, and the way he smells, and the way he says my fucking name, and the way he can go from classy mofo to sex beast." I rubbed my hands all over my head, trying to mold these thoughts into something I could understand. They were like Shock and Awe answers: raunchy as fuck but making no sense. "Isn't there a goddamn chair in here?"

Greg pushed over a stool. He was always the all-knowing, all-wise big brother when we were in college. There was never a problem he couldn't help me and the other guys get out of, whether it was about an impossible professor or a girl giving mixed signals.

"You're in quite the conundrum." He pushed aside some of the pots and sat on the table, making sure it wouldn't collapse before he put his full weight on it.

"Greg, how did you know?" I asked. "You were the ladies' man at Browerton, and then it was like, all of a sudden, you're gay and dating Ethan."

It had been a weird kind of whiplash. I remembered being in the common room of our frathouse when Greg came out to me, telling me as if he were recounting another wild story of his. But he was serious. At first, I thought it was just a phase. He'd gotten bored hooking up with girls, so he decided to try something new. Yet once he was with Ethan, that was it. They'd been together ever since, and it was like his heterosexuality was something we'd all dreamed up.

"Did you always know you were into guys?"

"On some level, yes. Looking back, there were signs. Little crushes I had as a kid that I made up excuses for. But I considered myself straight."

"How did you and Ethan get together then?"

"We were in the same law class. My dad made me study pre-law." Greg rolled his eyes. "Ethan was this uptight straight-A student. He was so annoying. I found this sick joy in getting under his skin because he took shit so seriously, as you saw tonight. One time in class, we were bickering as usual, and I forget what we were talking about, but I whipped out my dick to shut him up." Greg threw an embarrassed hand over his face and laughed.

"Are you serious? Right in the middle of class?"

"We were in the back row, in my defense. What can I say? I was twenty and stupid. But then Ethan grabbed it and..."

"Right there in class?"

"Only for a few seconds."

Shit. I had pegged Ethan all wrong. He apparently had a wild side. It reminded me a little of Julian giving me a blow-and-run.

"We met up in the library stacks and continued what we'd started in class. It was the hottest thing. And then we kept hooking up around campus, still finding each other annoying as shit, but that only made things hotter." Greg looked up at the glass ceiling, a nostalgic glint in his eye. Man, I thought my college days were wild. Greg (and Ethan!) had me beat.

"I wasn't thinking about whether I was gay or straight. I was just thinking about Ethan and how he made me feel."

"I think I'm the same. I mean, the physical stuff is amazing, but now I'm thinking about more than that."

"The physical's always good. I'm sure if most straight guys were offered free blow jobs from gay guys, they'd be able to get hard and come. We're simple creatures. But at some point, for some guys, the physical leads into the emotional. That's how it was with me. It was physical with Ethan at first, until the emotional side crept in. Then it became about more. Things got deeper." Greg scratched at his face. "Fuck, am I making any sense?"

"You are."

"Do you feel that way about Julian? Or are you just on a very strong sex high? Basically, are you thinking about Julian with your head..." He pointed to my dick. "Or your heart?" He jammed his fingers against my chest.

"What are you guys doing out here?" Ethan opened the greenhouse door. "We're ready to continue playing."

"We are? I thought that was more of a permanent break," Greg said.

"We can't stop now! I'm only two answers away from beating Ashley, despite her rule fudging. Nevertheless, *I'm* persisting."

I let out a laugh, low and snickering like I was trying not to get caught by the teacher.

"What's so funny?" Ethan asked.

Greg glanced at me, prompting me to keep my mouth shut. Was this Ethan really the same Ethan who'd jerked off a guy in the middle of class, and then fooled around in public? Love and sex made people do some crazy shit.

"Were you guys talking about me?" Ethan darted his eyes between us.

Greg hopped off the table, cool as a cucumber, and slid an arm across his husband's lower back. "We were just saying that you deserve to win and wipe the floor with Ashley. She obviously doesn't understand the rules of Shock and Awe."

Ethan rested his head on Greg's shoulder. "I'm glad we're on the same page. Let's go!"

15

JULIAN

Sundays were for grocery shopping and feeble attempts at meal prep. I usually started off the week on track, but by Wednesday, I was tired of what I'd made and would order in. I had a spoiled tongue that craved variety.

Going through the motions of grocery shopping helped me not think about Friday night. How was I going to face Seamus in school on Monday after my drive-by blow job? He had to think I was certifiable, although judging by the way he'd exploded in my mouth, he'd seemed to enjoy himself.

And so had I. I'd thought that blow jobs were only for the enjoyment of the receiver, not the giver. I had to be an exception because I wanted to do it again. I wanted to make Seamus moan, wanted to hear him call me baby. It wasn't infantilizing when he said it.

I stood in the canned goods aisle trying to be my best self. I strummed my fingers against the shopping cart. Buy food. Make food. Stick to routine.

Nope.

"I need some wine," I said aloud.

I strolled out of Market Thyme and walked over to In Good Spirits next door.

In Good Spirits was like a library with tall, intimidating stacks, but instead of books, they had bottles. I felt like Belle in *Beauty and the Beast*. Bonjour, indeed!

What was I in the mood for? I needed a wine that was dry, sharp. Something to take the edge off and stop me from thinking about...

Seamus.

He was one row over, looking lost as ever.

Maybe if I blushed enough, I'd blend into the row of reds behind me.

"Hey." He waved, giving me no time to duck.

"Hi. What a surprise to see you here." In Good Spirits was my safe space. Seamus was invading my safe space with his charm and sex appeal and fitted ringer tee.

"I pass this place all the time but I've never gone in. When I needed wine in the past, I just went to the supermarket."

The supermarket wine selection was sparse and depressing. People raved about Market Thyme's three-dollar wine, but it tasted like expired grape juice someone scooped out of a dumpster, in my humble opinion.

"You don't want supermarket wine. In Good Spirits has the best selection." I waved to the rows of wine. I didn't peg Seamus for someone who opted for wine, though. He was a crack-open-a-brewsky kind of guy.

He looked around, very much overwhelmed. "I just need a bottle of wine."

He grabbed the bottle closest to him, a thin bottle of prosecco.

"What do you need it for?"

"I'm going to a housewarming party with Greg and Ethan. They tasked me with picking out a bottle of wine to bring as a present."

"You're bringing prosecco?"

"Is that bad?"

I seesawed my head, trying to be diplomatic.

"I just grabbed it because it was next to me."

Prosecco was essentially off-brand champagne that tried and failed to replicate the magic of champagne. I might prefer the three-dollar wine to that.

"It's not bad, but I don't know how many people like it. If there's going to be a few wine options at the party, do you want yours to be the one that doesn't get opened?"

Seamus shook his head emphatically no.

"You want yours to be the one that people rave about and snap pictures of the label so they can buy it for themselves." That had happened with me on multiple occasions, not to brag. I might not know how to have sex, but I knew how to pick wine.

"So, which one do we choose?"

"First, we have to think about the person. Whose house are you warming?"

"I don't know this person that well. She's friends with Greg and Ethan. I'm mostly going for the food." Seamus rubbed his head bashfully.

"I'd do the same. You're going to wow your friend of a friend."

I pivoted on my heel and began our trek through the magical aisles of In Good Spirits. I loved a wine-based challenge. "So tell me about this friend of a friend."

"Her name is Lorna. She works in public relations. She broke up with her fiance a few months ago and after living with her parents, she just bought a condo in the meatpacking district."

I fed each new piece of information into my wine processing brain as I scanned rows of bottles, ideas beginning to form.

"What is she like? Have you met her before?"

"A few times. She and Ethan are close friends. We all went to college together. She was a regular at frat parties, just one of those people who knows how to have a good time. I guess she's perfect for PR because that's all about parties. Aren't girls into rosè? That's a thing, right? I think they sell it in six-packs."

"I'm not letting you walk into a party with rosè, and definitely not rosè in cans." Friends didn't let friends drink wine from beer cans. "What kind of condo? Tell me about it."

"From what I heard, it's really nice. It's a new building, super snazzy, amazing views of the Hudson. Pricey real estate. How about this sparkling white wine? What do you think of that?"

I recoiled and almost retched. Sparkling white wine was what they served in the pits of hell. As I was about to shut it down, the shit-eating grin on his face told me I didn't need to.

His laughter took over his whole face. Damn, this guy could smile.

"I'm kidding," he said.

"Thank God."

"I just wanted to see what your reaction was. It was very entertaining." He gave my ass a soft pat that threatened to turn me as fizzy as sparkling wine. "What about some Yellow Tail?"

He was egging me on, fucking with me yet again. Yellow Tail wine was known for being very inexpensive.

"There are some varieties of Yellow Tail that are good. I'm not against cheap wine, just bad wine."

"Sure, Jules." There was that pleased grin trying to make me melt. "Why don't I get that for the party?"

"Lorna deserves better. She's getting over a breakup."

Seamus walked backward, facing me as we ambled up the aisle.

"This is fun."

"Wine shopping?" I asked.

"Making you outraged." His eyebrows lifted in delirious glee.

"I'm not a snob. There are certain items where I prefer quality.

I eat McDonald's." I didn't become fat by eating free range, organic meals all the time.

"Man of the people! Do you know what my favorite wine is?" He leaned close to whisper in my ear. "Box wine."

Those two words sent a chill down my spine. Boxes were for Amazon shipments, not beverages.

"You are one twisted individual," I said, suppressing a laugh.

"I'm going to ask if they sell Franzia." He turned to go up to the cashier, who would likely toss him out the door for such a question.

"Don't!" I grabbed his sleeve to pull him back. "You'll have me banned for life."

"Fine, fine." He effortlessly took my hand in his and gave it a light squeeze, a nonchalant moment that burned within me.

I was a virgin with little-to-no dating experience, but...was Seamus flirting with me? The teasing, the smiling, the playful touching. That was flirting, right?

Or was this how he was with all of his friends? Seamus was a happy-go-lucky, friendly guy, the kind of person who could bond with anyone.

I stopped myself from falling down an analytical rabbit hole and returned to the topic at hand: wine.

"So what's Lorna like?" I asked

"She's cool."

I waved my hand in a circle to prompt a deeper explanation.

"She's always launching into a joke or an impression of someone she doesn't like. Oh my God is she funny. She's always reposting memes on social media and talking about causes we should be paying more attention to. She seems like one of those people who likes to unwind after a long day with a martini. She's in no hurry to get back into dating, according to Ethan. I think she enjoys being on her own. Oh, and she got a dog. Her fiancè was allergic, so the week they broke up, she got some little dog from a breeder."

"You seem to know her well," I noted.

"Social media helps."

My brain crunched all the data. "She strikes me as someone who would prefer a dry red. I don't see her drinking white wine."

I pointed at Seamus to put down the prosecco that he was still carrying. He hurriedly placed it on an endcap as if it were a bomb.

"Now that I think about it, I think she does prefer red over white," he said.

"If she likes a martini, then she probably goes for something especially dry, maybe one with a bouquet that includes hints of grapefruit and oak. Yes, oak. It has to be oak. Something a bit masculine as a way of sticking it to the patriarchy."

"Oh yeah. She's always talking about the patriarchy! I used to think that was a nickname for the government, but let's keep that between us."

He wasn't far off.

"Yes, Lorna relaxing on her designer couch at the end of a long day, martini in hand, gazing at the river in silent meditation, savoring everything she's built in her life. She'd go for an older blend. Definitely a cabernet," I said as we arrived in the cabernet aisle. I plucked a bottle from the top shelf with a gold label. "This is from my favorite winery in Napa. They ferment the wine in aged oak barrels that were imported from France and are nearly half a century old. Lorna will be able to tell a wine that was aged in an industrial steel container and one aged with care in oak. The flavors of the barrel seep into the wine, infusing it with a crisp, powerful taste."

I handed Seamus the bottle. His eyes were wide and awed, staring at me like I was a mystical shaman. Our fingers touched, sending a current of heat up my arm.

"Damn, Jules." He kept looking at me, staring at me with those dazzling blue eyes, his lips parting slightly, making it very hard to not think about wanting to kiss him. "You are incredible."

I shrugged. "I just know about wine."

"You are the smartest person I know. You are...wow. Thank you." Seamus stepped forward, and then his arms were wrapping around me in a hug, squeezing me tight. I inhaled his woodsy scent because I loved to tease myself.

Seamus also loved to tease apparently, because he gave my ass another slap with a squeeze tacked on. Baseball coaches might've slapped their players' butts, but they did not squeeze. Fortunately, I was wearing a thick pair of jeans, but my dick was still pushing their limits. I was hopeless against the power of Seamus's hands on my body.

He stepped back and gave me an awkward smile, kind of owning what had just happened but kind of not.

"Listen, I'm sorry about Friday night." Why the hell was I bringing that up now? My timing could not have been worse, but maybe it was something I had to own. I couldn't let Seamus heap praise on me without clearing the air. "I was...I probably should not have been driving, we'll just say that."

Lie. A total lie. I was one hundred percent sober.

"I had a good time." Seamus blushed.

Same. If only all nights could end like that.

"I don't know what got into me." I still didn't. I had a cute, smart gay musician who wanted to take me back to his place, and yet I chose the straight guy who wanted to stay friends. "I was just looking to move onto the next session. Time's a ticking and all that."

"No need to apologize." He stopped me from blathering anymore apologies and excuses. "I meant what I said. Use me for my body."

"Will do!"

He clapped me on the shoulder in the most bro-friendly manner imaginable then walked up to the counter to pay.

At least I knew where I stood with him. Seamus was happy to offer up his body; his heart was off limits.

Seamus handed the cashier the bottle.

"This is a good one," the cashier said.

He turned back and gave me a wink.

"That'll be seventy-six even."

"Seventy-six dollars?" Seamus asked.

The cashier nodded yes.

"Cool." Seamus's hand shook slightly as he pulled out his wallet. "It's quality wine. The good stuff."

Fuck. I should've asked if he had a budget he wanted to stick to. I'd got so wrapped up in picking the best bottle.

"We can go fifty-fifty," I said.

"Nah, I'm good. I got it." He shoved his credit card into the reader. Over his shoulder, I spotted a red X on the machine.

"It says insufficient funds," the cashier said.

"How about that?" Seamus stared down at his wallet, searching for another card as red traveled up his neck and ears.

I felt like an asshole. Why couldn't I just let him pick out what he wanted?

I went to put my card in the reader. Seamus pushed it away.

"What are you doing?"

"I, uh...wanted to help."

"I got it, Jules. I took out the wrong card by accident. As we say in my classroom, no problemo!" Seamus whipped out a new card from the depths of his wallet.

I held my breath until it went through.

"Thanks for the wine help. I'll let you know how the party goes." He spun on his heel and made a break for the front door.

16

SEAMUS

It was only Tuesday, and the week was already a shitstorm. I had one student break down crying to me because she got a D on the latest test, which made me feel like an asshole. I shot two videos for my account, and accidentally deleted one of them. But what hit me most of all was that I'd been avoiding Julian.

What had happened at In Good Spirits was more embarrassing than the time a kid pantsed me on the playground in fourth grade. My deepest, darkest secret was flung out in the open, in front of a good friend, a friend who I'd been having more-than-friendly thoughts about.

I didn't want Julian asking questions. I didn't want his pity. I didn't want him to see my mess.

When my last marker ran out of ink that afternoon though, I had no choice but to slink over to his room to borrow a fresh one in between classes. Because of course I didn't have my shit together to have extras on hand.

"Hey, do you have an extra marker? I don't have time to run to the supply closet." I held up the dud one.

"As they say in your language, no problemo." Julian handed

over a green marker. He mustered a half-smile. It seemed as if the week had been a little shitbag to him, too.

"Thanks. How's things?"

"Not the best." Julian stepped closer so the students filtering into his class couldn't hear us. "The tent rental company for my grandparents' party called and said they had to cancel. One of their tents was damaged. And the weather forecast has a forty percent chance of rain. Then, after health class this morning, I had a student ask me if having anal sex hurt. He was being genuine. I had to make up an answer which I hoped was accurate. Fortunately, my friends are big oversharers, but I hated having to lie to him."

"I'm sorry, bud." I gave his shoulder a quick rub. I was becoming addicted to touching him, like I had in the wine store. It was no bueno.

"It'll be fine. I called around to a few other tent rental companies. My mom was too stressed about the situation to help." He rolled his eyes. "But yeah, long week so far."

"What did you tell your student about the other thing?"

"I said it did hurt, but then you get used to it. I feel like that's the standard answer with anything sex related."

"Sounds like we're both having a crap week." I wished I could keep talking to him. We had less than a minute until the bell rang, and who knew what my students were doing in my unattended class.

"This too shall pass."

"What are you up to tonight? I know a fun way to blow off steam."

"Oh?" His face perked up with a knowing smile.

"Not that. Though it does involve balls."

"Batting cages?" Julian asked when we rolled up to the facility that night.

I shut off my car and unbuckled my seatbelt. Julian remained strapped in.

"It shouldn't come as a surprise to you that I'm not athletically gifted. Sports and I do not get along."

"You don't need to be athletically gifted to hit some balls at the cages. I love coming here to blow off steam. It's been a week, and it's only Tuesday." Two days of not getting to hang with Julian was surprisingly rough. I hadn't realized how much he was part of my day. "Trust me. Bashing the shit out of a baseball is a very satisfying feeling."

The cages were arranged in a big circle with the pitching machines set up in the center. Our cage was cordoned off with nets. On one side of us was a father and his young daughter, and the other had a group of twentysomething friends, beers in hand and music pulsing, enjoying a batting cage happy hour.

I got Julian fitted with a helmet. The brim came down to his eyes and smushed his floppy hair. As if this guy wasn't already adorable. Next, we picked out the right bat for him.

"All this work to blow off steam when we could've just gone for a jog," he said, balancing the end of the bat on his palm.

"Yuck. Jogging." Though I liked to stay in shape, I wasn't one of those freaks who enjoyed running. There was nothing pleasurable about jogging in freezing cold weather or putting undue stress on your knees. "Would you prefer if we went for a run?"

"God no."

I chuckled. At least we were on the same page about that. "Trust me. This'll be worth it."

"There's a studio in Sourwood where you can smash plates and glass as a stress reliever."

"They charge people money to break glasses? Man, rich people will find anything to spend their money on. Let's go."

I led us to our cage. The pitching machine stood at the far end, primed and ready. Julian was the lord of the wine store, but this was my domain. I was excited to be the smart one in this situation.

"First, we want to get you into proper hitting position. Step up to the plate. That's this thing down here."

Julian rolled his eyes. "I know what home plate is."

"Just making sure."

He put his feet up to the plate and hoisted the bat on his shoulder, as if he were a hobo carrying his belongings.

"You don't want to rest the bat on your shoulder. Hold it higher and bend your knees. You'll want to put your body's full force into swinging."

"Like this?" He lifted the bat way over his head. A caveman ready to catch lunch.

"Too high. Here." I stood behind him and positioned his arms in the proper form. Then I positioned his hips to point toward the ball. Then I had to readjust my crotch because all this touching was going straight to my dick.

"Give your hips a little bend. Stick your butt out."

"Are you sure?" he asked, bending down slightly.

"Yes. Your butt is very strong. You derive a lot of power from it, which will help make your swing stronger. People think that a swing is all about the arms, but it should involve the entire body."

Julian stuck his butt out. My eyes feasted on the sight. Since when did a guy's ass elicit that kind of reaction from me? I looked up to make sure the party at the cage next door didn't catch me gawking.

"How's this?" he asked.

"G-good." I gave his ass a little slap, something I did for my players all the time. A coachly butt slap. But only with Julian did my whole body sizzle upon contact. *Every day with Julian is my birthday because damn, that is some cake.*

I stepped back, so Julian could hit and I could reel myself in.

"This feels weird," he said.

"It hurts at first, but then you get used to it," I said with a wink. "Ready?"

He gave his butt a wiggle, signaling yes. *Unhhh.* I had to readjust myself.

The first ball zoomed down the path. It was a swing and a miss.

"That's okay. You're getting warmed up." I clapped my hands, making him stay positive.

The next ball came down. Another whiff.

"I told you—"

"You told me nothing. You think Babe Ruth hit a home run his first time ever at bat? That machine is full of baseballs. You get lots of chances. Focus, Jules."

He nodded and turned back to the plate.

On the next ball, he got a piece of it. The ball went about a quarter of the way down the row.

"How'd that feel?"

"My whole body vibrated on contact," he said, amazed.

"Keep going. Think of each ball as another orb of stress that you don't need in your life. Tent company. Boom. Awkward health class questions. Boom."

Julian made contact with the next few balls, but nobody would confuse them for hits. They'd be foul tips or easy outs in a baseball game. It seemed like he was holding back. He wasn't giving them a full swing with full force. He was being his polite, polished self. Where was the animal he unleashed in private?

The round ended. Balls littered the ground. Julian was flushed and glowing with sweat, his hair matted down in a vulnerable style that made his eyes shine.

"How was it?" I took the helmet and bat from him.

"I don't know how much better I feel." He shrugged.

"You were improving by the end. Let's get you one big hit, one true crack of the bat, before we leave." I firmly believed everyone had one home run in them.

He did not share that belief. "I think I'm good. I appreciate the effort, Seamus."

Julian sat on the bench by the door and drank his water. He then pulled out his phone and began scrolling, a clear signal to me that we could wrap this up. Thing was, I didn't let my players quit.

"You got some water?" I asked.

"Uh huh."

"Good. Now get up, Bradford." I used my stern coach voice, the ones that my players knew not to mess with. "We're not done yet."

I handed him the bat and had him get back to home plate. I had to make sure my own bat was under control while I adjusted his arms and hips into the proper batting position. We were going to get at least one smash out of him today. Coaches didn't give up on their players, whether they were hitting balls or having sex.

"What are you thinking about when the ball comes at you?"

"I'm thinking that I should hit it before it hits me," he said.

I stood in front of him, my eyes laser-focused on him, making sure he heard me. "What is the ball? What do you need to knock out of your life?"

"I mean, the tent stuff is annoying, but I'll figure it out. And the health class stuff is what it is." He shrugged.

"What else?" I let the silence brew until he filled it, because there was always more.

His facade slowly crumbled away. He heaved out a heavy sigh. "Everyone's fucking expectations of me. Sometimes, I feel like I can't even get to live my life on my own terms."

His face hardened with deep frustration, the kind that calcified over a lifetime.

I stepped aside and turned on the ball machine. Julian's hands tightened around the bat.

The first ball flew out. Julian gave a ferocious swing, a whoosh of wind following in its wake. Strike. Resolve formed in his eyes.

"What do they expect of you?"

"Be thin, Julian. It's easy. Just eat right and exercise. Can't be much simpler than that."

On the next ball, Julian's bat made glorious contact, sending it into the side net.

"Be a good son, Julian. Be the responsible friend, Julian. Be a role model for your students, Julian. You're almost thirty-five, Julian. The clock's ticking. The clock's *always* ticking."

Crack. He smashed the ball to the furthest reaches of the cage.

"Yes! Nice! That's what I'm talking about!" I threw my arms up.

Julian got a few more cracks, each ball another expectation on his life. I watched him free himself, just for a few moments, his veneer slipping away and the real Julian, the one just as scared as the rest of us, coming into view.

Maybe it was time I stopped being scared, too.

IT WAS dark when we left. We were one of the last cars in the parking lot. Julian collapsed into the passenger seat, his hair still adorably matted down.

I strummed my fingers on the steering wheel.

"You were right. That was fun," he said. "And very cathartic. I may have to come back here."

I only managed a half-smile, my mind distracted.

"Did you want to grab a drink somewhere?" he asked.

"Jules..." I exhaled a breath. *Here goes nothing.* "I want to explain what happened at the wine store, with my card."

It was a struggle to push out each word. I looked down at the wheel, not yet ready to see his reaction.

"My financial situation is really fucked-up. I barely have any money because it's all going to clean up the mess I've made."

I flicked my eyes his way, and he seemed confused about whether this was a joke or not.

"Every week, I go to Gamblers Anonymous meetings at the MacArthur Center. I used to have a really bad problem with online poker and sports betting. It started in college. Everyone I knew was doing it. You could make a little money. But unlike my friends, I couldn't stop. I wanted more. I was always on the cusp of victory. I saw it as another sport that I could get better at with practice." I shook my head, disgusted at all the excuses I'd used on myself over the years, all the lies I'd told myself and others.

"I maxed out my credit cards. I borrowed money from friends and family to 'fix my car,'" I said with air quotes.

I looked up and blew out a huge breath. I was about to get to the worst of it. This could be the end of my friendship. He was about to find out his friend was a full-on, undeniable walking shitstorm.

"I had a serious girlfriend. Lauren. She trusted me completely. She trusted me so much she agreed to combine finances." I held onto the steering wheel until my hands turned white. "And I wiped her out."

"Seamus," he whispered. My name had never sounded so pitiful.

"So yeah, Jules. I have a good body. When I go out with my bros, I get checked out. But I also have crippling debt, a gambling addiction, wonderful people whose lives I've hurt. I'd rather be a thirty-five-year-old virgin than a thirty-year-old fuckup."

I slumped in my seat, staring out the window at the empty cages. Silence hung heavy in the car. I was too scared to look over at Julian and see his first reaction.

"Anyway, that's my baseball I'm trying to hit." It was hard

having Julian look at me like I was someone special, someone worth being on a pedestal when I deserved to be in the gutter.

A hand glided onto my shoulder and rubbed out some of the tension, a tourniquet for my wounded self. Each second that passed without him saying anything seared my gut.

"I guess some stories we tell ourselves are easier to believe than others. Thank you for sharing this with me."

"Jules, you look at me like I'm something special, and I'm not. I'm just a guy who's terrible with money."

"That's only one part of you. A small part."

"And so is your weight." I turned to him, let my fingers linger in his hair, which was fast becoming one of my favorite things. Tonight, it was a balm against my shame.

"Maybe we're not the terrible things we believe about ourselves," he said.

I hoped. I had bared my terrible, ugly secret and Julian hadn't run away screaming.

Our eyes locked on each other, and there was a change in the air. I wanted him. I wanted to connect with him in a way words couldn't.

I kissed his neck. His skin was sweaty and salty, fire on my tongue.

I kissed his cheek. He shivered under my touch.

Next stop was his mouth. But I remembered his rule. A kiss on the lips was for love, and as close as we were in this moment, something held me back. Could I fuck up Julian's life like I'd done to the last person I loved? I couldn't bear to hurt him, especially as I was nowhere near finished figuring my shit out.

So I went south instead. His dick pressed against his jeans. I unzipped and unleashed him. He was hard and leaking pre-come. His breath hitched.

"Seamus," he gasped out. Was he telling me to stop? Warning

me that we were in a parking lot? Begging me to keep going? All of the above?

I disappeared his cock into my mouth. It was hot and pulsing. Julian vibrated under me. I licked his salty shaft, flicked my tongue over his engorged head.

"Oh my God. Holy shit." His voice shook with want.

I bobbed on his dick, finding myself surprisingly adept at giving head. I couldn't get enough of how much I turned him on. I stroked him as I tongued his balls. Julian grabbed at my hair. He wanted to push me down but hesitated. He was too polite to be rough.

I put my hand on his and pushed, giving him the green light. Julian didn't need another nudge. With a fistful of my hair, he pushed me down and up, making his dick fuck my mouth. Jesus, this was too hot. I could come in my jeans. Feeling Julian shuck off his proper self and unleash his animal need sent every nerve ending in my body on high alert.

"Fuck. Don't stop. Don't stop." He bucked his hips up. His cock hit the back of my throat, making me gag.

"Sorry," he said.

"Don't be fucking sorry. This is so hot, baby." I took him all the way until he filled my entire mouth. I strained over the center console, which dug into my ribs. I pushed through the discomfort of the position. Sex was a full-contact sport, after all.

"I think I'm gonna come. Wait no, I'm gonna come."

I smiled, a difficult task with a cock in my mouth. Who was thinking right now? My brain had checked out, and I was gliding on impulse and lust.

"Give it to me, baby." I slid my tongue across his head.

Julian clenched under me, then filled my mouth with hot goodness. It was such a bolt to my senses. I swallowed, eliciting another moan from him.

His breathing calmed down. I sat up and wiped my mouth on

my sleeve. Julian glowed beside me, his skin and eyes glistening with life.

"First blow job." I made a check mark with my finger.

"I don't know how another guy will top that."

I laughed at the joke, but a spark of jealousy hit my stomach. *Of course there will be other guys, Seamus. That's the fucking plan.*

We sat in a different kind of silence than the one that had preceded the blow job. I held Julian's hand over the center console. My mind played a highlight reel of what just happened. I…liked giving head. Or maybe I just liked giving head to Julian, which presented a whole set of complications.

Julian brought my hand to his mouth and gave me a peck on my knuckles. The world shut down around us.

"So what's next on the list?" I asked, trying to distract myself.

"There's only one thing left," he said.

We both took a deep breath.

Sex.

The final frontier.

17

JULIAN

It was eight days until my grandparents' anniversary party. Nine days until my birthday. Countdowns upon countdowns.

I was never a math person, but all I could think about was numbers. I spent Wednesday and Thursday night doing a deep clean of my apartment and finding a new tent vendor, all while fantasizing about Seamus deep throating me. I also bought a twenty-four pack of tissues. I would need them for all the jerking off I was doing over my straight friend.

On Friday, South Rock High held a pep rally for the basketball team, who were off to some divisional playoff. All these sports and their playoffs. Too much foreplay. Why couldn't they just skip to the championship game?

I walked my eighth period French class to the gym, where we promptly disbanded. Students found their friends, and so did I. Our spot was the corner of the bleachers all the way off to the side where we could chat in semi-privacy.

Amos, Chase, and Everett watched me climb up to join them.

"There he is," Amos said. "I feel like we haven't seen you in forever. What've you been up to?"

"Cleaning and party planning."

"Exciting," Everett deadpanned.

"Cleaning can be exciting," Chase said. "I've found many a lost object."

"You go on with your bad self." Everett rolled his eyes, then turned back to me. "We tried calling you last night. You didn't pick up." He leaned forward, and I knew what was coming next. "Did you have a hot date?"

It was on the tip of my tongue, everything that'd been going down between Seamus and me. I wanted to tell my friends. That's what friends were for! But I was so far down this lie, I couldn't catch them up. I didn't know where to start.

"I had a hot date with Dr. Frasier Crane."

"J, this is your third binge rewatch of *Frasier* in the past year. Do we need to have a *Frasier*vention?" Amos asked.

"What can I say? It's a great show. As I get older, I identify more with Roz."

"You should've gone out with us," Everett said. "We went axe throwing! It's half-off on Wednesdays."

"As in, Everett almost sliced off half his finger," Chase said.

I shuddered to think about my friends wielding deadly weapons. None of us would survive in a post-apocalyptic world.

"How was it?" I asked.

"Awesome! I let out so much rage about Cyllabus," Amos said.

The batting cages were also good for letting out rage. I wanted to tell them that I'd hit a few balls—actually hit them—but that would lead into the big, bad secret I'd been keeping.

"Cool," I said.

"Chase was the best of the bunch. I still don't know how that happened," Everett said. "But we're proud of you, Chasey." He rubbed Chase's head, blond hair going everywhere.

"It's quite simple. Throwing any object is merely about calculating its velocity and parabola of trajectory. Skill is secondary. But for the sake of this discussion, I easily whooped all your asses." Chase fixed his glasses, smiling in victory.

"It was a spur-of-the-moment thing. Hutch found a gift card he'd won in the Christmas party raffle that expired that night. We had to use it or we'd lose it," Amos explained. "I texted you, but you didn't answer. Too ensconced in the ashes of Must See TV."

Amos had texted while I was at the batting cage, but I'd promptly silenced my phone. I was paranoid my friends would be able to see where I was. Still, axe throwing sounded fun.

"You didn't even text me back, which isn't like you," Amos said. He crinkled his brow. Wheels were turning in his head.

"I was just really tired," I said, another twist in my gut.

"Everyone, shush." Everett fanned his hands to halt our conversation. "The pep rally is starting."

Everett used to hate pep rallies like they were his mortal enemy. He used to hate anything related to sports. Until he started dating South Rock's football coach.

The bleachers erupted in cheers as the basketball players jogged onto the stage erected at half court, Raleigh following behind them.

"Why is Raleigh up there? He doesn't coach basketball," I said.

"Because he gives good pep," Everett said, swoony eyes fixated on his boyfriend.

Raleigh strode up to the microphone. Some people would rather boil in a vat of oil than have to speak in public. Raleigh was not one of those people. Come to think of it, neither was Everett. They really were a perfect match.

"What's up South Rock High? Make some noise!" Raleigh commanded.

Everett yelled and clapped so loud I thought I went deaf in one ear.

"Hey, guys, remember when Everett hated these things?" Amos asked.

"I never hated pep rallies. I simply misjudged their entertainment value."

"Is that a euphemism for playing with Raleigh's graphing calculator?" Chase asked. We'd developed a code language to talk about sex in school so as not to scandalize the students. But frankly, this wasn't the Enigma. Most teenagers could probably decipher what we were saying.

"Chase, I can't reach. Can you smack your head for me?" Everett zinged.

"Coach Robolard is out sick today, so I'm here to get you pumpcited. Pumped and excited. Our South Rock basketball team is headed to the regional playoffs this week. They've had an amazing season."

"Yeah they have!" Everett yelled out.

Chase, Amos, and I traded a look. It was official. Raleigh's dick had possessed our friend and was slowly turning him into a jock.

"Everett, if you start calling any of us 'bro,' that's grounds for ex-communication," Amos said.

"Now we're in the crunch time." Raleigh paced on stage, holding the school in the palm of his hand. I wondered if Everett gave him tips to up his stage presence. "Our guys are facing the toughest games of their basketball career. Against North Point High."

The crowd erupted in boos, Everett the loudest of them all.

"North Point sucks!" Everett shouted.

"Everett!" I whisper-yelled. "We're not supposed to encourage bad sportsmanship."

"I didn't say they sucked ass," he shot back, as if that made a difference.

"This is the first time in four years that South Rock has made it to the playoffs. It's been a long haul, but our men have worked incredibly hard. They've logged the man-hours, the grit, the sweat.

We could be looking at state champions," Raleigh said, Everett mouthing along.

The bleachers went wild, and it swept me up, too. I whooped and hollered, throwing up a fist. I supposed I was part jock, too. I wanted South Rock to kick ass just like everyone else. Our students worked hard; they deserved to taste victory.

I felt eyes on me, that instinctual prickle at the back of my neck. I turned around and found Seamus on the top bleacher. He had a charming smile and cocked an eyebrow, as if he was enjoying the show.

I had no choice but to swoon.

I shrugged, letting him know that yes, I had pep. A buzz zipped through my chest. It was only a day ago that he'd had his face in my crotch. But also, it was only a day ago that he revealed his secret pain and made me hold back every instinct to kiss him. Seamus was no longer just a crush that I'd put on a pedestal; he was real, achingly real. A man I wanted to hold and protect and love.

"Could you be any more obvious?" Amos wore a perfectly pleased smile.

"Technically, he could be more obvious, but not by much," Chase added.

"What are you talking about?" I asked, playing it cool.

"Your moony eyes at Seamus," Amos said.

"They were not moony eyes. He's my friend."

"Oh, please. You want him to stuff your Trapper Keeper so badly it's not even funny," Everett said. "Actually, I take that back. It is funny."

"I'm starting to think our code language is more transparent than we think." Chase scratched his head.

"It wasn't moony eyes," I said, compelled to defend myself. "We were just..."

But why was Seamus looking at me? How long had he been staring at me? Was he the one giving moony eyes?

"An inside joke. About pep rallies and never having eighth period. Remember how you used to hate pep rallies because of that, Everett?"

Everett rolled his eyes, refusing to admit I was right and refusing to admit he liked pep rallies now because of his boyfriend.

"Leave him alone, Everett," Amos said.

"Thank you." At least one of my friends was cool.

"It's not his fault he's got a crush on his friend. The heart wants what it wants." Amos chuckled.

Heat coursed up my neck.

"I don't have a crush."

"Seamus is merely a coworker who makes you blush," Everett said with full sarcasm.

"Will you guys shut the fuck up!" Fire spewed from my lungs.

Fortunately, my outburst occurred right after Raleigh said something inspirational, so it was drowned out by the cheers of the student body. But my friends definitely heard it.

They stared at me, white-faced and speechless.

"Just shut the fuck up. You guys can be real assholes."

I got up and left my stunned friends to wallow in their shock. Again, my timing was great as everyone in the bleachers stood up at that moment to do the South Rock cheer. I slipped out unnoticed.

The halls were empty. My footsteps echoed as the rumble of the gymnasium became more distant. I passed a large bulletin board advertising the plethora of student clubs and wished for it to swallow me whole.

"Jules! Wait up!" Seamus jogged down the hall. He was slightly out of breath by the time he caught up to me. "Are you cutting class, sir? I'm gonna have to see a hall pass."

Did attractive, charming people ever realize how attractive and charming they were, or were they completely oblivious?

"I was just going to the bathroom."

"Riiiiight."

"Since you're here, that means you're cutting class, too. Bailing on your fellow athletes. Tsk tsk." I shook my head, totally getting into our banter rhythm.

"It's only basketball. They're tall. They'll get over it."

"I won't tell if you won't."

"What's one more secret between us?" He zipped his lips shut. What did they taste like? What would they feel like on mine? That was something I'd probably never find out.

"Did you run after me just to bust me?" I asked.

He checked his phone. "School technically ends in eight minutes. I want to beat the traffic." He took a step closer, checked to make sure we were alone. "Single digits, right?"

"Excuse me?"

"Nine days until your big day, right?"

I would never not find it sweet that he remembered my birthday. But alas, he was just a man who stayed atop deadlines, that was for sure.

"Correct."

He tapped his wrist where a watch would be. *Time's a-ticking.* I had to give him credit for being so eager to get me through our sessions. Even though he was merely being an organized friend, it still made me get semi-hard.

"I'm free this afternoon."

Was that how it would happen? Officially losing my virginity on a Friday afternoon because Seamus had an opening in his calendar? When I started on this journey, I'd warned myself not to make sex a big deal. That was how I wound up in this situation. But now that it was here, the final item to check off, I started to panic.

Fortunately, I had an alibi.

"Unfortunately, I can't. I have to check out this band that we're looking to hire for the party."

"Your grandparents are having a band? Swanky."

"They love to dance." My grandparents cut a rug at all occasions, even when a familiar song came on in the grocery store. It was adorable, if embarrassing at times. "We were going back and forth about hiring a band versus using Spotify. But Grandma finally made the call that she wanted a band."

"Good for her! I prefer bands, too."

"And you're still cool with attending the party?" I'd told him about the fake relationship misunderstanding from the catering session, and he had agreed to play along so far.

"Of course! In fact, I can come with you today and help really lay the groundwork."

I gulped back a surprised lump in my throat. Mom seeing Seamus and I together would put to rest any suspicions about me lying. And Grandma would get a kick out of spending more time with him. She raved about Seamus whenever we spoke.

"Let's do it."

"For some reason, this makes me feel like a spy." Seamus rubbed his hands together. "My car or yours?"

18

SEAMUS

Because I never did anything half-assed, I was holding Julian's hand when we met up with his mom and grandma on the sidewalk.

"Grandma Judy! It's so good to see you again." I leaned down and gave her a kiss on the cheek. I wasn't trying to lay it on thick. Grandma Judy was a blast! We all needed a sassy grandmother in our lives.

"Seamus. What a nice surprise!" She gave me a wet kiss back, her perfume seeping into my skin.

Behind her was a woman who shared Julian's brown eyes, but instead of them being wide and warm, hers seemed to be playing defense.

"Mom, this is Seamus."

"Elizabeth Bradford." She stuck her hand out and eyed me up and down at least twice. "So this is Seamus."

"In the flesh." I gave her hand a soft, mother-approved squeeze. She had the faded-but-intact looks of a former beauty queen. "It's great to meet you."

"Let's get inside. It's cold out here. My nipples could cut my wedding cake." Grandma Judy tugged her coat tight. Both Julian and Elizabeth turned the same shade of red.

"Well, now I'm hungry for dessert," I said as I opened the door for everyone. I gave Julian a reassuring wink. I could fake boyfriend in my sleep.

Julian had prepped me on the band on the way over. Vance Vance Revolution was made up of twin brothers who couldn't have been more than twenty-two, yet specialized in playing jazz music from a century ago. They had us meet at their loft, which doubled as their rehearsal space. They'd done their best to tidy up their bedroom space and the kitchen; the effort reminded me of the mad scramble my frat used to do right before parents weekend.

"Welcome, welcome! I'm Hunter, and this is my brother Ryder." The Vance twins didn't help the situation by having the same identical shaggy hair cut and both wearing blue T-shirts.

"Do you boys have nametags?" Judy asked.

"We do, actually!" Hunter said. On cue, the boys pulled nametags from their back pockets and pinned them to their chests.

Grandma Judy squinted. "Who can read that? The letters are so small."

"It's okay, Grandma. We'll keep track of them for you," Julian said. He gave the boys the nod to continue their spiel.

"Cool, cool," said Hunter. It seemed that Ryder was the strong, silent type and that we wouldn't be hearing from him. "Ryder and I are going to play some tunes for you. We hope you like it and, uh, book us." A tuft of hair fell into his eyes when he nodded. "Um, and yeah...Here we go!"

Hunter pointed at the folding chairs set up for us. I squeezed Julian's hand again when we took our seats. Out of the corner of my eye, I caught his mom eyeing us again.

Despite how awkward the brothers Vance seemed, they were

talented musicians. Their first song was a familiar jazz song that I knew I'd heard plenty of times before. Julian informed me it was *Take Five*, but that meant nada to me. Ryder played upright bass, while Hunter dazzled on the piano.

I tapped my fingers to the beat on Julian's knee and kept trying to impress him with my chair dancing skills. He grinned to himself, his lips forming this sexy snarl that did things to me that should not have been happening.

Was I laying it on thick?

Knowing that Julian's mom was observing us like lab rats made me step my game up. She probably had very high standards for her son. She probably wanted Julian to wind up with a guy who owned a sailboat or was on the board of children's hospitals and museums. Good thing this wasn't a real relationship. If she ever got ahold of my bank statements, she'd die of shock.

Grandma Judy was really getting into the music. She tapped her feet and swayed in her seat. This woman was made to groove.

"Judy, would you like to dance?" I held out my hand.

"I thought you'd never ask."

We glided to the empty space between the brothers and our chairs. My siblings and I had never understood why my mom insisted we take dance lessons as kids, but now it clicked. Knowing how to dance would always come in handy.

"This kid's got moves!" Grandma Judy exclaimed to her family members as I spun us around the floor.

"You ain't seen nothing yet," I said as I dipped her—slowly. She was an old woman. I had to be gentle. One wrong move, and we could have a broken hip on our hands.

Julian's mom shuffled her seat closer to her son. He rolled his eyes for a split second, which made me laugh. They got lost in conversation as Grandma Judy and I got lost in the art of the dance.

"What was your wedding song?" I asked.

"My husband was a big Beatles fan, so we went with 'Something.' Cliché, I know. I wanted 'Ain't No Mountain High Enough,' so I'm no better."

While my mom had made us get dance lessons, my Uncle Albie had made sure all Shablanski kids were well-versed in The Beatles.

"'Something' is a classic," I said, the guitar riff playing in my head.

"It wasn't a classic when we got married. Just another song by those funny-looking Englishmen." Her eyes lit up with memory. Under that brash demeanor was a woman with a big, bursting heart. "I can't believe it's been fifty years. It doesn't feel that way. You'll realize this as you get older. Time may be passing. My tits may be drooping to the floor. But in my mind, I still feel like I'm thirty. Getting older can be cruel in that way."

"It helps to have someone to grow old with."

A wistful smile flitted over her lips. "It was a bit of a scandal when I married George. Being thirty and single wasn't normal back then for women. And I was divorced. I might as well have sewn a scarlet letter onto my clothes." She peered at the floor in a moment of seriousness. "I felt so much shame. I carried it around with me. Nobody gets married expecting to get divorced. Life happens, but some people can't see beyond their narrow version of life. George was the first man who saw *me*, not my age or my marital status. Being with him made the shame disappear."

I nodded, a lump stuck in my throat. Maybe one day, I could meet someone who would lift this cloud of shame. What if I'd already met him?

"You two are a beautiful couple."

"You've only met me so far," she said.

"It's a gut feeling I have."

She sped up her dance steps as the song changed to an

uptempo number, and I quickly followed suit. I knew how to keep up with my partner.

"I also have a gut feeling." She beamed with a knowing smile as she glanced at Julian, then me.

"Your grandson is a special guy."

"You two are crazy about each other. I can tell."

We were good fakers. But even as friends, I was crazy about Julian in my own way. I loved hanging with him, and our sex sessions were mindblowing.

"I'm really happy you found each other." She gazed again at her grandson with all the love in her heart. "Julian's a good person. He's very smart, but he can be so unsure of himself. You've helped him be more confident and come out of his shell."

"I have?" And more importantly, how could she tell? She'd only seen us together for a few minutes.

"He's different around you. He smiles more. He seems more relaxed. As a mother and grandmother, you can easily notice a change in your offspring. It's this feeling like the change in temperature. Julian's a sweet man, and sometimes, I worried he was too sweet for this cruel world."

"I won't let anyone hurt him."

She cupped my face in her wrinkled hand. "I know you won't."

The song wound down. Hunter hopped off the raised platform where they were playing.

"So, uh, what do we think of, like...everything?"

At this point, I was curious to hear Ryder speak. He couldn't be much worse than his brother.

"How's the music sounding?" he asked.

"Delightful," Grandma Judy said. "But I may need to hear a few more tunes just to be sure."

She gave me a wink. The woman wanted to dance.

"Yeah, cool, cool. We love playing, so it's no problem."

Julian and his mom joined us. Grandma Judy and I gave them a thumbs-up.

"You guys sound great," Julian said. His mom nodded politely in agreement.

"I hope you boys are available a week from Saturday," Grandma Judy said.

"Totes! Oh, that's awesome!" Hunter high-fived his brother. "Do you want to like sign a contract?"

"Sure." Grandma Judy laughed to herself. If only all business negotiations could be this easy, yet also this awkward.

While Julian and Grandma Judy worked with the Vance boys to hash out details for the anniversary party, I used the bathroom. The shower curtains had lines of cellos on them, a cute touch.

I couldn't stop smiling at what Grandma Judy had said. Was I making Julian a more confident, more relaxed person? He seemed in better spirits, less serious. He joked around more. But was that because of me or my dick? Either way, a win was a win.

When I exited the bathroom, Julian's mom was waiting outside, her observant eyes fixated on the sloppy paint job.

"It's all yours."

"Thanks," she said, but didn't move. "We haven't really had a chance to talk. Julian says you two have been together only two months."

"We've been friends for a lot longer, so it made the transition pretty seamless."

"I think it's wonderful. How did it all happen? What made you decide to take that jump?"

"It was something that we decided together. And I don't know...Julian's pretty fantastic. I don't know why I resisted realizing that for so long."

My fictional story was beginning to blur with reality. I just hoped it matched Julian's version that she'd likely asked him about.

"That's how my husband and I got together. Our friend groups overlapped, and we wound up at the same gatherings all the time. And eventually, he asked me out."

"Yeah. You see the same guy across the hall for two years, you spend all the time with him at department meetings and faculty functions, and then suddenly you're like 'Whoa. I think I like this guy.'"

"Right." Something about the way her eyes moved between Julian and me was unsettling, but I couldn't put my finger on it. "I'm excited that you two are together. Hopefully, being with someone like you will give Julian the impetus to finally get his weight under control."

The sweet talk about love came to a record-scratching halt.

"Huh?"

"You're an athlete. You take good care of your body, seem to eat right. Your good habits will be able to rub off on him."

Julian's diet ran circles around mine. I leaned on our cafeteria pizza and hamburgers far more than I should have, while Julian brought Tupperware full of home-cooked meals.

"If anything, Julian's good habits will rub off on me."

An icky feeling hit the back of my throat. She opened her mouth to speak again, and I dreaded what would come out.

"You're being sweet. Julian says he eats well and exercises, but I don't see it."

"He does. He is healthy." Lord knew he had good stamina and endurance during our sessions, not to mention being able to stand in front of classes for six hours a day.

"I just want him to be healthy."

"He is healthy. I just said that." Ickiness coalesced into anger.

"You know what I mean, though? We get it." We? We were a we? Because we were both slim? "He's having trouble losing the weight, but you can get him on the right track."

Fury fumed within my chest. But yelling at my fake boyfriend's mother would not be a good move, so I went for a different tack.

"I don't want him to lose a pound. Your son is fucking sexy. I mean, have you seen that ass?" I bit my lip as I snuck a peek at Julian's luscious backside. "Your son is hot exactly as he is. He better not change. But don't worry, Mrs. Bradford, I'm making sure Julian's getting *pa-lenty* of exercise, if you know what I mean."

I winked at her and left her in my sex-tinted dust. I walked up behind Julian and gave his juicy ass a big, loud, for-the-cheap-seats grab. He yelped in surprise.

"What was that for?" he asked.

"Because you're the sexiest man in here. Sorry, twins."

Hunter and Ryder turned a deep shade of red.

I nuzzled my nose against his neck, planting a soft kiss on his collarbone. I sure as hell hoped his wretched mom was observing *this*.

Grandma Judy handed the boys the signed contract, pleased by my very public display of affection.

"One more song please," she requested.

"You got it!"

I didn't ask Julian if he wanted to dance because there was only one answer I would accept. I clamped a hand on his waist and led us in a slow dance, our bodies leaving no room for the Holy Spirit. Turned out dancing with a guy was no different from dancing with a woman.

"What's gotten into you?" he asked.

"You." I tucked a lock of hair behind his ear. "Hey, you're sexy just as you are."

"You're really leaning into our facade."

"I'm serious." I locked eyes with him until he realized I wasn't fucking around. "You don't need to change a fucking thing about you."

He nodded, his gaze never leaving me. I stared into his dark orbs, my mind and heart swirling with all the feelings that had been brewing deep within me and could no longer lie dormant.

Who was faking here?

"Let's go back to your place after this."

"Okay," he said.

19

JULIAN

All I could think about on the car ride home was, *I'm about to have sex.*

There was no way around it. Not after the dark, lustful stare he'd given me during our slow dance. I had been feeling something growing between us, but that might've just been friendship. The negative voice in my head, honed from a lifetime of rejection, insisted that he merely wanted to go back to his regular life and be done with these sessions.

We reached my building. My stomach clenched as we ascended the stairs to the apartment. *I'm about to have sex. Why am I feeling scared?*

In the apartment, I opened a bottle of wine, a savory French malbec that knew how to relax me.

"We'll cap it at one glass," he said. "No drunken sex."

"Agreed." I didn't need Seamus dragging me into my own bed.

I poured two glasses. We clinked and drank.

"What were you and my mom talking about?" I asked. She'd been quiet for the rest of the afternoon and whisked off with Grandma as soon as the audition was over.

"Nothing really. Baseball stuff. Your grandma is wonderful, by the way."

"She's the best. I feel closer to her than I do my immediate family. Is that weird?"

"Nope. She's family. That's all that matters."

"You sound like Vin Diesel in the *Fast and Furious* movies."

"You watch those?"

"Everett made us watch the first five during the blizzard we had in January when school was closed." The Raleigh effect was far-reaching on my friend. "What's your family like?"

"Loud. I was raised in a big family. Two older brothers who gave me shit, and a younger sister who was treated like an angel. I love my family, though. We give each other a hard time, but it keeps things interesting. They all still live in Staten Island, but I needed to get out. I needed to find my own way, y'know?"

"Yeah. My parents and siblings are so similar. All athletic and very right-brained. When I was young, I used to wonder if aliens dropped me off at this house by accident." I snorted a laugh. I hadn't thought of that memory since I was ten, back when I believed storks were aliens.

"To being our own people." Seamus held up his glass again for a toast.

"Cheers to that."

He downed most of his glass and closed the gap between us. He rubbed my sides, which was becoming one of his favorite things to do. "You ready?"

"Yeah," I said while my heart pounded in my chest.

This was it. Sex. The big enchilada. No pressure.

We had been building toward this. But then why did it feel so all-of-a-sudden?

Seamus took my hand and led me to my bedroom. How did he seem so calm, and I was a nervous mess?

"Nice bedroom! Damn, this bed looks comfortable."

I'd splurged on a king-sized bed and fancy dark red bedding. I wanted one area where I treated myself like a king. Since it looked like I was going to spend the rest of my life sleeping alone, I figured I better make it comfortable.

Seamus collapsed on my bed, the thick comforter billowing around him.

"We should've been fooling around on this thing from the start." Seamus rolled around like he was a dog. "Why'd we ever waste time on my bed?"

I liked his bed. There was something charming about the tight quarters and scratchy Ikea sheets that he'd likely picked out because they were on the showroom bed.

Seamus ambled to my nightstand and opened the drawer. He shuffled around pads and pens and old receipts cluttered inside.

"Are you looking for something?" I asked.

"Where do you keep your supplies?"

"Supplies?"

"Condoms and lube."

A sinking feeling hit my stomach.

"How do you know what those are?"

"I'm secretly in your health class." He cocked an eyebrow. "It's the twenty-first century. Straight guys know what lube is."

"I...don't have any." I hung my head. Reason 5,431 why I was still a virgin: I was forever ill-prepared. I had such low hopes for having sex that I didn't even bother to have lube and condoms on hand.

"Okay," he said, deflating a little. "Not a problem. We can improvise. Do you have olive oil?"

How much research had Seamus done on gay sex?

"I do, but it's this expensive truffle oil from Tuscany. Not really butt appropriate."

"I guess I can run out to the store."

My nerves continued to amplify inside me. I pushed them down. Why was I scared? Why was my body revolting?

"Hey." Seamus had me sit on the bed. "You don't look so good."

"I'm fine."

He rubbed my knee to soothe me. "We don't have to have sex today."

"That's the plan, though?"

"Fuck the plan, Jules. You are bugging out."

I threw my head into my hands. Why couldn't I be a normal horny person? Why did my brain have to get in the way?"

"I'm sorry. It's just all happening, like, right now. We were dancing, and then you were like, 'Let's go back to your place and fuck.' The 'and fuck' was implied, but that's what you meant. Which is great. I just...I think I need a little more time. And then there's the whole naked thing of it all." I was full-on spiraling. If Seamus wanted to drive me to the nearest mental institution, I would understand.

But instead, he hugged me close and softly shushed me, the shhh of his deep voice calming me down.

"Jules, it's okay. We don't have to have sex today, or tomorrow, or the day after that. Whenever you're ready."

"I'm kind of ready, but not completely ready. Does that make sense?"

He tipped his head to the side.

"Yeah," he answered, though his face said the opposite. "Honestly, I was kinda nervous, too. We're here, finally. It's game seven of the World Series. I want this to be a good time for you. I don't want this to be one of those games where it's a blowout right away, and you wind up turning off the TV in the sixth inning because the other team can never catch up."

To my credit, I got what he was saying. I'd gotten roped into watching enough baseball games over my lifetime to understand the boredom that came with a one-sided game.

I appreciated that he wanted this to be a great night for me, yet it only added to the pressure. I wanted him to have a good time, too. Well, as much as a straight guy could enjoy fucking a man.

He licked his lips, a thought percolating in his mind.

"What?" I asked.

"Huh?"

"You seem like you were about to say something."

"Yeah." He scratched the back of his head. "You know, if we want to make this a true-to-life sexual journey, there's one step we could do first. We could dry hump."

I broke out into a laugh. At least Seamus hadn't lost his sense of humor during this weird moment.

"I'm serious."

"You are?"

"Most couples who've done the deed have dry humped first. It's like a dress rehearsal."

What was more surprising? That Seamus suggested frotting or that he used a theater reference?

"It usually happens when people are making out, but we don't have to do that."

Because of my *Pretty Woman* rule. That rule was the rickety dam holding me back from completely falling in love with my straight friend.

"I thought dry humping was for awkward teens who didn't know what the hell they were doing."

"So is losing your virginity." Touché. "Awkwardness is the key ingredient for your first time."

There'd been little awkwardness in our sexual encounters thus far. Once we got into it, we really got into it, and everything flowed naturally.

I laughed some more. I couldn't help it. I was an educated, thirty-something young professional who was about to dry hump.

"I promise you won't hate it," he said.

"Maybe we'll dry hump so hard we'll rip a hole in our pants and inevitably have sex."

"Crazier things have happened." Seamus leaned on his arm and winked at me. "Are you ready for me to dry hump the fuck out of you?"

"Can we call it frottage? It's classier."

"Is that the scientific name for it?"

"Better. It's the French name for it."

"Ooooh. Then the Spanish name must be el frottage."

"The Spanish are way too sensual to dry hump," I said.

"What about the French?"

"Give them wine and a cigarette, and they'll do anything."

He pulled me down next to him, our faces side-by-side. It was a perfect kissing moment, and I wanted to lunge forward and plant one on him. Yet I couldn't break my own rule.

Seamus rolled on top of me. He lifted my legs and spread them. I was wearing dress pants and underwear, and yet I still felt exposed. I let out a groan as his weight pinned me down. His thickening cock pressed against my opening.

His muscular arms rested by my head as he stared down at me with a goofy, mischievous smile.

"You ready to ride the Frottage Roller Coaster?" he asked.

"My hands and arms are inside the ride."

My laughter stopped when he thrust his crotch against me, his cock making contact with my most sensitive area. A jolt of lust electrocuted me.

Four layers of clothing separated us...but they also didn't.

Frottage was no joke.

Seamus rocked his hips into me in a steady rhythm, the outline of his dick hitting my hole in a regular cadence that made my cock swell. I leaked pre-come. So much for keeping this dry.

"I can't believe we're dry humping," I said.

"The only thing that would make this better is if we were doing it on your childhood bed." Seamus lifted my left leg and threw it over his shoulder. He thrust harder against me, somehow hitting a new angle and a new pleasure center.

"Holy shit," I cried out, surprised that dry humping could feel this good.

"Penetrative sex is for losers, am I right?" Seamus wiggled his eyebrows. How he could be silly and ridiculously sexy at the same time was an incredible feat.

"Intercourse can go fuck itself. I should get that printed on a shirt." I devolved into wild laughter, tears prickling at my eyes. Seamus collapsed onto my chest, similarly in stitches.

Did all people laugh this much during sex? After our other activities had turned serious, it was a welcome change being relaxed with him.

"This actually feels good. I might be sore tomorrow." I rubbed a hand over his chest, his muscles flexing under my touch.

"Baby, you ain't seen nothing yet." He grabbed my wrists, pushed them over my head, and held me in place as he dry-drilled my clothed hole. His cockhead hit me in just the right spot, an unrelenting tease.

I unleashed moan after moan. "Fuck yes. Dry fuck me, Seamus."

We laughed at the command. We really did sound like awkward teenagers. I wouldn't be surprised if one of our parents walked in on us.

"You like getting dry fucked? Are you a frottage slut?"

I threw my head back, moaning and laughing.

"Are you the star of Jim Henson's new show *Frottage Rock*?"

"That's too far. You're ruining my childhood," I said.

Seamus pounded against me, grunting and thrusting. His arms flexed over me, muscles corded and clenched as his grip tightened on my wrists. I writhed under him, shifting my angle to feel him in different ways.

Lust hung heavy in his eyes. Those blue orbs bore into me ravenously, but they also had a caring glint to them, like he wanted to tear me apart but then put me back together. Was this the way he gazed at girls he had sex with?

Soon, the laughing died out, replaced with pure hunger. He slammed against me, his erection hitting my hole and lighting me up.

"Seamus," I panted out.

"Are you okay?" Concern immediately filled his voice.

"Yeah. Don't stop."I wanted to kiss him so badly, but I couldn't violate my own rule. I bucked my hips to meet his thrust, imagining him plunging deeper inside me.

The friction of our jeans mashing together could start a forest fire.

"Fuck yes," he grunted out. He curled a finger through my hair, a soft caress amid all this heat. "I think…I'm actually going to come."

"I think…I am, too." I was a leaking mess under my jeans. My dick was hard and aching with want from not being touched. I silently begged for relief. Please God, let Seamus's hand slip and accidentally land on my crotch. The slightest touch would be all I need to finish.

"I want you to come so bad. Soak your fucking jeans," I dared him. "I can't wait for you to do this for real. Stuff my tight hole with your thick cock. Fuck me until I can't breathe. Fill me with your hot come."

Since I couldn't find relief through touch, I got it through amping up the dirty talk.

"Holy fuck! I love your filthy mouth, baby."

I was about to continue when Seamus collapsed on top of me and mashed his lips onto mine.

Rule shattered.

Obliterated.

Pretty Woman? I don't know her.

His kiss sent me to another planet in another solar system. His lips were warm, a bit salty, everything I'd dreamed about. His tongue slipped into my mouth, flicking against mine, sparks and heat combusting inside me.

He groaned against my lips as his body clenched, every muscle in his back tight. He thrust once more before unleashing a primal grunt. Seamus's pants were suddenly anything but dry.

"Shit. I can't believe I came like this."

I wasn't there yet, but I was painfully close. My body squirmed in glorious torture.

"Put your hand on my dick," I pleaded, a desperate madman. I grabbed his hand and shoved it onto my crotch.

"Come for me, baby." He rubbed my erection, glaringly visible through the denim.

I cried out at his touch, relief like no other. Waves of come flooded my boxers. Seamus reached inside and ran a finger through my mess.

"Damn, you came a lot. It's like the time of Noah down there."

I threw a hand over my face. I didn't know ejaculation levels could be a cause for embarrassment, but here we were.

"I'm no better." He pushed my hand into his jeans, and I immediately was covered in him. "Maybe next time we dry hump, we should wear adult diapers."

We burst out laughing, our glee filling the room. I'd always thought that sex was supposed to be awkward and serious. People weren't supposed to laugh. Yet here we were, and it was the most natural thing in the world.

"If that was frottage, then I can't wait for the real thing."

"Man, I should be dry humping more often. That was hot." His cheeks flushed with color. "Hey, I'm sorry about kissing you."

"Oh." Even though we were clothed, I felt oddly exposed.

"I just got so into it. I was close, I needed something to push me over the edge. I broke your *Pretty Woman* rule. I'm a bad prostitute."

"That's okay. Things happen in the heat of sex, or so I've heard," I said, deflated. I wished his kiss had been real rather than a means to an end. It would be hard to forget.

"You're a good kisser, by the way." He smoothed a thumb down my cheek. For a moment, I thought (and wished) he would kiss me again. "Next time, it's the real thing. Get ready, Jules."

For the big event, I would lock up all feelings for Seamus deep in my chest and resist the urge to swoon at his heat-of-the-moment kisses. We would have powerful, amazing, emotionless sex.

I would be ready.

20

SEAMUS

The weekend flew by in a flurry of baseball tryouts and picking up extra shifts at the soul-sucking real estate data entry job. Julian and I texted throughout the weekend, but we were both too busy to meet up. Julian was in the thick of finalizing party stuff.

A part of me was admittedly dragging things out. Once Julian and I had sex, our arrangement would be over.

On Monday, all the South Rock coaches had a mandatory meeting with the athletics director for the school district. He liked to call these meetings, where nothing of value was discussed but he got to stand at the front of a room and bloviate for forty-five minutes about how we were training the next generation of athletes.

Hutch, Raleigh, and I traded looks throughout the meeting, trying to make each other laugh. After it was over, we unanimously decided that we needed a drink and headed to Stone's Throw Tavern.

We grabbed a booth by the big windows in the back which

overlooked the river. Sure, there were other watering holes in town we could try, but none of them could compare with this place.

"You guys, we're not ordering drinks, we're finding and nurturing the next generation of winners," Hutch said in mock seriousness.

"I think Johnson misses coaching," Raleigh said. "He's the administration now."

"He's still a tool." Hutch rolled his eyes and scanned the beer selection at the bar. He was still raw about how Johnson had tried to railroad Amos last year for failing one of South Rock's star athletes.

"And if you're going to monologue at us, at least punch up your script," Raleigh said.

"Monologue?" I raised my eyebrows.

"This is what happens when you date a theater nerd. You learn a whole new vocabulary. Apparently, blocking in theater doesn't mean protecting your lead actor from getting tackled." Raleigh checked out the tap menu on the wall, big wooden planks with beer names on them.

I glanced at the tap menu like I'd done before, but there was nothing that called out to me. I scanned the menu.

"Are you getting apps?" Raleigh asked.

"Nah. Just looking for something to drink."

The waitress, a redhead named Penny, approached. Her bangs fell into her eyes. Usually, I would find a gal like this attractive, but tonight, I felt nothing. My dick was still asleep from that meeting.

"Evening, gentlemen. What are we thinking about for tonight?"

"I'm going to take the Pilsner IPA," Hutch said.

"I'll do the Goose Island," Raleigh said, double-checking his selection on the tap menu. "Yeah, the Goose Island."

"Great." Penny scribbled it down. "And you?"

"What kind of red wines do you have?" I asked.

Hutch and Raleigh turned to me in unison, reacting as if I'd just spoken Mandarin out of nowhere.

"Excuse me?" Penny asked.

"Do you serve wine?"

"Wine? Um, I think so. It's not really our specialty. I'll grab you a wine menu," Penny said, unsettled by my question. She darted off.

I spun a coaster on the table, not looking at my colleagues.

"Wine," Hutch said.

"Red wine." Raleigh nodded his head.

Penny came back menuless. "So we don't have a wine menu. We have a merlot and a cabernet. And for whites, we have a riesling, chardonnay, and pinot noir."

"I'll take the cabernet. No, the merlot. What vintage is it?"

"I don't know." Penny bit her lip. "It's probably old because we don't usually serve wine."

"Let's do it. I'll take a pint."

"It comes in a wine glass."

"Right. I'll take a glass of your merlot." I nodded, confident in my decision.

She left one menu on the table in case we wanted food. Raleigh and Hutch continued to stare at me, amused and confused.

"In the mood for wine tonight." Hutch smiled to himself then looked under the table. "Yep. Seamus has on his fancypants."

I flipped him the bird. "A lot of people drink wine."

"Sure." Raleigh traded a look with Hutch.

"Because I'm a jock, I'm supposed to only drink beer? You fuckers can be really small-minded."

Penny returned with our drinks. She delicately placed my red wine on the table, the round, stemmed glass a sharp contrast to the sturdy pint glasses.

I held the stem between my fingers and swirled the wine around. My friends thought this was the funniest shit they'd ever seen.

"You're supposed to swirl the wine around to let it breathe and oxygenate it, you assholes." I held the wine up to my nose and breathed in its oaky aroma. "This is a good one. Good vintage."

I had no fucking idea if this was good wine or good vintage, but I wanted to show up Raleigh and Hutch.

They held up their pint glasses to their noses and sniffed.

"Mmm, yes I can really detect the hops in this," Raleigh said.

"Yes, the bouquet is magnificent." Hutch used a posh accent.

"And a hint of grain. This vintage is making my balls tingle." Raleigh took a sip and let out an exaggerated moan. People at neighboring tables looked our way, but Raleigh was born without shame.

"When you're done with your beer, you fellas can kiss my ass." I took a sip of my wine.

Hutch held up his pint, and we three clinked glasses.

"You guys are missing out. This is some good wine." I held back from chugging it. Wine was not beer. It had to be savored.

"What is up with you? Has baseball practice started up?" Hutch asked, wiping foam from his lips.

"Next week."

"So you haven't been busy with practice?"

"No, not yet. Why?"

Hutch looked at Raleigh before answering. "We've barely seen you this month. Usually, we'd go out for a regular happy hour drink during our off-seasons. But you've been booked solid."

"I've been logging more hours at my data entry job for extra cash." And when I wasn't busy with that, I was getting busy with Julian.

"And now you're drinking wine." Hutch nodded at my glass.

"What's wrong with wanting to expand my palate?"

"Nothing, but you've never been a guy who's said shit like 'expand my palate,'" Raleigh said.

The guys were more intrigued than concerned.

"And it's great that you do," Hutch added. "Palates are cool. But yeah, just a turnaround from the Seamus we knew in February."

Had I really changed that much? What kind of effect was Julian having on me?

"Guys, can I talk to you about something?"

They leaned forward. Now they were more concerned than intrigued.

"Is everything okay?" Raleigh asked. "Did you need a kidney? My organs are in tip-top shape."

"No organs needed. I appreciate it, though." These guys could give me shit, but they were good friends who cared about me. I was lucky that I'd wound up at South Rock. "If I tell you something, can you keep it a secret?"

They nodded yes. I hoped to God they were telling the truth.

"Since the beginning of March, I've been fooling around with this guy."

Raleigh slammed his hand on the table and pointed at Hutch. "I knew it. Toldja."

"We knew something was up with you." Hutch shrugged.

"I got a little bit of a wholesexual vibe from you," Raleigh said.

"A what vibe?"

Hutch smacked a hand on Raleigh's chest to keep him from elaborating. "Ignore him. Who's the guy?"

"I don't want to say. I want to protect his privacy." Considering I was talking about Julian to his friends' boyfriends, I had to tread lightly.

"That's cool. I get it." Hutch had been in the closet when he first came to South Rock. Julian had told me that he and Amos secretly hooked up in high school, and it took him a full decade to work up the nerve to be openly gay. He understood all about privacy.

"We'll call him Bert, in honor of Bert and Ernie," Raleigh said.

Between this and me uttering *Frottage Rock* to Julian, no childhood memory was safe.

"Fine." I rolled my eyes. "*Bert* and I have been fooling around for the past few weeks. He wanted more experience with a guy, and I was like, sure."

"Why did you say yes?" Hutch asked.

"What was your motivation? All characters are driven by motivation." Raleigh smiled proudly, another theater tidbit Everett had likely ingrained in him.

"Bert was self-conscious about not having much sexual experience. I didn't want him to find sketchy guys on the internet. We've been having fun running the bases."

"What was in it for you?" Raleigh asked.

I stammered for an answer. "I was being a good, bicurious friend." I didn't want to dig into this line of questioning more because my logic at the time seemed fuzzy now. "Look, is there anything that comes before sex that we missed?"

I listed off what Julian and I had done so far. I was a bit embarrassed to be asking for sex advice when I was thirty, but in my defense, same-sex sex was a whole new frontier for me.

Raleigh smacked his hand on Hutch's chest to beat him to the punch. "I'll answer this. I'm technically the gayest person at this table."

"Says who?" Hutch asked, shoving his hand away. "We're both bi."

"But I've been with more guys than you. Probably more girls, too." Raleigh licked his thumb and smoothed out an eyebrow.

"I wouldn't brag about that."

"Way to sex shame, Hutch. You are sex negative, my friend." He turned to me. "I can field your sex questions. Give it to me."

"Is there anything that we're missing? Any big milestones?"

"Rimming," Hutch shouted out.

"I was going to say that." Raleigh shot him a playful glare. "Rimming. It's the best equivalent to eating out a girl."

I nodded, the term clicking. My subconscious seemed to grasp this faster than my conscious brain. I looked down and found my finger was circling the rim of my glass. "Huh, I didn't know guys would be into that."

"We are," Hutch and Raleigh said at the same time, startling each other.

"Giving, receiving. Both good." Raleigh gave it two thumbs up. I appreciated his lack of filter.

"Agreed," Hutch said more demurely.

"Your boyfriends are into it? Did they need convincing?" I asked.

"I don't lick and tell," Raleigh said.

"Uh, same I guess." Hutch drank his beer. "But I will say that it's…it's an incredibly intimate experience. More intimate than sex can be."

"Really?"

"When you're receiving, you're putting yourself in the most vulnerable position a guy can be in. With sex, you and your partner can be face-to-face. With rimming, you're asking a guy to put his face up close and personal with you. Does that make sense?"

I nodded yes. Somehow, it made crystal clear sense.

"You need to innately trust your partner," he continued. "And when you're giving, you have to respect that your partner is letting themselves be in this incredibly vulnerable position."

"I couldn't have said it better myself. Well, I probably could have. I am great at public speaking, but Hutch hit the nail on the hole. I mean, head." Raleigh downed the last of his beer.

"Interesting." I looked at my wine glass. The thought of being that intimate with Julian was scary, but exciting. This whole arrangement had been scary but exciting.

"If you're already doing all that other stuff with your male friend, then add this to the list. It's hot," Hutch said.

Raleigh raised his empty glass. "Carpe dat ass!"

21

JULIAN

This was a week of lasts. If all went according to plan, then this would be my last week as a virgin. And currently, I was standing in front of health class for the final week before Mrs. Stockman returned on Monday.

"Let's talk about sex," I proclaimed.

Kids reacted as expected, with giggles and looks down at their desks. I didn't feel as nervous. While I hadn't had full-on sex, I was much closer than I had been on the first day.

The lesson went smoothly enough as we discussed consent and the different kinds of penetrative sex. I remained as clinical as possible. Kids needed the facts.

"Sex is a major milestone in your lives. You want to be prepared physically and emotionally."

Meanwhile, I was doing my best to prepare for my first time. That rule-breaking kiss, and the way he looked at me every time we got physical, made me believe that there was a real connection there. Maybe Seamus was more than straight, and we were more than friends.

"Actually, it's not that big of a deal," said Front Row Menace, whose name turned out to be Cale. No wonder he was kind of a jerk. His parents named him after a vegetable.

"Sex isn't a big deal?" I asked.

"I mean, it's great. Don't get me wrong. But it's just like whatever, you know?"

Not even the world's foremost expert on grammar could untangle that sentence.

"Sex is just what mammals do. The only reason we make a big deal out of it is because of our puritanical roots," Cale said, confident in his grasp of American culture. "In Europe, sex is no big deal. You teach French, Mr. Bradford. In France, everybody has sex all the time. It's like doing the laundry."

I cocked my head to the side.

"I'm not sure that's accurate, Cale."

"Cale has a point," said Ella, the cool girl one row over with jet black hair who always wore killer boots. "It's like adults and society put all this weight on sex and losing your virginity, that it's some big milestone, but really..." Ella shrugged. "It's just sex. You do it for the first time, it hurts a little, it feels good a little, and then you go on with your life. By calling it a major milestone, it just puts all this pressure on us."

"Yeah." Cale pointed his thumb at Ella in solidarity. "Like, why is it so important who we have sex with for the first time? It's only one time. My first time was with a girl I worked with over the summer. We weren't dating or super close. I'll go ahead and like some of her Insta posts, but I'd never comment on them."

"The whole virginity conversation is so toxic anyway." Ella brushed her hair out of her eyes. "Like women are supposed to remain untouched for their husbands so they can be pure."

She rolled her eyes with the trademarked teenage mix of disdain and detachment. Other kids nodded in support.

"But you know, women shouldn't be having sex with like *tons* of guys," Cale said.

"Cale, shut up." Ella shot him a glare that had the tiniest bit of playfulness at its core. "The point is, you can have good sex with no feelings involved. We're told that sex is all about soulmates and love, but it can also just be fun."

"What she said." Cale nudged his head at her. "Like, in the moment, you can have a connection with someone, but it's not anything real. It's just a..."

"A sex haze," said Ella.

"Exactly." Cale snapped, happy that she took the words out of his mouth. The student behind him added a *yup*.

"A sex haze?" I asked. Sex haze wasn't in the lesson plan.

"You can pretend like you have this connection when you're in the middle of sex, and a part of you may even believe it, but once it's over, the high wears off and you're like 'Oh, no way am I into him.'" Ella shuddered, making me wonder how much experience she had with the sex haze. (No judgment!)

"Yeah, you come to your senses once you...come." Cale bit his lip, probably curious whether "come" was appropriate for sex-ed class.

"Huh." I refused to let Ella and Cale believe they'd spouted off anything insightful, but my stomach got queasy wondering if they were right.

"I think the only emotional preparedness someone needs is realizing that it's not always that emotional." Ella shrugged, her face softening as she likely read the tumult on my face.

What if I had it all wrong with Seamus? If my students could enjoy fucking on a purely physical level, then why couldn't he too succumb to a sex haze?

Like he loved to say, it was friction.

———

Seamus texted me afterschool. He wanted to come over tonight and try rimming. I might've been more scared of that than actual sex. I said yes, then proceeded to take a very thorough shower.

"What's that?" I pointed to the small box in his hand when he arrived.

He stepped inside and walked right into the bedroom, ignoring my question.

"Did you want a drink?" I asked.

"No, I'm good." He shut the blinds, an unnerving confidence in his actions. The box remained in his free hand.

Seamus sat on the bed, while I stood in the doorway.

"We're getting naked tonight," he said, as sure as the sky was blue.

"We don't both need to get—"

"We are."

Nerves jangled through me. I held onto the doorway. I couldn't handle a Seamus this certain.

"What's in the box?" I asked.

He opened it and removed a candle.

"Mood lighting?" I joked.

Seamus creased his brow in determination. He leaned forward and took both of my hands. "I know you're scared, Jules. I know you're going to try to talk your way out of this, but I won't let that happen. You are a beautiful man, and you shouldn't be embarrassed or ashamed of how you look."

He stood up and placed the candle on my nightstand. He took out a pack of matches from his pocket and placed it beside them.

"Here's what we're going to do tonight. We're going to turn off the lights and undress in the dark. We'll be naked together, but I won't be able to see you. Only touch you. Taste you."

My breath hitched. My dick immediately went full mast.

"The candle will be on the nightstand. If you get to a point where you feel comfortable, light it."

I gave a terse nod. My body trembled for all different reasons. Lust, need, fear.

I was going to lie naked with Seamus, the man my heart longed for.

"You ready?" he asked.

My throat was thick with nerves, but the kind of nerves that hit me at the top of a roller coaster. I was tired of looking up from the ground. I was ready to fly.

"Hit the lights." He pointed behind me at the lightswitch.

I gazed into his crystal blue eyes as he disappeared into the darkness.

I heard the rustling of Seamus's shirt shucking off his frame, then the zip of his pants.

My heartbeat pounded in my ears. I exhaled a shaky breath as I unbuttoned my shirt. But to my surprise, my fear turned into a rush of exhilaration. The pitch blackness snuffed out my insecurity. Off went my shirt, cool air hitting my naked chest. Then went my pants, and finally my boxers. My hard cock stuck straight out, loving the open space.

I moved closer to the *pwop* sound of Seamus kicking off his shoes, the clanging of his belt as he stepped out of his pants.

Seamus was naked.

I was naked.

I was walking around naked in my apartment, something I never did. I stayed in a T-shirt and underwear up until the very last second before I darted into the shower. I pulled on a towel and avoided looking at the mirror when I stepped out of the shower before beelining to my dresser to put clothes on. In other words, I was only naked for maybe three minutes per day.

"Marco." Seamus's disembodied voice cut through the silence.

"Polo," I called back.

We had no right to be making a game out of this. Our laughter filled the dark.

"Marco," he said again, this time his voice closer, a playful chuckle.

"Polo."

According to Chase, my resident science guru, when one sense was dulled, the others were heightened. That had to explain the sheer surge of heat, unlike anything I'd ever experienced, when Seamus's hands found me.

The tips of his fingers landed on my chest, sliding through the curls of my hair. Nobody had ever touched me there. I didn't have firm pecs like he did. They were unshapely mounds leading down to a protruding stomach.

What if he was grossed out? What if he snuck out?

I shushed those thoughts. Seamus wouldn't do that. He wasn't like the guys on Milkman writing me off as a fatty, refusing to see the human underneath.

He let out a low, raspy moan as he moved up to my shoulders, his strong hands cascading over my skin. He gave them a massage, letting out the tension. My head dipped back.

"Relax," he whispered.

He moved down my chest and gave my nipples a pinch, turning them into spears. He took one in his mouth, his tongue flicking over the most sensitive part. A hungry gasp escaped out of me. I should have been touching him back, but my arms were immobile, turned to jelly.

He shifted to the other nipple, his tongue doing wonders. I moaned at the pleasure coursing through me.

Seamus nuzzled between my pecs, or what counted as my pecs, and buried his face in my chest hair, his stubbly beard making me shiver. He grunted his approval.

"You're warm," he said. "I can feel your heart racing."

Seamus drifted down to my belly, kissing down my furry trail, his hands fluttering at my sides. I didn't have a happy trail, but he had no trouble finding the way. He moved up and ran his hands over my back, sending rows of goosebumps in their wake.

There was that alarm button in my head—bright red, waiting to be pushed, waiting for Seamus to bail. I couldn't tell if he was just being a good friend, but judging by the way he hungrily grabbed at me, I chose to believe he was a happy customer.

"You're so sexy," he whisper-moaned as his lips dragged down my chest. I fought back a lump in my throat that was close to turning into tears. I never thought anyone would call me sexy. When society kept saying you were fat and ugly, at some point, you had no choice but to give up and believe them.

He went lower, kissing down past my belly button until he took my dick in his mouth.

"God, yes," I cried out. I would never not melt at his mouth enveloping me. It was even hotter not being able to see, not knowing what he would do next. I ran my hands through his soft hair.

He took me to the base, licked my head, and cupped my balls, hitting every pleasure center I had. I reached out for the wall to get my balance. I wished I could see him, wished for a glimmer of those blazing blue eyes staring up at me.

"Feels so good. I want you so bad. I'm yours." In the black void, I lost my nerve. Darkness emboldened me.

"Baby." Seamus groaned against my cock.

"I want you, Seamus. I want you."

"Get on the bed," he commanded, his voice low and thick.

A few steps backward, and I lay flat on my comforter. I could make out the slightest shape of his body hovering over me. I decided that Seamus was drinking me in, hungry for the rest of me. Not because he was a chubby-chaser or a dutiful friend. Because he wanted me. I let myself believe that and was rewarded with a flood of fresh confidence.

I...was sexy.

He lifted my legs up. I held onto them and jutted my hips forward to give him a better angle. Was my ass in the fucking open, welcoming visitors like it was a SuperTarget?

His warm tongue circled my entrance, making me shudder and clench at the new sensation.

"Yes. Yes, this is fucking amazing," I yelled. Fuck if my neighbors heard. If they'd ever been rimmed, they would understand. "Don't stop. Eat that fucking hole. Fucking take it."

Who was this person dirty talking like this? It couldn't be Julian Bradford.

I was unleashed. Was this what it was like to feel sexy and confident? To know that you were wanted? To know that you were someone being *lusted* over? Greetings from the top of the fucking world.

"Give it to me. Fuck, just like that." I pushed his head farther into my hole.

Seamus moaned against my opening, currents upon currents of heat surging through me.

"Play with my hole. Finger me," I said, a general ordering his troops. To repeat, I *never* spoke like this. My God, I didn't even say please! Yet the more I said, the less self-conscious I felt, and the more Seamus went to town on my ass.

He slid a finger inside me, filling me up.

"More," I said, back arching off the bed.

Two fingers.

"Baby, you are so goddamn tight. I'm gonna stretch you out with my cock."

"Yeah, you fucking are."

Seamus played my hole with his fingers and tongue like I was a fucking clarinet. I moaned and panted from his touch, lust breaking my brain.

And then, before I lost all ability to function, I sat up.

"Is something wrong?" he asked, immediately switching back to concerned Seamus.

Without saying a word, I grabbed the matchbook, struck a match, and lit the candle.

Let there be light.

22

SEAMUS

I had worried that I'd be freaked out by seeing another guy naked. I mean, I'd seen plenty of naked guys in the locker room, but I always averted my eyes. You found a point on the wall and focused on it.

This time, I stared. I soaked it in. I *wanted* to see. My fingers and mouth had had all the fun. Now my eyes got to have a turn.

Guys' bodies usually didn't do it for me, but there was something about taking in Julian's big frame that hit a primal urge in my gut. It wasn't just any body. It was attached to this wonderful person. This guy who was intelligent, but also had a wildly dirty mouth that made my cock stand up at attention.

I stood over him, feasting on the sight of his curves aglow in the hazy flame. He might've been on the bigger side, but he was strong, too. I could see it in his thick arms and broad shoulders. A big bear, all for me.

At least, for this month.

"Wow," I said, damn near awestruck.

Julian propped himself on his elbows and stared into me, eyes overflowing with lust. "You still have work to do."

Holy shit. I *really* liked this bossy Jules.

I gave him the captain's salute and got back on my knees. I flicked my tongue over his hole, taking in the musky scent making my head spin. I wasn't totally sure what I was doing, but I leaned on my experiences going down on women, and it seemed to do the trick. I aimed to please, and I had one satisfied customer. I'd thought I would be freaked out because it was a guy, but again, because it was Julian, I was hungry for it.

Julian writhed under my touch, his breathing getting more intense, more labored.

"Eat that hole."

Fuuuuuck. Julian's filthy mouth was such a turn on. I gripped the backs of his legs tighter, tiny leg hairs tickling my palms.

Julian began stroking himself, letting out more guttural moans in the process. I was dizzy with heat. I dragged my tongue up to take a ball in my mouth.

"Don't fucking stop. Suck that dick."

I licked up to take his cock to the back of my throat, then released just as he was getting into it.

"You fucking tease," he gasped out.

Mm-hmm.

I stretched his hole with my fingers. He fought against me, clenching as the orgasm whirled through him.

"I'm so close, Seamus. Make me come."

I freed up a hand to jerk myself. I had to give myself some release or else I'd have to be rushed to the emergency room.

"Fuck, I want you, Seamus. Don't stop." He huffed above me, begging for more.

Each time he cried out how much he wanted me, it hit me in the heart. Julian had done a fucking number on me.

Julian let out a borderline scream as his hole clenched up and he exploded across his stomach and chest. I had to hold up his legs to keep him from collapsing and sliding off the bed. My man was spent.

"Jules?" I peeked up. He was absolutely dazed. He'd taken a big hit off nature's most powerful drug.

"Present," he said while catching his breath.

"Damn." I wished I were more eloquent in this moment. "That was...wow."

Nice one, Seamus. Damn. Wow. My, you're so well-spoken.

Julian sat up, stars in his eyes, face flushed. He didn't try and cover himself up.

"Do we need to take care of you?" he asked.

"I'm good."

He looked down at my crotch, where I was absent-mindedly stroking my ragingly hard cock. No wonder I could only speak monosyllabically. All my blood had left one head and gone right for the other one.

Julian wrapped a hand around my cock, a plan clicking together on his face.

"Get on the bed." He nudged his head, and I didn't need to be told twice.

I lay down, expecting a masterful blow job, but instead, Julian lifted my legs, just as I had done to him. My body tensed up.

"Is this okay?" he asked.

"Um, yeah?" I thought of what Hutch had said, how this was the most vulnerable position a guy could be in. He was one hundred percent right. "We can check it off your list."

He stood up and sat beside me on the bed.

"Forget the list for a second. We don't have to do anything you're not comfortable with."

I squeezed Julian's hand. "I'm comfortable with you."

He was someone I wanted to be vulnerable with. I had already shared my deep, dark secret with him, and he hadn't run.

I rolled backward and threw my legs in the air. Julian got back into position.

And then I lost consciousness. Was it possible to black out from sheer pleasure? His tongue swept over my hole, unlocking new levels of desire. Now I got why he was a squirrely, panting mess minutes ago.

"Whoa." I slammed my head back as Julian went to town on my ass. Everything I'd done to him, he was doing to me. Plugging me with his fingers, slicking me with his tongue.

I saw every damn star in the galaxy, and in a few minutes, I was going to shoot out the Milky Way.

"Jules. Holy shit." I pulled my legs against my chest to give him the best workspace possible. Goosebumps blanketed my body.

Why were straight guys so afraid of anyone coming near their butts? They were missing out.

Julian fucked me with his tongue. My balls tightened, and like a maniac, I jerked myself with both hands. I put my foot on the accelerator and raced to Climax Town.

He reached up to my dick until he saw I had it covered. I fucked my fist as the orgasm took full hold of me, making every cell tense.

"Come for me," he said.

I let out a groan that emptied all the air from my lungs. I shot so hard, I gave myself a facial.

"Wow." Julian handed me the tissue box on his nightstand.

"Wow," I said definitively.

If rimming was this life-changing, then what would sex be like?

We lay there in silence. Time didn't exist. Finally, Julian got up and swiped a robe hanging on the bathroom door.

"What are you doing?" I asked.

"Putting on a robe?"

"Why?"

"I don't know. I'm probably going to shower."

The thought popped up in my head of soaping him down, which caused my dick to spike up, already ready and willing for round two. He gave off strong *I want to shower alone* vibes. Showering was something you couldn't do in the dark. Baby steps, I told myself.

I should've been taking baby steps, too. A month ago, I was ardently heterosexual with a smidge of bicuriousness. Now I was clamoring to take a shower with my friend whose ass I'd just eaten like it was a grocery store sheet cake.

"You don't need a robe to go into the bathroom." I bit my lip, hoping for a show. "Drop it. Let me see that fine-ass body."

"You really want to see it?" he asked, confused and intrigued.

I made my eyebrows do a double raise.

"Before we have to go back to clothes."

"Seamus, have you ever thought about living in a nudist colony?"

"Only old people go to those. You're stalling, Jules." I pointed a finger down. *Drop the robe.*

Julian clenched his eyes shut, took a deep breath, and released the robe from his hands.

There, in the yellow glow of the candle, was one beautiful man.

"That's what I'm talking about."

I nodded in delight, my eyes refusing to blink. Those shoulders, the pouch of his stomach, his thick legs. All day long, we were bombarded with guys with six-packs and not an ounce of fat. What a pleasure to get to see a real body. How lucky was I?

I whistled at him like I was a construction worker.

Julian waved off my catcall and waltzed into the bathroom, no robe needed.

After we cleaned ourselves up, showered, and dressed, we collapsed on the couch with a bag of microwave popcorn and *Frasier* reruns. I had trouble focusing on the Crane brothers; all I could think about was wanting to tell Jules that I was really into him, that I might be falling in love with him. The words were on the tip of my tongue, but I was too scared to pull the trigger.

Julian rested his head on my shoulder. I stroked my fingers up and down his forearm. We were natural, comfortable.

When the episode ended, a message popped up on screen asking if we were still watching.

"Rude," I said. "Why do streaming services need to be passive-aggressive like this?"

"If we didn't want to keep watching, we'd shut it off."

"What time is it?"

I checked my phone and couldn't believe it was past ten. Even though I had to be at school early every morning, it didn't stop me from going to bed around midnight. Somehow, being a working adult had trained me to survive on less sleep.

"It's late," Julian said.

Was that my cue or was he merely stating a fact?

"I should get going." I clapped my hands on my knees, the universal signal that the party was over and I had to get my ass off the couch.

I stood up and stretched. I wanted so badly to kiss him. My heart vibrated in my chest.

"Thanks for tonight," Julian said.

"You're welcome?" It was weird to be thanked for making someone come. The thank you was the orgasm itself.

"For the candle idea. Thank you for pulling me out of my comfort zone."

"You don't seem that comfortable in your comfort zone."

He shrugged. "It's the only place I know."

I fingered a lock of his luscious hair.

"Jules, I hope that one day, you see what I see."

He stood up and pulled me into a tighter-than-expected hug, then gave me a kiss on the cheek. Was that my cue to kiss him back for real or was he merely being nice?

There had been a time when I knew how to be suave. Not tonight, it seemed.

I strolled to the door. "There's only one thing left. We can't avoid it now."

"Sex." He breathed out a sigh.

"Nervous?" I asked.

"Isn't everyone nervous before their first time?"

"True." I was nervous, too, but not for the reasons I should have been.

I massaged his hand with my thumb, clinging to the last bits of physical touch.

The time was now. My heart was begging me to kiss him and gush every feeling I had for him. Was I gay? Was I straight? I'd figure it out in the morning.

The batter couldn't stand at the plate forever. He had to take a swing.

"Jules. Tonight was incredible. Truly. You are...so wonderful." My nerves wanted to swallow me whole, making my throat go dry. "I...am having trouble talking tonight."

"I get it. It's the sex haze."

"The what?"

"The sex haze. Our brains get all fogged up in the heat of sex. We get discombobulated and emotional."

I wondered if a sex haze was the same thing as the sex high Greg had mentioned in Ashley's greenhouse. Was sex really that much of a brain fogger?

"You feel out of sorts?" he asked.

"Yeah. A little." I'd eaten a guy's ass and loved it. Out of sorts didn't begin to cover it.

"The same thing will happen when we go all the way. We have to remember that sex is a physical act, that's all. It's not emotional. We're just two friends who are going to have sex, and that's that. Two guys fucking around. Nothing to be nervous or awkward about."

He held up his hand for a high-five, which for some reason felt like a punch in the gut.

Still, I was never one to turn down a hi-five.

I couldn't explain why, but I left Julian's place soulcrushed. The high was replaced with a pang of hurt lighting up my chest. I stood on the stoop, taking in the chilly air, the rustling of naked branches on the maple trees lining his street.

We're just two friends who are going to have sex, and that's that.

23

JULIAN

Three days until the anniversary party. Four days until my birthday.

And less than four days until I lose my virginity. But who was counting?

Seamus and I hadn't met up since that magical, candlelit night. Life was determined to get in the way, what with party planning, lesson planning, and BlingBling video planning. We still managed to sneak quick chats and smiles across the hall in between classes.

He was constantly on my mind. That night with him had begun to transform something inside me. Instead of bundling myself up in a robe the second I got out of the shower, I let myself air dry for a few minutes. I didn't obsess over getting dressed right away. I walked around in my underwear first. I checked myself out in window reflections in school. Was I becoming a vain teenager?

Each time I looked at myself, I saw a little bit more of what Seamus saw.

And each time I thought about the way Seamus gazed at me, my heart did a fluttery jump. I told myself what I told him: our sex would be purely physical, not emotional. *Keep your emotions out of it, Julian. That way lies danger.*

Sure, it might seem like Seamus really cared for me, like maybe there was something more there, but I was too scared to find out. If I brought up how I felt, and my feelings weren't reciprocated, if Seamus said that it was all the heat of the moment and nothing more, I would be devastated. And I would lose one of my closest friends.

If only I could talk to my other friends about this. But I was in too deep. Tangled under too many lies. And I didn't want them turning my feelings into tawdry gossip or a joke. They were too raw.

I stayed after school on Thursday to help one of my freshman students struggling with the intricacies of French grammar. Outside, the air was cold and the teacher's lot was nearly empty. As I walked to my spot, Raleigh's car pulled into the space beside mine.

"Julian! How's it going? Whatcha up to?" he asked when he got out.

"I'm doing all right. I have to meet my mom at the flower shop." The florist had called and said that freesias would no longer be available for the anniversary party. We had to come up with a plan-B fast.

"What's in the bag?" I nodded at the shopping bag dangling from his fingers.

"Ev is stressed with auditions for the spring musical, so I ran and got him some snacks."

"You're so thoughtful."

"Eh, kinda. He gave me a list of what he wanted and told me if I didn't run out and get them ASAP, then he would quote 'devolve into a brokedown version of himself from which he might never recover.'"

Oh, Everett. Never change.

"But I added in a few healthy things, too. I got him some fruit chews so he gets his Vitamin C. We don't want him getting sick."

Sick Everett was the ultimate drama queen. The last time he'd tried to go to school while sick, he spouted off the "Not Personal" monologue from *Erin Brockovich* when we made him go home.

As much as Raleigh and Everett bickered, one could get a toothache from how sweet they were with each other.

"Wish him luck on choosing the right actors for me."

"He says you've been like a ghost recently."

The comment stuck to my ribs.

"I've just been busy planning this party."

Raleigh nodded. I was unsure what he believed. He put a comforting hand on my shoulder.

"Hey, there's something I think you should know." Raleigh's voice got low. His face creased with concern.

My stomach clenched at his ominous statement. "What's wrong?"

"Look, I remember our conversation from the Christmas party. You were a little tipsy and secretly admitted to me that you're majorly crushing on Seamus."

My face got hotter than the Red Hots peeking from the top of his shopping bag. Neither of us had talked about that conversation since it happened. I'd wanted to believe it was a dream. I trusted Raleigh had kept my secret.

"What about it?"

"I'm usually not one for gossiping. That's more Everett's speed. But I think this is something you should know, and it's better you hear it now rather than Seamus springing it on you." He rubbed the back of his head, then spat it out: "Seamus is seeing someone."

And there it was. The cord snapped, and I was in an elevator hurtling to the ground. Confirmation that my feelings for Seamus were a lost cause.

"Oh."

But why didn't Seamus say anything to me? Why would he keep this from me?

"I know you were into him. I'm sorry."

"Who is she?" I prayed she didn't work at South Rock. I couldn't see them in the halls. I'd have to transfer.

"So, actually, fun fact: it's a he."

My head darted up. "He? Are you sure?"

"Yeah. It's kind of a weird situation he told us about. He and this gay guy have been experimenting with each other over the past month, running all the bases. He asked me for sex advice last week because he wanted to make it really good for this guy."

"Who's the guy?"

"He wouldn't say. I'm assuming they met on an app. No judgment here. The thing is, it started with them fooling around with each other, but the way Seamus talked about this guy, he has it bad for him."

"Bad?"

"Real bad. He couldn't stop smiling and blushing. He was practically levitating off his seat. He really likes this guy, whoever he is. Really, really likes him." Raleigh's shoulders slumped. "I'm sorry, Julian."

It was then I remembered I had to act sad. I fought back the grin spreading across my face.

"Thanks for telling me, Raleigh."

"I wanted to warn you. And hey, I've had my heart broken, too. It sucks."

"It's such a shock."

"I know. Who would ever dump me?" Raleigh shook his head, mystified. "Who would dump these?" He held up his shirt and pointed at his abs.

Rumor had it that he'd walked in on his fiancé in bed with the rival football coach at North Point High. No one could escape heartbreak.

Except for me right now. I did an internal happy dance.

"It all worked out, though," he said. "I'm with Everett now. And you'll find that special person."

It turned out, maybe I already had.

I had third-party confirmation. Seamus really, really liked me!

AT THE FLORIST, I was a smiling fool as I searched for a backup flower. My grandparents couldn't have cared less about whether the flowers matched the tablecloths. They were happy to be alive and together still. My mom was a different story.

"What about lilies? Can we do lilies?" she asked, almost desperate. Being naturally indecisive and on a time crunch was never a good mix. "Or maybe we go in the total opposite direction and choose sunflowers."

The florist cocked an eyebrow at me, perhaps wondering why I hadn't committed my own mother to an institution.

"How could they not have freesias? We settled it weeks ago," she said. It was one of the only things she had settled on before I was called in to intervene.

"Our supplier's crop got infested with aphids."

Mom's face transformed into disgust. She whipped her head toward me. "Why are you so happy about this?"

I turned away, willing my smile to go away for a few moments. It was a tall order. I was swept up in a wave of pure joy.

An idea came to me. I rubbed her arm in an attempt to soothe her. "What about orange roses? They're classic, but also colorful like sunflowers. It could be a good compromise."

"I do love roses."

"Could we do orange roses?" I asked the florist.

"Those I should have. Let me go check." He went into the back, while Mom took a deep breath.

"Crisis averted," I said.

"I'll be relaxed when I have a glass of champagne in my hand on Saturday." She heaved out a breath while checking her hair in the mirrored wall because that was the type of multitasking Elizabeth Bradford excelled at. "Is Seamus coming with you?"

The mention of his name made me break out in another ear-to-ear grin.

"Yep. I can't wait for everyone to meet him."

Mom studied me with a curious glint in her eye, as if the wheels were turning in her head for some inexplicable reason.

"Is that okay? I accounted for him in the guest list."

"Of course. Why wouldn't it be okay? He *is* your boyfriend." There was that unmistakable note in her tone, a blip of disbelief and condescension that had been honed over a lifetime of being the mean girl.

"What's that supposed to mean?"

"Nothing."

The florist came back out and gave us the thumbs-up on our orange roses order. Mom went ahead and filled out the updated order form while I stood there in contemplative silence. I wished her words and tone didn't get stuck in my head, but that was the power a mother wielded over her son.

She was in high spirits when we left the florist shop. We walked to the community lot where we had parked. She clicked her remote to unlock her car, while I hung back. This time, I was the one studying her.

"Did we forget something?" she asked.

"You think I'm lying," I said.

"Lying about what?"

"Seamus being my boyfriend."

"Don't be preposterous. I saw you two together with my own eyes."

The outside world might take her statement at face value. I

was versed in her passive aggression, though. The look of utter surprise when I had introduced her to Seamus stuck in my head.

"Just come out and say what you're thinking. How could a guy like that be into a guy like me? Why would he ever want to be with a fat piece of shit?"

"I never said that."

"But you're thinking it. Come on, Mom. You're never one to hold back your opinions."

"I enjoyed meeting him, and he seems to really like you. You got lucky."

And there it was. Of course there it was. Like she would ever be able to help herself from slipping a comment in. Years of those comments boiled inside me, fire for my rage furnace.

Perhaps it was the knowledge that Seamus liked me. Perhaps it was the leftover confidence of being naked, but that was the moment when I was finally, one hundred percent over her shit.

"I got lucky? Lucky that a guy like Seamus is giving me a chance? Lucky that I landed someone with a great physique who can save me from being a fat, lonely loser?"

She fixed her coat, appalled that I was saying the quiet part aloud.

"I know you think I sound shallow, but this is how the world works, Julian. I have girlfriends with wonderful hearts and personalities that are perpetually single because men want someone hotter, younger, *thinner*. While I'm no expert, I'm fairly certain those rules apply in your world, too. Sweetheart, I want you to be healthy—"

"I am healthy. You can call my doctor if you want."

"Fine. I want you to be *slimmer* only so you can have more opportunities in the world, more confidence, so that people will treat you with respect. You're almost thirty-five, and this is the first time I've heard of you dating someone seriously. All of a sudden, on the eve of a big party where our entire family will be present, you introduce us to your hunky, athletic boyfriend. I'm happy to play along with this charade if that's what you want, but at some point, you're going to have to face the truth."

The only truth I needed to face was that my mother and I would never have a healthy relationship. She gave a voice to every negative thought in my head. A speech like this was bound to happen someday, her frustration and disgust for my life reaching a breaking point.

Well, I also had a breaking point.

"You got lucky too, Mom. You're lucky that you found a man who's been taking care of you your whole adult life, because God knows you're too stupid to spend one minute on your own. You're lucky that you have two kids who are 'healthy.'" My air quotes were as sharp as daggers. "Who cares that your daughter had to be hospitalized with an eating disorder and your athletic son is so shallow that he cheated on the mother of his kids with his nineteen-year-old nanny? All that matters is that they're thin. What a small life you live."

Tears rained down my face.

"It kills you that I'm happy. How dare I be fat and walk down the street with a smile on my face. How dare an athletic guy find me sexy. How dare he want to be my boyfriend. That goes against your whole world order. What would you and your cheerleader friends have called me behind my back? My life may not look like yours, but it's mine, and I love it, and that eats you up inside. Because your life is empty and meaningless."

I yanked my car door open, shooting her one last final glare.

"I am lucky, Mom. I'm lucky that I'm nothing like you."

24

SEAMUS

"Jules, there's something I want to talk to you about. I was too scared to come out with it the other night, but I can't sit on my feelings any longer. The thing is, when we started our sessions, I was straight. I really saw it as helping out a friend, because you deserved to have a good first time. But I like you, Jules. I really like you, as more than a friend. I think about you all the time. I guess this means I'm bi, which is cool. I don't care what the label is, just as long as I get to be with you."

I looked up at the two sets of eyes watching me from the couch. "How was that?"

Greg started a slow clap, just like in some sports movie. Ethan joined in as it got faster until it became a round of applause.

Was that the reaction I'd been hoping for?

"I'm proud of you, son," Greg said.

Ethan squeezed his husband's hand. "Our boy is growing up."

"Guys, the dad/son stuff is still weird," I said.

"I remember when he was just a little, lost frat boy scrubbing barf off the front steps. Excuse me." Greg turned away and dabbed at his eyes.

"Have you ridden this joke until the wheels fell off yet, or did you need to circle the block a few more times?" I asked with my typical annoyance before curiosity got the better of me. "Was it good?"

"It was great," Greg said.

"This is so wonderful. I was telling Greg how much I liked Julian."

"This is weird, right?" I paced in the living room. "I was mostly straight in February, and now I'm totally gay in March?"

"That's how these things happen sometimes," Greg said, putting his arm around his husband. He and I had talked about it earlier today. He'd shared more of his process of coming out, which made me feel better, and saner. "It's not a straight line, no pun intended. If you look back, there were probably moments growing up that you ignored or straight-up repressed. Again, no pun intended."

"I remember the third baseman on my Little League team. I had this major urge to be his friend and go out for pizza together. I thought I just wanted us to be friends, but maybe...I had a crush on him?"

"Could be." Greg scratched at his chin.

It was as if my life had a twist ending, and I was going back and sifting through the clues. There were no gay role models growing up, no gay uncles to light the way. Manhattan was a much different world than Staten Island. Until Greg, I thought that only guys in the arts could be gay.

"I'm...bisexual. I am a bisexual man. Okay." I sank into the armchair opposite my friends.

"Welcome to the party!" Greg gave me a thumbs-up.

"Coming out is strange for everyone. You're basically informing the world about who you like to have sex with," Ethan said.

There was only one man I wanted to have sex with.

"Do you think Jules is going to freak out?" I asked. "The other night, he said this was all just physical and nothing more."

"Greg used to say that all the time about us hooking up in college." Ethan rolled his eyes.

"It started off that way," Greg bickered back.

"Please. You were a goner for me the first time we met up in the library stacks."

"Agree to disagree," Greg shot back at Ethan with a knowing wink. They locked eyes in a cute moment. Would Jules and I be this mushy for each other in a decade?

Ethan turned back to me. "The point is, I promise you it's not just physical. If being intimate with Julian has conjured up all these feelings for you, then he has to be feeling the same way. He's probably as scared as you are. I mean, he still assumes you're straight. Gay guys falling for their straight friends is like a rite of passage."

I mashed my fists together like they were defibrillator paddles, something I'd done since I was little when I was concentrating hard.

"Okay," I said at the end of my thinking. Maybe it was time that I got off the bench and let my heart have another shot.

I texted Julian for us to get together tomorrow night. It would be a night of firsts. His first time having sex. And my first time telling a guy I liked him.

My nerves were on fire for the rest of the evening. I channeled my energy into editing a batch of videos and scheduling them, as well as researching other popular content creators with sponsored videos. My follower count continued to swell, which had to mean something to brands.

Sometime after eight, Greg knocked on my door.

"Someone's here to see you."

"Jules?"

"No, some guy named Vince."

"Vince?"

He shrugged. Vince sounded familiar to me, but I couldn't place it.

A minute later, it all came back to me. I stepped onto the front porch where Lauren's brother Vince, a large, beefy guy with a shaved head and a seeming inability to smile, waited for me.

"Hey, Vince. Long time no see."

"I wonder why that is."

I'd met Vince a bunch of times while dating Lauren. He'd been a welcome presence during happy hours and holidays, his stern outer shell hiding a wicked sense of humor. We were just starting to bond as everything blew up between his sister and me.

"Good to see you," I said, matching his seriousness. "Considering you came to my home, there must be a problem."

"Listen, man, Lauren's been real patient with you, but she needs the rest of the money you stole from her."

"Stole? I didn't steal from her."

"What would you call it?"

My throat went dry. Maybe the word was accurate. I didn't consider what I did stealing, but I was going too easy on myself. Was that how she described it to others?

"I'm working on paying her back. I have a plan in place."

"You've been paying her back for two years, and you're barely halfway there. You're stringing her along."

"I'm working on it." Free cash flow wasn't in the cards for me at the moment.

"Maybe borrow from friends and family? Looks like they can afford to help you out." Vince gave a chilling glance at Greg and Ethan's beautiful house.

I'd never told my family about what happened. I couldn't bear to tell them the truth, and it wasn't like they had extra money to send my way. Only Greg and Ethan knew the truth, and they'd already helped me so much. Julian also knew, but I wasn't going to ask him for money. I wanted to do this on my own.

"Lauren and I have an agreement in place. I've been sticking to that schedule. I've never missed a payment. I'm working two jobs trying to pay her back."

"She needs that money. She and her fiancé want to plan a nice honeymoon. They're saving up for a house. The market's gone crazy, interest rates are up, and they have to come up with more money for a down payment."

A wave of mixed feelings struck me. Lauren was engaged and househunting. I was happy that she'd been able to move on, but it also reminded me how stuck in place I was.

"She wants to move on with her life, but you're making it impossible. It's not fair. You've had enough time to get your shit together." Cold-blooded anger ringed his dark eyes.

"I'm sorry. I'm so sorry about what happened. I hope she knows how sorry I am," I said.

"She doesn't know I'm here."

He was in full protective mode for his baby sister. I couldn't fault him for that, especially when everything he was saying was true.

"I'm working on it. I promise."

"Are you, though? Lauren's a good woman. She's been patient with you, even though you put her through the fucking wringer. That money was important to her. She had to cut back and make sacrifices because of what you did. She's missed out on girls' trips and driven around with a busted bumper that she can't get fixed." Vince gulped back a hard lump in his throat. "Her fiancé Adrian is a great guy. He told me that he was crazy about her from the start, but it took Lauren three months to agree to go on a date. She was so closed off. You know what she told me? She was *terrified* of letting someone in and having them hurt her like you did. Everyday, in the back of her mind, she feared that Adrian was lying to her, that the rug would get pulled out. She was upset that you wiped out her bank account, but she hates what you really stole from her."

His jaw trembled with barely contained hurt for his sister, hurt that I'd caused. I could blame it on my addiction all I wanted, but it was me. I was the one responsible.

"She was in pain, man, a lot of pain. And then you're out there making your stupid little videos, having a ball...You're an asshole, Seamus."

I had no rebuttal. I'd thought when we came up with the payment plan for my debt, things would be fine. I'd ignored the hidden costs of my actions. I'd wanted to believe that paying the money back would be the only thing needed to clear my conscience. But did I make a real effort to pay her back sooner? Did I ever check in with her to see how things were going?

Vince was right. I was an asshole.

"It's a miracle she was able to trust anyone after what you did."

"I'm working to make things right."

"I need you to make things right *now*. Do whatever you can to get that money so she can move on." Pain infused his demands. I wasn't the only person feeling guilty about not being able to help Lauren.

"Are you dating anyone?" Vince asked.

Not wanting to open a can of worms about my sexuality, I simply shook my head no.

"Thank fucking God for that."

"I'm really sorry," I said, my voice cracking.

"Your apology is worthless to me." He shoved me against a column, his expression a block of ice. His hand pressed against my neck, making me gasp for air. "I want my little sister made whole by the end of the month. Are we clear?"

I nodded as best I could. He let go and stomped back to his car. Breath flooded back into my lungs.

What the fuck was I going to do?

25

JULIAN

I woke up Friday morning determined. I would prove Mom wrong. I would prove our whole society wrong.

Fat guys could be loved.

I was tired of shrinking away. I was going to walk into South Rock High and confess my feelings to Seamus. I was done with dancing around this delicate topic. When we met up tonight for our final session, we would be two men making love. Physical *and* emotional.

I entered South Rock High, my heart buzzing and my stomach dealing with so many butterflies it could've been mistaken for a nature conservatory. Seamus was already in his classroom, busy toiling away on Cyllabus.

Now that I had confirmation that Seamus liked me as more than a friend (correction: *really* liked me), I should've had no problem being around him, right?

Wrong. Very wrong.

Nerves pummeled me.

I knocked at the door with a shaky fist.

He looked so damn good in a polo that hugged his freckled

shoulders. How did I know they were freckled? Because I'd seen him naked. Multiple times.

"Hey, Jules." He stood up. His polo showed off his flat stomach, a stomach that I had also seen in the buff multiple times.

"Hi. Happy Friday."

Hey Seamus, so I heard that you like me. Really like me. Well, I like you, too.

That was all I wanted to say, the only train on my one-track mind. The words were on the tip of my tongue ready to parachute out, yet they refused to move.

What was I more scared of? Raleigh being wrong, or Raleigh being right?

And if Seamus did like me, then what was stopping *him* from proclaiming it?

Something about his posture seemed unusually rigid, a tenseness that I couldn't blame on Cyllabus.

"Still having trouble?" I pointed at the computer.

"Always." He rolled his eyes and leaned back in his chair. "I thought teaching meant I didn't need to be on the computer all day."

"What's the problem? I can help."

Seamus kept his hand on the closed laptop. "It's okay. I can figure it out. I should figure it out on my own."

There was a heaviness to how he said it that made me paranoid he wasn't merely talking about grading software.

"Oh. Okay. Well, I'm right across the hall." I pointed behind me, as if he'd forgotten where my classroom was, which only made things more awkward.

"Cool," he said. The mood between us seemed tense.

"Great. Have a good Friday!" I turned on my heel and retreated into the hall.

Dammit, what was I doing? I kept thinking of that quote that all my jock students were fond of: *You miss one hundred percent of the shots you don't take.*

I marched back into his classroom and shut the door.

"Actually, can we talk for a second?" I fought to stay calm.

"Sure."

He leaned against his desk and fixed his icy blue eyes on me. It was now or never. One small sentence for Julian. One giant leap for Julian's love life.

"Seamus, before we go forward with our grand finale session tonight, I have to be honest with you. I don't want this to be the grand finale. I want it to be the start of something." My eyes initially shifted to the floor, but I found the courage to meet his gaze. "I like you. I really like you."

Where I should've been petrified, I felt oddly exhilarated. An epiphany came to me: moments like these, where we dared to be true to ourselves, were what life was all about.

"I've always had a little crush on you, Seamus, but I kept it tucked away. When we started our sessions, I told myself you were doing this as a good friend. This was only about physical stuff. But this past month has been incredible, and it's made me open my heart in ways I didn't think possible. You make me feel like I'm sexy and powerful and someone special. I like who I am with you." I exhaled a breath. "I like you. As more than a friend. And tonight, I want to lose my virginity to a man I am in love with."

Whoa, did I say LOVE?

I did.

And I meant it.

I was totally, unmistakably in love with Seamus Shablanski.

Was this my first romantic declaration? My first grand romantic gesture? Should I have used cue cards like the guy in *Love Actually*? My body was on fire, alive in a way I'd never experienced.

Until I took a second to read Seamus's face, which lacked the same excitement. His reaction belonged at a funeral, not a love declaration.

"Jules, I...I'm flattered."

He was flattered. That was never a good sign.

"You mean a lot to me, too. But not in the same way." He spoke slowly, his voice strained. "You're one of my best friends, Jules."

Friend. Another f-word that was a terrible sign.

"I thought that you liked me as more than a friend." I wanted to haul Raleigh in here and explain himself.

Now Seamus was the one looking at the floor, making his hair fall into his eyes in a cruel tease. His hand gripped his desk until his knuckles went white.

"I did. I mean, we've been doing so much together, how could I not?" He looked at the blinding white of the markerboard. Anywhere but in my eyes. "But I was caught up in the moment. The sex haze. It's best that we stay friends."

Cupid's arrows turned to poison-tipped spears slicing through my chest.

"I'm sorry, Jules." He kept shaking his head. "I'm sorry for getting things all confused between us. I wanted you to realize you're worthy of everything you want in life."

I didn't feel worthy.

"There's a guy out there for you who's got his shit together."

"I don't want some guy out there." *I want you.* An alternate version of us, where we were kissing by this point, slipped from my hands.

"It's probably for the best that we don't have our final session either," he said, adding a vat of salt onto my open wounds.

"It's for the best," I said, fighting back tears. I wasn't going to cry and make this moment even more uncomfortable. "Thanks for...all your help."

He bowed his head, watched his shoe trace a circle on the tiled floor.

I stopped at the door, a surge of anger finding its way to the surface. But who was I angry at? Him or me?

"You know, at least the guys who reject me for being a fatty are being honest."

"You don't want me, Jules. Trust me. You can find someone better. You deserve someone better."

I left his classroom and walked past my own as fast as I could without actually running. I needed to get away from people. I was in no state to be a leader, a mentor, a role model. How could I teach when I couldn't even speak?

26

JULIAN

March was supposed to go out like a lamb, but today's weather didn't get the memo. Wind whipped across the roof in sharp spikes.

What kind of teacher was I to abandon my class because I was so confused about a quasi (though not really) relationship? I was acting like one of my students. I could teach the mechanics of safe sex, but when two people came together in an intimate, vulnerable way, it would never be safe. All the condoms and IUDs couldn't protect against hurt.

I wish my friends were here.

"There you are!"

My heart lifted at the sound of Amos's voice. I turned around and found Chase, Amos, and Everett coming toward me. Chase even carried my jacket. Had prayers ever been answered that quickly? God really was pro-gay.

I got emotional, choking back tears. I couldn't help it. Almost thirty-five years of zero boy drama had made me unprepared for my first wallop.

They surrounded me like angels, putting my coat over my shoulders.

"J, what's going on?" Amos knelt in front of me, his sparkling eyes a safe harbor amid all the craziness swirling in my head.

"I'm fine. I just needed to clear my head."

"Okay, that's it." Everett stood up and stomped his foot. "I've had it with whatever is going on with you. You've been MIA from the group chat. You stormed out of the pep rally. There is something going on with you that you just aren't telling us, and now we find you shivering in the cold by yourself crying, and you're telling us everything is fine. I never thought I'd be one of those gays who used honey, but *Honey*, what the fuck is going on?"

I opened my mouth, but he stopped me.

"And I swear, if you say the word 'fine' again, I'm going to have an aneurysm. There's only one four-letter F-word I'll be tolerating up here." Everett pulled my hat onto my head making sure it got below the ears.

"I'm having guy problems," I told them, feeling the dam break.

"We had a feeling," Chase said. "We ran a statistical analysis of potentially troubled areas in your life and surmised that your family life, professional life, and health wouldn't generate the same level of caginess you've displayed this month."

"What Chase is saying is that it's obvious you've been having guy problems, but we don't understand why you're hiding it from us," Amos said as he pulled the gloves from my other coat pocket and slipped them onto my hands.

"It's because this is the first time I've ever had guy problems." I looked up to the clear blue sky and released the weight of this deep, dark secret. "I'm a virgin."

They didn't snark or laugh. If anything, they seemed confused.

"I don't understand. You've regaled us with tales of former lovers..." Chase began before Amos and Everett each put a hand on his shoulder. The truth clicked for him. "Oh. I see."

"I was embarrassed. I'm the oldest one in our friend group with the least experience. Make that no experience. So I made up stories. You guys are my closest friends. I didn't want to feel left out."

"We would never leave you out." Amos rubbed my knee. "You're not our friend because of how many guys you've been with. Who cares about that?"

"It's not something I planned. You wouldn't understand. You're all thin and in shape—"

"Hold the fuck up. First off, I wouldn't call any of us in shape. Do you remember when we tried to run that Zombie 5K?" Everett said.

A smile came to my face as I recalled us all huffing and puffing and getting passed by kindergartners. One of the zombie actors had chastised us for signing up for a race without doing the proper training. Everett didn't have a stake on him, so instead, he told the guy to fuck off.

"I can't remember the last time I was inside a locker room, not counting the time when Hutch and I roleplayed."

We swiveled our heads toward Amos, whose cheeks flared red.

"We're still working through our high school trauma," he said.

"Trauma. Sure." Everett rolled his eyes.

"Why would you think that our thinness or physical ability would have any bearing on our friendship? Those variables have nothing to do with each other," Chase said. "This isn't a wrestling team. There's no weight limit required."

I listened to myself. My obsession with how I looked had completely taken over my mind and seeped into every corner of my life.

"And maybe you're the smartest one of all of us for being a virgin," Everett said. "You've escaped the hell of bad sex."

"Who's the guy?" Amos asked.

I exhaled a stifled breath. Saying his name would be hard. "Seamus."

"What?!" my three friends yelled in unison.

I spilled my guts on our whole arrangement, speaking fast since our time up here undisturbed was limited.

Everett scratched his head. "When you say you've done everything except the big one with Seamus, you mean..."

"Everything," I answered with a definitive nod of the head.

"Everything," he repeated, shocked. "Damn. Nice job."

"I didn't know how to tell you any of this because then I'd have to go into my virgin status, and you guys kept teasing me about my crush on Seamus."

"We're sorry," Amos said.

"It was only for fun. We didn't know any of this was going on," Chase said.

"I'm not completely sorry. I'm like forty-three percent sorry," Everett said. "Part of the reason why I liked to give you shit about your crush was because I wanted you to *do* something about it. You liked Seamus, and whenever I saw you two together, I always wondered. You two had some kind of spark."

"Considering how many coaches at this school have turned out to be gay, the odds were statistically in your favor." Chase shrugged. "I wonder if correlation equals causation in this case."

Tears broke down my face. I cried into my knit gloves.

"Chase, I told you to cool it with the science talk," Everett said.

"It was math talk."

"Oh, whatever." Everett pulled me against him as Amos and Chase rubbed my arms and back. "J, talk to us. What happened?"

"I thought we really had something special, but it was all in my head. I told him I was in *love* with him. How could I be so dumb?"

"You weren't dumb. You were honest," Chase said matter-of-factly. "Telling the truth is never dumb."

"God, I'm such a cliché. I fell for my straight friend."

"In all fairness, that was after you two fooled around multiple times. That would mess my circuits up, too," Amos said.

"I was so certain, too. I felt something between us." The heat of his kiss, the way he stared at me, wanting me. Was the sex haze really that powerful? "Doesn't matter now."

"His loss." Chase rubbed my knee.

"But your gain."

I popped my head up and stared at Amos. Did he misspeak?

"What?" I asked him.

"You might think you're in the same place you were a month ago, but you're not, J," said Amos. "You've gained all this experience. You dared to confess your feelings to a guy you love. You let yourself be vulnerable for once."

"What does that mean?" I wasn't sure whether or not to be offended.

"You keep things in. You work so hard to be this stable, reliable person, the friend we can all count on. You're always wearing a poker face, and you don't even realize it." Amos took my tear-stained, gloved hands in his. "It's okay to fall apart sometimes."

This was uncharted territory for all of us. I was never the one who needed support. I spent my life supporting others, being there for them when they needed a shoulder to cry on, or advice, or help with party planning, or assistance with grading software.

"I'm sorry you're going through this. Let us be your rock this time," Everett said. "You don't have to keep secrets from us or worry about what we think of you. We love you, J. We'll always love you. You're a mess like the rest of us."

I leaned into my friends. They shielded me from the harsh cold and everything else that life tried to throw at me.

"This hurts," I said, plain and simple.

"I know." Amos ran a soothing hand through my hair.

We sat like that for a minute before Aguilar found us. The pain slowly began to subside, and a feeling of gratitude overtook me.

Gratitude for everything I got to experience. Gratitude for the strength that would eventually come. Gratitude for the people who would be there with me along the way.

Apparently, the guys had put on movies to entertain their classrooms, but it hadn't taken long for their students to seep into the halls. Aguilar, seeing my red eyes, asked if I needed to take the rest of the day off. I declined.

I didn't have Seamus, but I wasn't alone.

27

SEAMUS

I told Aguilar I was sick and needed to take the rest of Friday off. My body was a wretched mess of sharp aches and queasiness. Could a broken heart make a person physically sick?

As I left school, I glanced into Julian's classroom where he was in full French teacher mode. He shot me a disinterested flick of the eyes before returning his attention to his class.

At home, I collapsed on my bed and let streaming services numb my pain. The first show to pop up under *Shows you might like*:

Frasier.

Like the mature, grown-ass adult I was, I threw my pillow at the TV.

I went through the motions the rest of the day, and by the motions, I meant ordering takeout and binge-watching old episodes of *Fear Factor*.

It sucked to let Julian go, but it was the right thing to do. Who said I wouldn't do to him what I did to Lauren? Julian was smart and interesting, and I was watching a show where people ate bugs for money. He deserved a real stand-up guy, someone who wouldn't run the risk of ruining his life. I hoped our time together had given him the confidence to get back on the dating market and find himself Mr. Right. He didn't have to worry about sexual inexperience or not being attractive to guys. He had experience, and damn was he attractive inside and out.

Doing the right thing was hard, but that was how we became better versions of ourselves. Maybe it wasn't too different from *Fear Factor* contestants chomping on spiders. No challenge, no reward.

Greg charged into my room sometime that night. The hours had faded into one mushy blob of time.

"Make yourself pretty. We're going out."

"I don't really feel like it."

"Let's go out. Ethan's working late. It's Friday night."

"It's okay. I'm good here." I would let the TV be my friend tonight.

"What happened? Rough day?"

I stared at the TV, which was off. The thought of Julian was a sledgehammer to the heart; Greg quickly picked up on my pain.

"Shit. I'm sorry, dude. What happened?"

"Don't feel like talking about it."

Greg sat on the edge of my bed. "Why don't we get some fresh air? We'll go out, have a few drinks and a few laughs. You haven't left your bed since you came home."

"You don't know that." I dug deeper into the comfort of my bed.

"Educated guess. Come on, man."

"I'm good. Not feeling it." I threw the covers over my head. I preferred darkness. It matched my current mood.

The floor creaked, which I assumed meant Greg was leaving me in peace. A moment later, the ground shook under me, and I tumbled onto the floor.

"What the fuck!" I yelled. Greg stood over me, mattress in hand. "Did you flip my mattress?"

"Moping does nobody any good." Greg squatted down to my eye level. He mastered the no-nonsense stare that dads around the world used on their kids. "Get up, get showered, and get dressed. Don't make me carry you into the bathroom."

WE WENT to a bar on the water with a wide-open view of the river. It was the first warm Friday of spring, and the rooftop balcony was open. Flirty single ladies mingled in the crowd. My dick had no response.

Greg faded into the crowd to get us a round of drinks. I leaned against the railing, wondering what Julian was up to. Was he out with his friends? Meeting someone new and quickly forgetting about me?

"I think we need to skip beers and go straight to cocktails." Greg put two vodka sodas on our high-top.

I swiped the glass that had a teeny bit more drink and took a healthy, cleansing gulp, letting it burn all the way down.

"Easy there, slugger." Greg sipped his drink like a normal person. "I'm sorry again about Julian. At least you took your shot."

"I didn't. Jules took the shot, and I swatted it down." I wiped a finger around the glass, condensation slicking my grip.

"Huh? But I thought..."

I kept quiet about my altercation with Lauren's brother. My guilt was too strong, and I didn't want Greg trying to be my white knight and bail me out.

"It just wasn't the right time," I said quietly.

"You don't like him?"

"No. I love him, but it wasn't the right time."

"Holy shit," Greg said. "You love him?"

Sadly, yes. I loved him. I loved Julian Bradford. I loved every shy blush, every smile, every lilting word out of his mouth.

I chugged the rest of my cocktail, the vodka burning my throat.

"I'm gonna get another one," I said.

Greg blocked my way. "Have a seat there. Maybe getting smashed isn't the best idea."

"I won't get smashed."

"Dude. Remember when you got dumped junior year by that girl on the volleyball team? You did kegstand after kegstand at our party and then tried to serenade her outside her dorm to...what song did you use?"

I hung my head. "'Best of Both Worlds' by Miley Cyrus, a.k.a. Hannah Montana."

"Huh. I still don't understand the connection there."

"She was studious, and I was a frat guy, and together we had the best of both worlds! Plus she had blonde hair like Hannah."

Greg cocked an eyebrow at my explanation. Despite how I sounded on the video a bystander had secretly recorded and uploaded to YouTube, I thought I'd nailed it. Her loss.

"Let's leave the singing to Miley this time."

He was and would always be my big frat bro having my back, making sure I didn't make an ass out of myself. Greg poured a little bit of his drink into my empty glass.

"So you love him." He nodded, processing. "And I take it he felt the same way."

"Yep. But he deserves better than me."

"That's bullshit. Are you still hung up on what happened with Lauren?"

"I shouldn't be anyone's boyfriend."

"Isn't that up to Julian to decide?"

Anger rose in me. Anger at Greg for not understanding, for thinking things could be this cut and dried. Anger at myself for perpetually not having my shit together and hurting good people.

Years later, and my actions were still continuing to derail Lauren's life.

"You wouldn't understand," I muttered and left.

I stalked to the bathroom, cutting a path between bargoers enjoying their Friday night without heartache. The sinks had automatic sensors that seemed to be taking the night off. It took waving my hand like a lunatic under two of them until one of them gave me water to splash on my face. The cool water refreshed me.

I looked at the man in the mirror.

"I did the right thing." I loved Julian, but I couldn't risk derailing his life. Because no matter how many bad things I might do because of my gambling addiction, he'd always search for the good in me, and that simple fact broke my heart.

I swung open the bathroom door and came face-to-face with Raleigh and Hutch, arms crossed and glaring like they were bouncers prepared to toss me on my ass.

"Evening, fellas." I laughed nervously. Had Julian's friends sent them to beat me up?

"What the hell?" Hutch asked.

"Correction. What the fuck?" Raleigh said.

"It wasn't me who clogged the toilet in there." I gave them a weak smile, but they weren't in a joking mood. "How did you know I was here?"

"Greg told us. He said you've been moping in bed. Come with us," Hutch said.

"Uh, if you're going to shove me in a dumpster, then forget it."

"We're going back to your table." Raleigh hustled me through the crowd.

Unless I could learn Kung Fu super quick, like the file that downloaded to Keanu's brain in *The Matrix*, then I had no choice but to do as they said. They were taller and more jacked than I was.

In silence, we marched up the narrow staircase that led back to the rooftop balcony. Greg had no reaction to seeing me return with two new guys, who now that I thought about it, he'd never met before.

"Gentlemen," Greg said to my South Rock friends. "Thanks for coming."

They nodded back.

"Nice to meet you, by the way." Hutch shook his hand. Raleigh followed.

"What is going on? How do you guys know each other?" My Browerton and South Rock lives had remained separate. Not by some master plan, but more of a work/life balance.

"We don't," Greg said. "Raleigh messaged me on Instagram."

"You'd talked about Greg before. I knew he was a close friend of yours. I put my masterful social media sleuthing skills to work," Raleigh said.

"Masterful." Hutch rolled his eyes. "Seamus is friends with only one Greg. Don't apply to work at the NSA anytime soon, pal."

Raleigh gave him the talk to the hand sign, straight out of the '90s. Hutch responded by high-fiving it.

I turned to Greg for some clarity.

"They reached out, rightly worried that you weren't doing too well. They told me what happened with Julian."

I whipped my head to Hutch and Raleigh. Of course their boyfriends had given them the scoop. And then they'd relayed the details of my devastating Friday to Greg.

I turned to my frat brother. "So this whole time, you've been playing me? Getting me to talk about what happened when you already knew?"

"Talking it out is good. I told them we'd be here tonight." He shrugged, as if it were all that easy. I appreciated that my friends had coordinated to check up on me, even if in the moment, I wanted to be left alone.

"We were going to sneak in wearing fake mustaches," Raleigh said.

"No, *we* weren't. *You* were going to. I talked you out of it," Hutch said.

"I think I'd look good with a mustache." Raleigh rubbed his fingers over his upper lip. "Go for the whole *Top Gun: Maverick* look. I already have the body for it."

"You must be very flexible to be able to kiss your own ass like that," Greg said.

We burst out laughing, me loudest. It felt good to laugh again. Good for the soul and all that jazz. Greg grabbed us another round of drinks.

"So Julian was the gay guy you were telling us about at Stone's Throw?" Hutch asked.

I nodded yes. It seemed a million years ago, back when I was more optimistic.

"Julian likes you, too," Raleigh said.

I sighed. "I know."

"Then I don't understand." Raleigh said as Greg handed him a fresh vodka soda. "If you like Julian, and Julian likes you, then why are you here moping with us and not bumping uglies with him?"

"It's complicated." I shrugged.

"Uncomplicate it for us because I'm confused," Greg said. "We have time."

It was three against one. The pain of my decision built in my chest.

"I wouldn't be a good boyfriend," I said.

"Why not?" Hutch asked, almost offended that I'd speak about myself in that way.

That was the problem with having good friends. Sooner or later, you'd have to share everything, all your dirty secrets.

"Because I have a problem." I shifted my eyes to Greg, who gave me a nod of support, forever in my corner. "I used to have a gambling problem. I probably still would if I didn't make myself stay away from online poker. It made me ruin the life of someone I loved."

"You didn't ruin her life," Greg interjected.

"I nearly did. She's still struggling."

"How do you..." Greg had a lightbulb moment. "Who was that guy that came over last night?"

"Her brother."

Greg nodded, things clicking for him. Maybe it was good that Vince had roughed me up. He'd stopped me from potentially hurting someone else I loved.

"She's going to have trust issues on top of financial issues for the rest of her life thanks to me. I can't do that to Julian."

I kept looking out at the river, as if the water could take me away or provide comfort. No matter what, no matter how broke and broken I was, the river would never reject me.

"Does Julian know about this?" Raleigh asked.

"Yeah. I told him everything a few weeks ago."

"You did? What happened when you told him?" Greg cocked his head to the side.

"Uh, well, we...we blew each other."

"Interesting. From what I've heard, that is the common response from loved ones when people share that they have an addiction," Greg said. "Interventions are basically giant orgies."

"You guys don't understand," I said, not here for their snarky bullshit.

"And just to be clear, after you revealed your addiction to Julian, he still told you he loved you?" Hutch leaned forward on the table.

"Yeah," I muttered. I was in a police interrogation. All three were playing bad cop.

The guys traded looks like a jury conferring.

"Stop! Whatever telepathic thing you're doing, just stop," I said. It was weird watching my friends be friends with each other.

"Julian wanted to be with you despite what happened. Why did you throw that away?" Greg asked.

"Because I'm damaged goods!" I shouted, cutting through the din of the bar. We got some eyes on our table, people thinking a fight was about to break out for a hot minute. "I nearly bankrupted my ex-girlfriend. I fucked up so bad. I'm going to be paying off debt until the day I die. Why would Julian want to be with a guy who is sucking at life so hard?" Heat flamed on my cheeks, angry at myself as I replayed my greatest fuckup hits. "What if I fell down the gambling rabbit hole and guilted Julian into lending me money? What if things were worse next time? What if I break his heart and make him unable to trust other guys? Jules is a good person. He doesn't deserve a guy with baggage. And so even though I would give my left nut to be with him, I don't want to hurt him."

I stormed from the table, weaving through tight clusters of happy bargoers blessed with normal lives until I reached the calm of inside. Down the stairs I went until I hit the exit. I kept walking until I hit the riverbank. A long dock stood along the edge with boats bobbing in the water, moonlight hitting their hulls. I took a seat on the smoothe slats of wood, letting my legs wobble above the water.

I'd worry about getting home later.

I shut my eyes and longed for the day when Julian would be fully out of my system, when my stomach wouldn't crumble when I thought of him. In Gamblers Anonymous, we talked about how our addiction wasn't us, only a part of us. I wondered how true that was. How many parts of myself were worth saving?

The dock creaked with footsteps. Hutch winced as he sat down beside me.

"Am I damaged goods?" he asked me.

"No. Of course not. You're awesome."

"I have a bum knee." He extended his left leg, provoking another wince of pain. "I was the star of South Rock. I was drafted into Major League Soccer. My whole life, I'd been training for this path. Then my knee gave out, and it all went away."

"I'm sorry, man." I'd heard whispers and rumors about what brought Hutch back to South Rock last year.

He winced once more from something deeper than physical pain.

"So why do I deserve to be with Amos?"

"What are you talking about?"

"I was supposed to be this big pro athlete. Now I'll never play again. I'm just a gym teacher with a slight limp who was living at home, and Amos is this brilliant, thoughtful history teacher who owns his own place. Why the fuck do I deserve to be with him?"

Raleigh sat down on the other side of me, his legs spread wide and dangling over the water.

"I have a really fucked up family. My parents were always fighting and drinking before they died. My brother is a drug addict who's in the wind. I haven't heard from him in years since he stole from me. When people ask me about my family, I get this pit in my stomach before I give them my standard bullshit answer about how they're a bunch of interesting characters, and I'm the best-looking one by a mile. Everett comes from a large, close family. His siblings are all super successful. They get together for holidays and send each other birthday cards. I'm hardcore damaged goods. Why should I date Everett and get him mixed up in my fucked-up family?"

Greg squatted behind me and gave my shoulders a supportive rub. "I'm married to a very ambitious and very successful man. I don't have that same ambition. I gave up a lucrative path toward being a corporate lawyer to be a middle school special education teacher. I'll never earn what my husband earns. When we go to his law firm's parties, I see people's faces when I tell them I'm a teacher. We're not like the other couples at the firm. We're not a power couple each making multiple six figures and living that glorious DINK lifestyle. Why should Ethan be with me when he can get some hotshot lawyer or doctor or hedge fund manager? How am I not bringing him down?"

We sat there in silence for a moment, listening to the water splashing against the echoey boats. A million thoughts and feelings swirled through my head. I had the greatest friends, and it hurt to hear them shit all over themselves.

"The truth is, everyone is damaged goods in some way," Greg said.

"How do you think Julian feels?" Hutch said. "He's a thirty-five-year-old virgin, something he was so embarrassed by that he asked a friend to pop his cherry. He probably thinks he's damaged goods, too. He probably thought the same thing you did, that he didn't deserve to be loved." Hutch scooted back and let his left leg lie completely on the dock.

"But he does. He's a wonderful guy," I said.

"So are you!" Hutch gave me a shove.

"Yeah, so are you, dingus." Greg slapped me in the back of the head, a classic move from our frat days. "So are all of us!"

"Nobody's perfect. Including me," Raleigh said. "Shocker, I know. Imperfect people deserve love, too. We're all just trying our best out here. Someone loves you warts and all. I wouldn't shrug that off."

When I was with Julian, he made me forget about my fucked-up past. We existed in the present, full of life and opportunity. I had been trying to make him more confident in his body, and he'd wound up doing that for me.

"Shit." I dragged my hands through my hair. "I fucked up."

"Pretty much," Raleigh said. He playfully kicked my leg, a sign of support. "But it's not permanent. Fortunately, you're able to learn from fuck-ups and fix them. That's the beauty of not being perfect."

"Thanks, guys. Shall we go back inside?" I stood up.

"Eh, I have a better idea. Who needs bougie drinks?" Greg found a nearby liquor store and got a six-pack, and we hung by the docks drinking beer, four imperfect guys having a night to remember.

28

JULIAN

In twenty-four hours, I would officially be a thirty-five-year-old virgin. First, I had to get through my grandparents' anniversary party with people asking me where my new boyfriend was.

It would be one hell of a weekend, emphasis on the hell.

I sat on the edge of my bed and put on my shoes. My bed was bigger and emptier with just me in it. Now that I'd had another guy in there, I knew what I was missing.

My phone buzzed with texts now that I'd reactivated the group chat.

Everett: I can pretend to be your boyfriend. I do a great Seamus impression.

Amos: I can strangely vouch for this. Don't ask.

Julian: Appreciated, but not needed.

Everett: We're here if you need us. Chase can create a diversion.

Chase: Why me?

Everett: You can use science to create a thick cloud, through which Julian can sneak out.

Chase: If I tried to point out all the flaws in that sentence, my thumbs would cramp up.

Everett: I've got more ideas if you need them, J.

I smiled at the screen. Why had I ever kept secrets from them? Not my finest hour.

Amos: How are you doing?

Julian: Hanging in there.

Amos: *Sends all the hugs*

Everett: *Sends all the martinis*

Chase: I believe what Everett is trying to convey is that we're here if you need us. We can all go to the party together. We've all met your grandparents. Your grandmother once suggested to me that I should have a threesome.

Julian: Oh my God.

Chase: She said I seemed flexible.

Julian: OH MY GOD.

I buried my head in my pillow. Grandma never knew the meaning of too much. If she ever knew I was a virgin, she'd disown me or drag me to the nearest sex worker.

Amos: I hope you manage to have fun today, J.

Julian: I will. It'll be good to see family.

In truth, I was an anxious wreck. People would likely ask about Seamus. Mom would likely say something that hit a nerve. We hadn't spoken since our fight. I had to be numb. I was there to support my grandparents, who loved me dearly.

Everett: I think your grandmother was right. Chase gives off major threesome energy.

Chase: I doubt that. The closest I ever came was in elementary school when I was dared to shove two Twinkies in my mouth at once.

Amos: But did you succeed?

Chase: Point taken.

My grandparents lived in a big house that they'd owned back when this town was mostly farmland. They had an expansive backyard decked out with tables, a buffet station, and a bar. The weather forecast was for a lovely spring day with bright blue skies. So much for fretting over finding a tent.

I'd bought myself a new outfit for the party. I wore a baby-blue button-down shirt with a tweed vest over it and matching pants. The vest did a great job of acting like Spanx, i.e., making my midsection into one solid block. For an accent, I pinned an orange rose to the lapel. Other people here wore suits and nice pastel dresses. I appreciated being slightly different.

Across the lawn, Mom and Dad were engaged in a fun conversation with family friends. Mom was aglow, loving the socializing and the attention. She looked beautiful, the type of effortless beauty that took loads of prep. She glanced my way, her stern eyes landing on me.

I turned away, suddenly feeling self-conscious about my suit, my hair, my shoes. Maybe she was right about everything. Seamus wasn't here, after all.

"You look so handsome!" Grandma pulled me to her and kissed my cheek. She stepped back to take me in, her eyes misting up. "My grandson. My wonderful, wonderful grandson."

"Happy anniversary." I kissed her back and shook my grandfather's hand. He was a man of few words, unless the conversation came to military history or the stock market. He'd let Grandma have the reins, and he was along for the ride.

Grandfather retreated into the crowd. Grandma stayed holding my hands and beaming into my eyes. She might've been eighty, but she was full of vitality. I wanted her to give a lesson to my students about how youth shouldn't be wasted on the young.

"This party is beautiful. Thank you, Julian. It would've turned into a barrel of shit if I hadn't had your help."

"I'm glad I could do this for you."

"Lord knows your mother wasn't able to help. She gets so frazzled about organizing things."

My stomach twisted at the mention of Mom. I wasn't used to fighting with her. Our relationship was built on her saying outrageous things, and me holding in my feelings.

"Where's the guy?"

And there it was. The inevitable question of today. The question of my life.

I had practiced my answer in the car on the way over, a diplomatic way of letting her know Seamus and I were over. Yet when I stared into Grandma's hopeful eyes, I knew the truth would put a damper on her afternoon. She was rooting for me. I didn't want to let her down.

"He had to help his dad with something. He'll be here later."

A lie and a false promise. That would be Future Julian's problem. Poor guy.

A smile stretched across her face. "I really like him. He's a good guy."

"Thanks," I said, my heart sagging.

"I mean it. I've been around for a while. I've seen my fair share of couples who didn't make it, boyfriends who we all knew were terrible from the get-go, but we had to keep our mouths shut. You got a good one, Julian."

My throat went tight, the air suddenly stifling. I nodded and kissed her cheek, then made my way to the bar. I couldn't bring myself to order a drink just yet, so I went with water.

I had to send an update to the group chat.

Julian: Well, my grandma asked about Seamus, and I said... he'd be here later. Party foul. I'm too stressed to drink.

Amos: I'm sure if you called Seamus, he'd show up and play along.

Julian: I'm not doing that.

Everett: The alcohol will be there later if you change your mind, but I suppose you're doing the right thing. Having a meltdown at a public party only works for ingenues in romcoms.

Chase: There was a study that said that certain forms of stress can mimic the effects of drunkenness on the brain.

Julian: So no matter what, I'll be smashed today?

A LITTLE WHILE LATER, lunch was served. It was a gorgeous buffet. The tray of short ribs looked as sumptuous as I remembered. People murmured their delight and kept saying how good the food was.

I took their word for it.

A full buffet was one of the most beautiful sights in the world. Delicious abundance. And yet I didn't have the stomach to eat. I was living on borrowed time. The bill for my Seamus alibi would be due.

The waitstaff wheeled out a replica of Grandma and Grandpa's wedding cake, three tiers of vanilla with strawberry filling. Usually I shied away from baked fruits, but all rules were suspended when it came to cake.

They cut a piece of cake but passed on feeding it to each other by hand. They used forks.

"I don't want to ruin my nails," Grandma told the party crowd.

My heart swelled as I watched them be adorable together, as they'd been for the past half century. Not everyone got to have that, myself included, and that was okay. Some couples could be a beacon of hope for the rest of us.

Grandma and Grandpa shuffled onto the dance floor set up by the band. Vance Vance Revolution started playing "Something." Couples filled the floor: my sister and her husband, my brother and his barely-legal girlfriend, my parents. I watched from my seat, a plate of lettuce in front of me, feeling lower than I thought possible. But I kept a smile on my face because I wasn't going to ruin this day for my grandparents.

I went to the bar for a drink, going with the fruity themed cocktail, The Lovebirds, which had been concocted for the event. I got roped into a conversation with one of my grandparents' neighbors, an older couple who really had some things to say about how teachers unions were destroying education. As if today couldn't get anymore stressful.

Grandma swooped in like a superhero, her perfume a calming force in my life.

"I'm going to borrow my grandson for a moment." She gave me an eyeroll once we were out of their gravitational pull. "If we didn't invite them, I'd never hear the end of it."

"They're charming."

"Bullshit. Speaking of charming, where's Seamus?"

My stomach dropped. As much as it hurt to keep lying to someone I loved, I was in too deep. "He's still helping his dad."

"Still? What are they doing?"

"Fixing a car?" That was something fathers and sons did. It was the top answer on an episode of *Family Feud*, from what I remembered.

"Tell him to take a pause on fixing the car. The party's going to be over soon." I appreciated how excited she was to see Seamus again, which only made the lie worse.

I rubbed my eyes, everything in my life piling to the forefront of my brain.

"I...I need to tell you the truth, Grandma."

Concern ringed her eyes.

"Seamus isn't helping his dad fix his car."

"Seamus didn't have an outfit to wear today."

The hairs on my neck tingled at the familiar, jovial voice. Seamus slipped his hand into mine. He wore the nicest outfit I'd ever seen him in. A full suit with a tie.

"There you are!" Grandma pulled him into a kiss.

"I didn't know the dress code, so I had to run out and buy a suit. I should have one, but the one I own is from when I was fifteen, and the pants are basically capris." Seamus lifted my hand and kissed my palm.

Fuck, he had never looked better. Dapper, sophisticated, damn sexy. His wild shag of hair was combed into submission. His beard was gone.

"You shaved," I said, wanting to run a hand over his smooth cheek.

"It's Judy and George's fiftieth wedding anniversary. How could I not?"

"You didn't have to go through all this trouble to get a new suit," Grandma said. "Although, for someone your age, you should have one."

"My bad."

"Eh." She waved it off. "Who am I kidding? The only reason old people have them is because of all the funerals we attend."

I was stunned into silence, both by Seamus's presence and how good he looked in a suit. It was torture, highly awkward torture. He flicked his eyes my way. I gave him a terse nod that tried to convey all the gratitude I felt.

Seamus snaked an arm around my waist. I let myself enjoy the feeling, even though this was all fake. Seamus would leave the party, and we'd go back to existing in some kind of gray area.

"Now Grandma Judy, you and your husband have been together for fifty years." Seamus leaned in. "Is the sex still good?"

Grandma leaned in, too, almost giddy. "It's incredible."

Vance Vance Revolution segued into another slow song, "The Way You Look Tonight."

Seamus turned to me, blue eyes ablaze. "May I have this dance?"

"Uh huh," I said stunned.

Seamus led us to the dance floor, where we got some looks. That was par for the course whenever two guys danced together, but I was Teflon at that moment, thinking only about how good this felt.

I was tongue-tied. I didn't know what to say. *Thank you for coming? Why are you here?* Whatever had brought him here, I didn't want him to leave.

Seamus didn't say anything either. It was a game of chicken. Who would break the silence?

"Jules, I'm so sorry about the other day. I was an asshole." He looked down, and I could sense how nervous he was. "When you said you loved me, I got scared and pushed you away. I'm terrified of relapsing and dragging you down with me. I don't want to hurt the person I care about most. I'm kind of fucked up, and a part of me feels like I'll never be good enough for you. But I want to try. I want to be the man you deserve. Jules, I love you."

"As a friend?"

He shoved us out of the friend zone with a heat-filled, yet party-appropriate, kiss. He slipped in the slightest bit of tongue that had me dying for more.

"Does that answer your question?" he asked.

AFTER ANOTHER ROUND on the dance floor, we went down the buffet now that my appetite was back. If people wanted to gossip about how much I piled on my plate, let them talk.

We dug into our food, and I forgot about everyone around us.

"This is the best meal I've ever had," Seamus declared. "This is like death row final meal food. Good job."

"Thanks?"

Someone cleared their throat behind us. Mom stood over us.

"Seamus. Good to see you again."

"Mrs. Bradford. Always a pleasure." He wiped his mouth and gave her hand a light shake. "Sorry I'm late."

"We're glad you're here."

Mom had an inscrutable look on her face. I wasn't used to this stare. There was no contempt, no hidden criticism. It felt like sadness.

"I'm going to get seconds." Seamus seemed to sense the vibe. He kissed me on the lips, stroking my cheek with his thumb before absconding to the buffet.

"Can we talk?" she asked.

I pointed to the empty seat beside me.

Mom sat down, her eyes heavy. "I wasn't a nice person growing up. I made fun of kids in school, especially the ones whose bodies didn't fit the conventional mode."

"The fat ones."

"And the very skinny ones or oddly shaped ones," she noted. "But yes, mainly the fat ones." Tears formed at the corners of her eyes. "All my life, I'd been told how pretty I was. That was the main—only—compliment my parents gave me. That was how teachers and friends and guys described me. I was never called smart or interesting or funny or kind. Just pretty. When I would get back tests with Cs and Ds, my teachers would tell me, 'At least you have your looks.' They thought they were being nice."

I guffawed at what teachers used to get away with.

"It taught me that looks mattered most. They were all that mattered. So when I saw you were having trouble with your weight, I thought I had failed as a mother. And I even thought...it was karmic payback for how I'd treated others." She wiped at tears rolling down her face. "You are such a wonderful young man, Julian. You *are* smart, interesting, funny, kind. All the things I wanted to be." She grabbed my hands. "I'm proud you are my son."

My anger at Mom dissipated, turning into pity. Mom and I had had completely different upbringings. She came from a world where a woman was only allowed to be pretty or ugly. It was hard to shake off the things that warped our minds when we were young. But it sounded like she was trying.

We hugged, and her warmth filled my soul.

"Have you tried the brownies?" she asked. "People have said they're to die for."

"I'll check them out."

Her eyes flicked up as Seamus rejoined us, a knowing smile on her lips.

"I'll let you boys eat. Seamus, welcome to the family."

I grabbed a brownie off Seamus's plate.

"I got there just in time. They're clearing things away."

Seamus put his hand on my knee and rubbed up my inner thigh, heat instantly pooling in my gut.

"Seamus." I shuffled my chair so my legs (and erection) were fully under the tablecloth. "What are you doing?"

"According to my phone, we have five hours until your birthday," he said in my ear in a raspy growl. "Maybe we should get going."

"That's plenty of time," I said.

He let his hand graze directly over my crotch. "You sure about that?"

My grandparents wouldn't mind me cutting out early. Grandma was no cockblock. Surely, she would be doing the same.

29

JULIAN

It was a very difficult drive back to my apartment. Concentrating on the road was difficult when I had a beautiful man in the passenger seat. Seamus found his suit to be stifling and uncomfortable, but damn if he didn't look runway ready, especially with his loosened tie. And the hungry look in his eyes was devouring me whole.

Additionally, driving with an erection was not something I would recommend. It diverted needed focus away from my brain.

We pulled up to the curb, where I did a horrendous parallel parking job. If I got a ticket, I'd go to court and plead with the judge to let it go because I was about to get laid for the first time, and really, wasn't that more important than being too far off the curb?

"This is it, Jules. Tomorrow, you will be thirty-five and no longer a virgin. Thank you."

"Why are you thanking me?"

"For letting me do the honors of deflowering you. It's something I don't take lightly," he said with all seriousness.

"I'm deflowering you, too. Your first time with a guy."

"This is true. Nervous?" He cocked an eyebrow.

A flutter of nerves expanded in my stomach. I was about to make love to the man I loved. Yeah, I was nervous.

"Taking someone's v-card is just as stressful as having the v-card. Everybody remembers their first time. You're going to remember tonight forever, for better or worse. It's going to be tens across the board."

"Don't fuck it up," I teased, knowing that would be impossible.

Once we got into my apartment, Seamus shut the door and took over, pushing me up against the wall until our cocks were aligned under our pants. Our lips came together in a rage of heat and need. My stupid *Pretty Woman* rule had kept me from kissing this man all month. Stupid Julia Roberts.

I pulled away to catch my breath. His lips were as red and flushed as mine likely were.

"This is the final exam, Jules. And like all final exams, you will be tested on all material studied over the course of the semester. I hope you crammed."

"I think you'll be the one cramming." I flashed him a wicked smile. Luckily, he seemed to be a fan of my dirty mouth.

He smashed our lips together in violent need, his hand skimming down to my rock hard dick. His tongue slid into my mouth, setting off fireworks. I mashed our crotches together, heat and friction pushing me closer to the edge.

"On your knees," he commanded, his voice husky.

I didn't need to be told twice. I looked up at him from the floor, his eyes deep pools of need. I stroked him over his dress pants, his erection thick and hard. And all mine.

Seamus could only handle so much foreplay before he whipped open his belt. He struggled with the clip to undo his pants.

"Fuck. Why do they make this shit so difficult?" he fumed.

"Why can't suit pants just have a button like normal jeans? Why do they gotta be so frickin' hoity-toity?"

"Allow me," I said, calm and collected. I'd worn lots of dress pants in my life. I unclasped and zipped down the fly, teasingly taking my time before everything fell to the floor. His cock flopped in my face, heavy and engorged.

Not to pat myself on the back, but I was a flawless student, expertly remembering our previous blow job lessons. My tongue lapped over the head and slinked down his shaft.

"Holy fuck."

"Good?" I asked.

"Very very."

"Because I'm a student that needs constant validation." I smacked his cock on my tongue.

"How's this for validation: I'm desperately trying not to come right now, but you're making it damn near impossible with that hot, pretty little mouth of yours." He threaded his fingers behind my head and fucked into my mouth hard.

"Baby, you are fucking fire. Take it," he said before being reduced to a puddle of moaning.

The heat of his length filled my mouth. I licked down to his balls, taking one then the other in my mouth.

"Stand up," he growled.

When I got up, I noticed his shirt had come off during the blow job.

"Your turn." Seamus leaned over to turn off the lights, but I stopped him. I didn't need darkness anymore.

I gave my first striptease. First came my tie and vest. Each button of my shirt that popped open was another rush of freedom and abandon. I waved it over my head and flung it behind the couch. Cool air hit my chest, but I wasn't done. I ran my hands down my chest, feeling a love for my body that had eluded me all my life.

"Yes, baby." Seamus watched while stroking himself.

I flicked open my dress pants, shimmying my ass until they fell off on their own. I pushed down my boxers, letting my cock hang free.

And there I was. Julian Bradford. Naked by his own hand.

Seamus feasted on the sight.

"I need to have you." He crashed our lips together, cocks tangling below. He grabbed my big ass and squeezed, pulling us closer.

"I need you to fuck me, Seamus. Make me scream and come for you."

He kissed along my collarbone, a tender moment amid the lust, reminding me that this wasn't just a sex haze. This was something special.

Seamus pushed us backward until we were in my bedroom, falling onto my bed. He moved south until my cock was in his mouth.

"Suck me. Yes. Take it all."

Seamus took me down to the base. I was lit up head to toe, practically levitating off the bed. The orgasm was dangerously close, surging through my body. Before I could push him off, he flipped my legs in the air.

"Don't stop. Oh my God. Eat that hole." My voice was a loud moan as if I were possessed. His tongue did wonders to my ass. I groaned with lust as heat braced my core. I heard the nightstand drawer open.

The cold feel of lube-covered fingers entered me, opening me up, sliding in and out and making me long for the real thing.

"God, yes, Seamus. So fucking hot. I want you to fuck me so bad. I can't wait to feel your thick cock stretching my hole."

He stared into my soul as his fingers went to town, making me writhe under his touch.

"Fuck me," I begged.

"Almost," he teased. "I need to be sure you're intimately familiar with the course material."

Seamus moved to the other end of the bed where my head was. He knelt over me, his pert, jock-toned ass in my face. Seamus had been a catcher on his college baseball team, and it showed. I grabbed a cheek in each hand and spread him open.

"Shit. That's the fucking stuff." Seamus heaved out a breath as he shook over me.

I circled my tongue around his pink hole, then added a finger. In and out it went, achingly slow, then dizzingly fast.

"Jules. This is fucking amazing. Work that hole."

He rocked his hips back, fucking into my fingers, letting out a guttural groan that emanated from deep inside him.

I slid out from under him, kissing along his muscled back.

"I want you to fuck me," I whispered in his ear. "Fuck me so good until I come all over myself."

"Yes, sir," he said in a husky, breathless voice.

Seamus took out a condom from the drawer.

"Wait," I said, thinking back to my horrific first day as a health teacher. "Can I put that on you?"

"Yeah," he said, excited.

Talk about your final exams.

"Let me know if it hurts or I'm doing it wrong." I ripped open the packet and placed the condom on his dick. I rolled it down slowly, gripping his thick shaft.

"You're doing great," he said.

I gave myself a silent cheer when I made it all the way down. I marveled at the sheathed cock with a surge of pride. Maybe it was merely nerves that made me stumble in class. Or that damn demonstration dick out to get me.

"A-plus," he said. "Now get on your back."

I looked up at the ceiling and threw my legs in the air. This was it. No turning back.

"Nervous?" he asked.

"A little."

"Me, too." He squeezed my thighs in solidarity. "At least we can be nervous together."

There was something sweet about that. Although, it would be one of the only sweet things about tonight, because the ideas kicking around in my head were not family appropriate.

He slipped a lubed finger into my opening. Seamus leaned over my spread-eagled body and planted a delicate kiss on my lips. It was everything. Romance and lust. Heat and heart.

"Ready?"

I nodded yes. His cock breached my opening, stretching me wide, flooding me with new sensations. It was similar to the number Seamus had done on my heart.

"Congratulations, Jules. You're no longer a virgin."

30

SEAMUS

This. Felt. Amazing.

This was my first time fucking a guy, and it sure as hell wouldn't be my last. My cock sank into Jules's tight hole, heat coiling around me.

I went slow, each of us experiencing a different kind of pain. Julian did his best to hide his discomfort, and I was desperately holding back from coming.

"Are you okay?"

"Yeah. I'll be good," he said. "This isn't exactly what I was expecting."

Uh oh. Not something a guy wanted to hear.

"It feels good, but strange," he said, slipping into his academic voice. "Everyone says that your first time hurts. They weren't lying."

"Did you want me to stop?"

"No. Keep going. Please. I'll find my way. It's like walking through a dark room and finding the light switch."

Even when he had a painful dick up his ass, Julian still knew how to be eloquent and produce a beautiful metaphor. Respect.

I went slow, pulling out, then pushing back in, each time reading Julian's face. I felt bad because *I* was in fucking heaven. I was seeing stars. Julian had cloudy skies.

"Keep going. God, this is embarrassing." He threw a hand over his face.

"Don't be embarrassed. This is life, not a porno. And don't cover up your sexy face."

"I promise I am liking this."

"Thanks for the reassurance. Let me know whenever you want me to stop." I applied more lube to my dick. You could never have too much.

Each time I thrust inside him, the pain appeared to subside a little bit more. His wincing faded to eyes rolling back in his head. I kissed along his neck to calm him, to let him know I was here and we were in this together.

Eventually, he began to moan for more, pupils blown open wide.

"Yes. Okay, now this feels good, really good," he said with growing realization.

"Good." I took that as permission to fuck him a little harder. I groaned each time I filled him up, willing myself to hold out.

We moaned at the same time, the pleasure of this feeling overwhelming us. I kept going, sinking deeper into his tight hole, feeling it clench around my cock.

"Wow," I said, because apparently that was the only fucking word I knew during sex.

"Wow indeed."

"You okay?"

"This is...wow." His hard cock flopped against his stomach. "I'm full of Seamus."

I slid the rest of the way in.

"Very full." He bit his lip as he unleashed a wild groan that bellowed in the room.

"Yeah, baby. This is heaven." I was stretching out every second of this moment, imprinting it in my brain.

And then he found the light switch. He flipped to his animal self, his eyes zeroing in on me.

"Just like that. Fuck, give me that big dick. Destroy me, Seamus. Yes." He threw his head back onto the bed, thrusting his ass up to meet my humps.

What happened next was a sputter of still images collected together, tiny moments I'd remember forever. I thrust into him, still slow, our bodies connecting in rhythm. I kissed him more, his cock pressing into my stomach, which only made me go faster. He dug his nails into my back. We were panting, sweaty messes, limbs tangled together, hearts locked in.

I ran my hands over his hairy chest, savoring being with a man.

"Don't stop. I'm so close," he said.

I'd been close since the moment we walked into the apartment. I pumped him faster, harder, heat and desire driving me. I reached between us and stroked his leaking cock, thick and pulsating.

"Fuck. That's it. Please don't stop, Seamus. Please don't stop. I'm coming. I'm coming." He sprayed out desperate words as his hole clamped around my dick and his release filled the close quarters between our chests. Julian let out an intense howl of need as he emptied himself.

I wasn't far behind. My balls drew up as my body went into overdrive, the orgasm coming fast. I emptied myself into the condom and collapsed onto his soaked chest, the electric smile on his face telling me he liked it.

Of course he did, my dirty smart man.

We caught our breath. I glanced at the alarm clock. It was 10:32.

"We did it. With just over an hour to spare until your birthday." I was a man who always got the job done. "How do you feel?"

He pulled me down to him for a kiss, his fingers slinking around my sweaty hair. His salty lips sent sparks down my sides.

"I feel like I'm going to want to do that again in a few hours."

A FEW HOURS LATER, we did it again, and then almost did it again in the shower. Soap did not make for good lubricant, yet we still found other ways to entertain ourselves.

I woke up the next morning with Julian in my arms.

I breathed in the clean scent of his back. Julian had tried putting on a shirt, underwear, and pajama pants when we climbed into bed for the last time. I strictly forbade it. I wanted to feel his bare skin against mine as we slept.

My morning wood poked into his ass, but I resisted the urge for a third round. Julian looked tired. Let the man rest.

I got up, slipped on my boxers, and crept into the kitchen. I had a feeling Julian would want me to have some clothing on near food. I poured myself a glass of water and got a pot of coffee brewing.

Our phones were charging side by side on the counter, as cute a couple as their owners.

My phone buzzed with an unexpected call. Lauren. Was it weird to speak to your ex-girlfriend after having sex with your new boyfriend?

"Uh, hey," I said, moving as far away from the bedroom as possible and keeping my voice low.

"Hey, Seamus. Sorry for calling so early." Lauren was also speaking in hushed tones.

"Don't apologize. I'm up."

"Actually, I did call to apologize. My brother told me that he went over to your place the other night and got a little physical.

I'm really upset with him for doing that. He went there behind my back."

"It's all good. He roughed me up, but I could take it," I said with a grin. The memory of the altercation shook me up, but she didn't need to know.

"I told him we have an arrangement for you paying me back. You've never missed a payment. He shouldn't have butted in."

"He was looking out for you." And Lauren was looking out for me, even after all this time. Guilt and shame washed over me. "I'm so sorry about everything, Lauren."

"I know. You've apologized so many times. I know how bad you feel."

"Why are you being so understanding?"

"Because you have an addiction. And you're working on it. Are you still going to GA meetings?"

"Yes. Every week." I didn't say much in them, but I was listening, and they kept me accountable.

"Good."

How could she not hate me? How was she able to show compassion after what I'd done? Her strength bowled me over. She had lost so much. Major milestones were delayed on my account. Yet she cared about my recovery. Why did I have to hurt such a good person?

In that moment, a sense of determination calcified in my bones.

"Listen, I'm going to pay you back everything by the end of the month."

"What? That's next week. And that's two years ahead of schedule. Seamus, you don't have that kind of money."

She was right. It was time I swallowed my pride and took up Greg and Ethan's offer to loan me the money. It wasn't what I wanted. But it wasn't fair to make Lauren suffer all so I could prove that I could pay back my debts all on my own. Just because I needed help didn't make me damaged goods. In a way, asking for help was a sign of strength.

"It's time both of us were allowed to move on."

I could feel the excitement build on her end.

"Seamus...I...Thank you."

"I'm sorry things didn't work out between us. But it sounds like you've found a great guy. Congratulations on the wedding and whatever comes next."

Chills rolled up my back. I liked being a responsible person. Julian was already rubbing off on me.

I put down my phone next to Julian's, which was blowing up with what looked like a group chat. I couldn't help scanning the texts flashing on the lockscreen. Everett, Amos, and Chase all seemed like straitlaced guys. They were preppy and cleancut. It turned out they had a hell of a raunchy side.

"Morning," Julian said from the entryway, also clad in only boxers. I soaked in the sight of his hot body.

"Your friends are freaks." I held up his phone. "This group chat is full of nasty."

Julian raced to grab his phone.

"And you can let them know that you don't need 'anonymous dick' for your birthday."

Julian flushed red, and then a deeper shade of red when he scrolled through the messages. "I haven't spoken to them since the party. I'll update them on my sexual status."

"And relationship status, too." Oh yeah, Jules was totally my boyfriend. There was no getting around that.

He smiled wide as he typed away on his phone. I came up behind and wrapped my arms around him, while making sure to give him and his friends their privacy. He felt so good in my arms, like he'd belonged there the entire time.

I slipped a hand into his boxers and squeezed his ass.

"What's that for?" he asked.

"Because I can."

The coffeemaker went quiet. I strode to the machine. Julian pointed out where the mugs were.

"Um, how do you take your coffee?" I asked.

"Half and half and sugar," he said.

"I feel like I should know that already." We'd spent countless hours hanging in the faculty lounge. I truly was oblivious. "Do you know mine?"

"A little bit of milk that you stir vigorously into the coffee." He bowed his head, embarrassed by the level of detail. "What can I say? Perks of having a crush on you for so long."

"Just you wait, Jules, because soon, I'm going to know all of your little quirks and likes."

"That sounds like a threat."

"It is. A loving threat." I pecked him on the lips as I handed him his creamed and sugared coffee.

I poured myself coffee with the requisite milk and checked the various apps that had a stranglehold on my attention.

"Holy shit." The mug wobbled in my hand as I read through the message at the top of my BlingBling inbox. "This educational company messaged me. They love my videos and want to talk about sponsoring one!"

"That's great!"

"Holy shit." Shock pummeled me. Was instant karma real? "I didn't know if I had enough followers. I thought stuff like that only happened with other creators."

"You still have to talk with them, see if it'll be a good fit."

"Yeah. I can't put the cart before the horse."

"Congratulations! You've been very diligent in making those videos. I love them."

"You helped me with them and gave me some good ideas."

"So you're saying I'll get a cut?" he asked jokingly.

"I'm excited to use most of it to pay down some debt. Is that the most depressing, adult sentence ever uttered?"

"Not at all! Being responsible is sexy." Julian put his mug on the counter. "I was thinking about what you said yesterday at the party. You're worried about relapsing and dragging me down. I won't let that happen. Yes, there might be a time in the future when you fall off the wagon, but we'll get through it together. I'm not going to bail. I won't let you drag us down. I'm going to fight like hell to lift us up."

My throat clogged with gooey emotion. How the fuck did I get so lucky? I wanted to be a pillar of strength for Julian, but deep down, I knew I'd have my moments where I faltered.

"Relationships aren't equal all the time. Sometimes, one person needs to lean on the other," Julian said.

"I don't want to be the only one leaning in this relationship," I croaked out.

"I've leaned on you this entire month. Thanks to you, I'm standing in my apartment devirginized and drinking coffee shirtless!"

Relief filled my chest. Maybe this relationship was more equal than I realized. I pulled him to me for another kiss, one of a million we'd have together.

I slipped my hand into his boxers and ran a finger over his dick. I pushed my arm down until his boxers fell to his thighs. "Oops. My hand slipped."

Naked Julian was very hard to resist.

31

JULIAN

Four wine glasses clinked in the center of the table.

"A toast to J. Happy birthday to a one-of-a-kind guy," Amos said.

"You are officially closer to forty than you are to thirty."

Not even Everett's math lesson could bring me down. This had been the best birthday in Julian Bradford history.

My friends had taken me to my favorite winery for my birthday. It was nestled in a stretch of temperate hills west of Sourwood. A large, gorgeous white house overlooked rolling fields of grapes. Inside was a restaurant, tasting station, and cozy fireplace. There was something especially calming about wineries. They didn't exist in the real world. The stresses of everyday life faded away.

But maybe that was just the wine.

"Oh this is good," I said, savoring the last drops of my pinot noir. I'd had us order a bottle of my favorite wine made here.

"Is it better than sex?" Everett asked. "Because you can answer that now."

"It's different," I said judiciously. "You can't accurately compare wine and sex."

"He is right. Wine and sex are two completely different items. How can you compare a liquid to a physical activity?" At least Chase backed me up.

"Fine, but I still think you're dodging." Everett went back to scanning the menu for a dinner option.

"Don't worry, Everett. Sex reigns supreme," I said. How could I not tell the truth? I finally was able to join in these conversations honestly.

"I'm surprised you didn't ditch us to spend more time with Seamus," Amos said.

"I'm surprised you're able to sit comfortably." Chase snapped a breadstick in two, while our jaws fell to the floor. "What? Why does Everett have a monopoly on saying dirty jokes?"

Chase might act all academic, but I could tell he had a wild side, just like me. He needed the right guy to bring it out of him.

"I wouldn't miss dinner with my friends. Sure, Seamus is hot, charming, and sweet. But he's not you guys."

Everett and Amos's snarky demeanors fell for a second as genuine love filled the table. I had a hot guy in bed waiting for me, but I'd rather be here, and my friends felt the same.

"I love happy endings," Amos said.

"It's a happy beginning," I clarified. "It's only been twenty-four hours. I wonder what it'll be like in school."

I was going to be working across the hall from the man I loved. How people managed having office romances was beyond me. Would I be able to concentrate? Would I be coming up with excuses to venture into Seamus's classroom? *Oh, I need to borrow a marker. Oh, I need a kiss.*

"How do you and Hutch and you and Raleigh manage?" I asked my friends.

"Fortunately, the red tape of public school administration

combined with the omnipresence of impressionable kids is a powerful anti-aphrodisiac," Amos explained. "Aguilar already caught Hutch and I going at it once. He'd probably fire us if he found us again."

"This is why it pays to be a drama teacher. I have access to a large auditorium with lots of nooks and crannies." Everett took a teasing sip of his wine, as if to say he didn't kiss and tell. But let's be real. This was Everett. It was more like kiss and monologue.

"Remind me to apply hand sanitizer generously the next time I'm backstage," I said.

Everett continued chugging his wine with a smile on his face. Maybe Seamus and I would beat him at his own game and sneak into the wings sometime for a quickie. Though, the thought of fooling around on school grounds made my stomach turn. I was no longer a virgin, but that didn't mean I was no longer a rule follower.

Before Everett could launch into more of his and Raleigh's tawdry usage of the auditorium, two vaguely familiar faces stopped by our table: one a short, stocky dirty blond with olive skin, the other taller and lankier with a dark, Middle Eastern complexion. The guys were in their early twenties and underdressed for the winery in smudged T-shirts and jeans. They looked to have a combined five percent body fat between them.

"Mr. Mathison?" said the blond one.

Chase turned to them, eyes alight with recognition. "Sebastian? Anton? What a coincidence running into you here! Although, if you're frequent visitors to this establishment, then it's less a coincidence and more of a numbers game."

"Great to see you, Mr. M. You're looking great," said Anton, the taller one. "You guys look familiar."

Chase turned to us. "Sebastian and Anton were students and on the wrestling team at South Rock. They graduated...two years ago?"

"Three years this June," said Sebastian, the dirty blond.

"We loved Mr. M.'s advanced chemistry class, even though we didn't wind up doing anything with it. We started a business selling and installing vending machines. That's what we're doing here. Excuse our appearance." Anton wiped his brow with his shirt, revealing tight six-pack abs. I felt guilty for admiring the body of a former student, but these guys hadn't been my students, so maybe it wasn't so bad?

"Why would a winery choose to install a vending machine? Isn't that a competitor?" Chase asked.

"They found that more families are coming to wineries, and kids need something non-alcoholic to drink. It's easier for them to use a vending machine than stock drinks themselves," Sebastian said smoothly, as if it were a regular part of his sales pitch.

"I guess that's better than slipping kids wine," Everett said.

"Exactly! Business has been going great. We're continuing to expand, and we may even start a podcast to talk about our adventures in the vending machine trade," Anton said, full of pep. Who knew vending machines could be such an enthralling career?

"If only you could install a new machine in our faculty lounge. The only way to retrieve a soda is by crossing your fingers and hoping gravity does its job," Chase said in a highly accurate description of our janky machines.

Anton and Sebastian laughed at his joke.

"How long have you guys been doing this?" I asked.

"A year," Sebastian said. He turned back to Chase. "Mr. Mathison, can I just say that I loved your class? I never thought I'd like chemistry."

"I feel the same way," Everett joked. The boys barely reacted.

"Mr. M., you're looking good. Have you been working out? I would've remembered those guns," Anton said with...was that a flirty smile?

I looked at Everett and Amos, who were thinking the same thing. Chase, bless him, was completely oblivious.

"Well, I do push-ups and light training with dumbbells every morning. It's the best way to maintain bone density," our friend said.

"It's working for you, Mr. M." Anton gave Chase another once-over, barely hiding his interest. Were this wine not extremely tasty and extremely pricey, I would've spat it out in shock.

"Anton, we should go. We have that delivery in Montgomery," Sebastian said.

"Cool. It was great meeting all of you and really good running into you Mr. M. Here's our business card if you wanted to talk about getting a new machine in your faculty lounge." Anton handed Chase the hand. "Make sure to grab a Coke on your way out!"

He waved to all of us, saving one last lingering look at Chase.

The boys left the winery, and we were left with some questions.

"Was that guy hitting on Chase?" I asked.

"Oh yeah. One hundred percent," Amos said.

"One thousand percent," Everett chimed in. "Chase, for the love of everything gay and holy, please tell me you're going to call him."

"Of course I will."

"Awesome!" Everett cheered.

"The faculty lounge is in dire need of a new vending machine. It's holding two of my Diet Sprites hostage."

Amos, Everett, and I let out a collective groan.

"Chase!" Amos pleaded. "Anton was hitting on you."

"And not subtly," I added.

"I think Sebastian was also a little interested, too." Everett sipped his wine.

Chase looked at us like we were crazy. "They're students!"

"Former students," we said in unison.

"Just because a student graduates doesn't mean I shirk my responsibility as a teacher."

"Chase, you have a responsibility to let a hunky wrestler have his way with you," Everett said. "Maybe two wrestlers if you play your cards right. It'll be like shoving two Twinkies into your mouth again."

Chase rolled his eyes and bit into a breadstick. He wasn't asexual—he'd shared stories of hookups. But now that I thought about it, I'd never heard Chase mention dating. Did he have a deep, dark secret like me?

"Can we go ahead and order some food?" Chase popped open his menu, hiding from us, and that was that. For now, at least.

On Monday morning, I walked into South Rock High as I always did. This time, when I reached my classroom, I didn't wave to Seamus from across the hall. I waltzed into his classroom and planted a kiss on him. He pushed me against the markerboard for a deeper make out session.

"Good morning," he said.

"Morning." Judging by the hardness of his dick digging into my leg, he was wide awake.

"We probably shouldn't do this." He looked down. "I don't know how I'm going to explain having a hard-on to my students."

"The students here are very sex positive," I informed him. "They get it."

"Thank goodness for comprehensive sex education." He kissed along my neck, setting me ablaze.

Principal Aguilar cleared his throat behind us.

Busted.

We turned from our tight embrace to our boss, standing in the doorway, thoroughly unimpressed.

"I take it this is a thing now," he said.

"Uh huh," Seamus said.

"Is there something in the water here?" He put his hands on his hips. Though, he was one to talk. He was currently dating the parent of a former student. "Please remember to conduct yourselves with decorum on school grounds."

"We will. I promise." I held up my hand. All that was missing was a Bible.

"I'll send over a congratulations cactus," Principal Aguilar said with zero enthusiasm and walked away.

"I should get back to my classroom." I didn't know how we were going to share the news with our fellow teachers and students. The gossip would quickly circulate. There would be people who thought we were a mismatch. But that was their problem.

I slowly walked backward. It became a struggle since Seamus refused to let go of my hand. The glint in his eye wouldn't let go of my heart either.

"I have to go, Seamus."

"Come here." He pulled me to him for one more earth-shattering kiss. "That'll get me through fourth period."

DURING MY FREE PERIOD, after dealing with the wonky vending machine in the lounge that made me fight for my Pop Tarts, I wandered into familiar territory. I knocked on the door of Mrs. Stockman's health class. She was mid-lesson, a cast on her foot.

"Mr. Bradford! Thank you for helping out while I was gone. Can I help you?" she asked.

"Mrs. Stockman, would you mind if I said something to the class quickly?"

"Sure," she said with a shrug. "We were just about to learn about gonorrhea."

I walked to the front of the class, where I'd spent the past month a nervous wreck, feeling like a total fraud. The students, including Cale and Ella, lit up with smiles of recognition.

"I wanted to say it was a pleasure subbing for this class. We had some really good discussions about sex. There's been something on my mind, though. We're always wondering why sex is so important. Is it because it's a major physical act? Is it because society puts this pressure on us to make it important? I think this is a question you need to answer for yourselves. For some of you, losing your virginity is just sex. And for some of you, it's a major milestone. Whatever path you take, make sure it's *your* choice."

I was emboldened with confidence as I gazed at each student. Not because I'd lost my virginity. Not because I had a boyfriend. But because finally, for the first time in thirty-five years, I had fallen in love with myself, and there was no better relationship in the world.

EPILOGUE - SEAMUS

A.K.A. ONE LAST THING TO CHECK OFF THE LIST

Four Months Later

I dove headfirst into the oncoming wave, submerging myself in the cold, salty spray of the Atlantic Ocean. Even in the heart of summer, the Atlantic was cold enough to freeze a guy's nuts off.

I jumped out of the water, flinging my hair back like I was in a photo shoot. Sunny skies and warm air greeted me. Was there anything better than a beach day?

Yes, there was.

There was my boyfriend, coming to join me in the water, his hot body on display for all the beachgoers. *Hands off, people. He's mine.*

He clenched his teeth as he waded into the water.

"Just run in like I did. It's the quickest way to adjust," I said, no longer freezing.

"I'm psyching myself up." He nodded to himself, as if he were saying some kind of motivational chant.

"You're dunking, not walking over hot coals and broken glass."

He held up the "one minute" finger. I had all the time in the world. The water was crisp yet delightful. It would be even more delightful when Jules joined me, and I could pull him close for an underwater sword fight.

Julian sucked in a cloud's worth of air and plunged under the water. He stayed down there a few seconds. Right as I started to worry he'd become a permanent resident under the sea, he bobbed up. His wavy hair wet and pushed back was a *very* good look on him.

"Still getting adjusted," he said, teeth chattering.

"Here." I hugged him for warmth.

"I thought the water was supposed to be warm by August."

"We had a rough winter." I gazed into his big, brown eyes. Whenever I looked into those eyes, I knew I was exactly where I needed to be. "What took you so long? My fingers are starting to prune."

"I was on the phone with my mom. We're on for tennis with her and my dad tomorrow."

"Excellent. I want a rematch."

Julian's mom was terrible at planning parties, but that was because she spent all her time playing tennis. The woman was a force on the court, and her husband was no slouch either. They wiped the court with Julian and me last time. If we were playing baseball or back alley stickball, it'd be a different situation.

The four of us had made a summer Sunday tradition of tennis and lunch. Each time, the ice between Julian and his mom continued to thaw. She'd stopped making comments about his weight and eating, and it allowed them to get closer. If she ever did let something slip, Julian knew I had his back. I had no qualms about standing up for my man.

We swam out a little so we were farther away from the crowds.

"I can't believe we start school again in a month," Julian said. "I'm not ready to wake up early."

"Think about all the coffee you get to have."

"I can have coffee now." We had our morning routines down. There was a fresh pot brewing every morning for Jules.

"My video views go up during the school year, so I'm selfishly not dreading the return."

"How did Cyllabus like that last video?"

"They loved it. And they loved the feedback you gave them."

Since my first sponsored post in March, I'd had a few more brands approach me to make videos. I tried to do them sparingly so that my feed wasn't all sponcon. When Cyllabus had approached me about making a video, Julian and I thought it was a joke at first. Had they been listening to our conversations about their product?

Once I got in good with them, I'd handed over some issues the South Rock teachers had been having with the software, and they'd actually made changes. It was a win-win for everyone.

But the big win was that the sponsored content enabled me to speed up payments to Greg and Ethan. I would pay them back completely by early next year. Things were still tight for me financially thanks to my other debts, but I was so happy I could do this for Lauren. She'd been able to get her dream house and go on her dream honeymoon. She was doing great.

I was spending practically every night over at Julian's place, and we'd recently broached the topic of cohabitation. Our relationship was moving fast, yet not by our own doing. It was natural. Nothing felt forced. We had already laid the groundwork through years of friendship.

Back in the ocean, I had Julian wrap his legs around my waist.

"Much better," I said.

"This is the only time you can do this."

"Not true. I can pick you up whenever I want." I kissed him, forgetting that we were in the middle of the water in the middle of a crowded beach in the middle of summer. Julian made me forget that time existed.

"Are you having a good birthday?" he asked.

"The best."

"How's thirty-one treating you?"

"So far, so good." This was the best birthday weekend. It was filled with my guy, good weather, good food, and good sex. And if all went well tomorrow, a very good victory over the Bradfords.

Julian got a curious look on his face, his lips curling into a mischievous smile.

"What?" I asked.

"I've been thinking. There's one item left on my list that never got checked off. I've never topped. And since today is your birthday, you are technically a thirty-one-year-old half virgin."

My breath hitched. Despite the cool water, I was flooded with heat. Getting topped by Julian had been a fantasy lingering in my mind for a while. As we got more comfortable with sex, I got more intrigued about what it felt like for him. Was the grass greener on the other side?

"I thought that you only wanted to bottom because you'd never mentioned otherwise," I said.

"I do enjoy it. But I want to try this. I guess I had it in my head that since you came from the straight world, bottoming was off limits."

"I'm not part of the straight world anymore."

"Is this something you might want to do?" he asked.

Getting railed by Julian?

"Hell yeah." I held up my hand for a high-five. "Let's do this!"

That night, we were doing this.

"Relax." Julian put a calming hand on my chest.

We sat on the bed in the hotel room sans clothes. In a first, Julian had gotten naked before me.

"I'm good," I said, but Julian could tell that was minor bullshit. "I'm just psyching myself up."

"You mean trying to unlearn all of the heterosexual messaging about how men are inherently weak if they bottom."

Man, he was smart. His brain was as much a turn on as his body.

"I'm going to set the mood." Julian began lighting candles around the room, giving the bed an ethereal glow. This might've been against hotel policy, but no fire alarms had gone off yet.

"You brought candles on our vacation?" I asked.

"I came prepared," he said as he tossed lube onto the bed. He turned to me, his strong body lit in soft light.

Our lips met in a hungry kiss that instantly revved me up. Julian pulled me to the edge of the bed and hugged me in a tight embrace, his lips never leaving mine. The man knew how to take the wheel, and he would make sure this was an incredible night for me.

He kissed down my chest, his lips firecrackers on my skin. My cock was in its full and upright position. Julian took me in his mouth.

"Fuck, yeah." I dipped my head back, soaking in the hot feeling of his tongue sweeping over my dick. He teased and tortured me with slow strokes that took their sweet time. I got lost in the heat of his mouth. Julian had that power over me. He had gotten more confident, more aggressive in bed thanks to all his experience. It didn't matter that he'd lost his v-card late. The man was a really fast learner.

"Shit," I cracked out as the world exploded around me. He slipped a slicked-up finger inside my hole as he continued sucking me. I hadn't heard him open the bottle of lube. He should've been in the CIA or a ninja. He was that stealth.

"You are so damn tight. I can't wait to open you up," he said, his voice husky and drenched in need.

"Break me wide open, baby." I fell back on the bed. My spine gave out from the overload of pleasure. Julian played me like a fucking violin. His fingers spread me open as his mouth took me to the base. Then his tongue drifted down to my ass and sent new shockwaves of heat through my body.

I let out moan after moan. And this was just foreplay. I was going to lose it during sex. I couldn't wait. My fear had been subsumed by desire.

Julian lifted my legs, my slick hole jutting in the air waiting to be stuffed like a Christmas stocking. He slapped his slick cock against my opening. We'd ditched condoms shortly after we got together. Julian hadn't been with anyone else obviously, and I hadn't been with anyone since Lauren. There would be no barrier between us.

"Are you ready?" he asked, circling his cockhead around my hole. Was he getting a perverse pleasure out of dragging this out?

"Give me a minute. I need to think about every important moment in my life that's led up to this."

"I don't have a minute," he warned. His thick erection pressing into me made that very clear.

"Do it." I gave him a firm head nod.

Julian leaned over me and kissed me on the forehead. "You're going to love it. I promise."

"I trust you."

"And I love you."

"I love you and I trust you," I said, not one to be beaten.

And then he was inside me. I had never felt fuller. It was tight but exciting, like reaching a new bench press personal record.

"Seamus check: How are we doing?" he asked.

I gave him a thumbs-up.

"No thumbs-up allowed in sex," he said.

"Keep going," I said with a groan.

Julian slid inside me, then out, then in again. His thrusts and grunts above me set me ablaze. It wasn't painful like I'd been expecting, or the pain was easily overtaken by the physical and emotional pleasure. In most of our previous sexual escapades, a tongue or finger usually found its way inside me, which probably helped to grease the tracks for tonight.

Watching Julian fuck me, that animal look in his eye, hurtled me into a new stratosphere of ecstasy.

"Harder," I said.

"Already?"

"Yeah. Give it to me."

Julian lifted my legs more and pumped me with greater force. Each thrust brought me closer to the edge. I jacked myself, high on our lust. I was naked, spread, and his for the taking. I felt totally free.

The orgasm building inside me was more intense than anything I'd ever experienced. Every part of my body tensed and battened down the hatches. I gripped the comforter until my knuckles went white. I was going to completely explode.

"Jules..."

He could sense what was happening. His gaze remained steady, leading me through this wilderness.

"Come for me," he said, his voice hitching. He was close, too.

A massive moan ripped me in two as I saw stars and God and everything in between.

"Damn." I looked at my soaked chest and stomach.

Julian dipped down and kissed me hard. He shook and clenched, his back tight as he emptied himself inside me.

His eyes were glassy, hair sweaty, skin flushed with color. I was probably the same.

"Fuck."

"What's wrong?" he asked.

"Why did I hold out for months on that? I'm such an idiot."

"We'll just have to make up for lost time." Julian kissed down my neck. Something told me we'd be doing this again after dinner. And I was A-okay with that. As long as I was with Julian, I'd be happy.

I held up my finger and made one final check mark.

Thanks for reading!

What happens when you combine a socially awkward science teacher and two beefy, former students?

You get Advanced Chemistry, the fourth book in the South Rock High series. The bunsen burner won't be the only thing turning up the heat!
Start reading today

You can read Greg and Ethan's college origin story *Out in the Open*, Book 1 in the Browerton University Series. You'll see exactly what happened in those library stacks all those years ago.

Sign up for my newsletter to get the first scoop on new books, read bonus stories, and get exclusive access to other cool goodies.
www.ajtruman.com/outsiders

Please consider leaving a review on the book's Amazon page or on

Goodreads. Reviews are crucial in helping other readers find new books.

Join the party in my Facebook Group and on Instagram @ajtruman_author. Follow me at Bookbub to be alerted to new releases.

And then there's email. I love hearing from readers! Send me a note anytime at info@ajtruman.com. I always respond.

ALSO BY A.J. TRUMAN

South Rock High

Ancient History

Drama!

Romance Languages

Advanced Chemistry

Single Dads Club

The Falcon and the Foe

The Mayor and the Mystery Man

The Barkeep and the Bro

The Fireman and the Flirt

Browerton University Series

Out in the Open

Out on a Limb

Out of My Mind

Out for the Night

Out of This World

Outside Looking In

Out of Bounds

Seasonal Novellas

Hot Mall Santa

Only One Coffin

Fall for You

You Got Scrooged

Written with M.A. Wardell

Marshmallow Mountain

ABOUT THE AUTHOR

A.J. Truman writes books with **humor, heart, and hot guys.** What else does a story need? He lives in a very full house in Indiana with his husband, son, and cats.. He loves happily ever afters and sneaking off for an afternoon movie.

www.ajtruman.com
info@ajtruman.com
The Outsiders - Facebook Group

Printed in Great Britain
by Amazon